The Thrice Named

Part III

Sasanian

The Thrice Named Man

Part III

Sasanian

by

Hector Miller

www.HectorMillerBooks.com

The Thrice Named Man

Part III

Sasanian

Author: Hector Miller

Proofreading: Kira Miller, J van Rensburg, Carly Weii

First edition, 2018, Hector Miller

Part III in the book series The Thrice Named Man

ISBN: 9781719909563

Contents

Contents (continued)

Contents (continued)

Chapter 1 – Governor (August 238 AD)

Hostilius turned in his saddle. "What in Hades is going on…?"

Marcus and I exchanged glances and we both shrugged, which just caused to worsen the Primus Pilus's scowl.

Hostilius was dressed in his Roman military garb, identifying him as the head centurion of a legion.

"Centurion", I said, "just to clarify. You are the only one among us who has military rank. Although we carry the orders from the emperor with his personal seal, it is not official until it is entered into the rolls of the legion."

Marcus nodded in agreement.

Hundreds of legionaries marching in ranks blocked the road that led to Sirmium and the camp of the Legio IV Italica. Hostilius spurred his horse and rode past the orderly column of soldiers until he drew level with a tribune riding close behind the vanguard of officers. He saluted, followed by a quick conversation. Hostilius trotted back to where we were waiting at the back of the column.

"The newly appointed governor of Moesia Inferior is on his way to his posting", Hostilius said. "Apparently there is trouble in the province. We are allowed to pass the column, in fact, I have been ordered to do so by the tribune."

We rode past, and as we skirted the vanguard I noticed a group of officers clustered around an older man dressed as a legate. It was good to know that the governor of Moesia was a military man, rather than a pampered administrator.

Free of the traffic, we increased our pace, keen to arrive at our destination. I sensed a rider approaching and halted my horse as the tribune galloped up from behind.

He nodded to us and addressed Hostilius. "Centurion, you and the civilians are to report to the governor immediately. Follow me."

We rode back at an easy trot and Marcus said: "Centurion, what did you do to antagonise the governor?"

Hostilius just shrugged, but he was acutely aware of the fickle nature of the upper classes. I could see the concern etched on his face.

The column came to a halt as the governor and his officers dismounted. We followed suit and left our horses in the care of a junior centurion. The governor had his back turned to us, deep in discussion.

As he turned to face us, Hostilius saluted and said: "Primus Pilus Hostilius Proculus of the IV Italica, reporting as ordered, sir."

The governor flatly ignored him and walked over to Marcus and me. He embraced us in turn, leaving our centurion standing at attention with a generally confused expression.

Governor Tullus Menophilus smiled broadly and placed his hand on my shoulder. "Gentlemen, I would like to introduce to you the two men who are the saviours of Italy. They fought alongside me on the walls of Aquileia even though they were guest-friends of my esteemed colleague Governor Crispinus."

At the command of Menophilus, we rode alongside him the rest of the way to Sirmium, with Hostilius looking decidedly out of place amongst the patrician officers.

"Lucius, tell me where you have been all the time since you left Aquileia", Menophilus said.

"As you know, Marcus and I were dismissed by the Thracian and we had no legion to report back to. I did the next best thing and married the beautiful lady who helped us to defend the walls", I replied.

"Yes, I recall her face", he said. "What was her name again?"

"Ulpia Severina, sir. She hails from Dacia and is from the line of Traianus."

"Yes, yes, I recall her name now that you mention it. It is a good choice, and a most noble lineage. Where are you heading with the grim-looking Primus Pilus?"

"We have received written orders from the emperors", Marcus replied. "Lucius and I have been given the option to take up senior positions within the IV Italica. Lucius will be prefect of the auxiliary cavalry and I will be tribune laticlavius. Our orders will only be effective once they have been entered into the rolls of the legion. As it stands, we are still civilians."

Menophilus smiled and pointed to the walls of Sirmium in the distance. "Then you had better go and enter the orders into the rolls. Report to me as soon as you have taken care of the necessary, and bring your surly Primus Pilus with."

We were out of earshot when Hostilius said: "Surly my arse. Bloody patricians. Someone has to explain the difference between serious and surly to him." He rode ahead, scowling.

The watch officer not only recognised the Primus Pilus, but also his mood. The gates to the camp were opened quickly. The guards all stood to attention and saluted smartly without making eye contact. Marcus and I immediately walked to the Praetorium to report, leaving Hostilius to go about his business.

The scrolls with the imperial seal ensured that we were given access to the commander of the legion without delay.

The legate looked up from the tablet he had been studying. "I have been expecting you", he said.

Marcus handed him the scroll. He read the document containing the orders from Pupienus, also signed by his co-emperor, Bulbinus. "Welcome back to the IV Italica", the legate said. "I will have my secretary take care of the records immediately. Report to me once you have been shown to your quarters. I will arrange for the quartermaster to issue the necessary gear. Dismissed."

Less than a watch had passed when Marcus and I reported to the legate as ordered, appropriately attired in military garb.

The legate informed us of the situation. "There is trouble in Moesia Inferior. Big trouble. The Carpiani has breached the limes. They have annihilated two cohorts of the V Macedonica based at Noviodumum ad Istrum, where the Danube flows into the Dark Sea. That is all we know for a fact. There have been many rumours, but one thing is certain, they will ravage Moesia Inferior, looting and killing as they go about their business."

We were still being briefed when Tullus Menophilus entered the quarters of the legate.

They clasped arms. "Forgive my unannounced intrusion, Legate", the governor said. "I have been in discussion with the procurator of Pannonia Inferior. I will be taking a vexillation of the IV Italica with me. The first and second cohorts as well as the auxiliary cavalry will join me. They will have tomorrow to prepare. We march at first light the day after."

He turned to face us. "Tribune Marcus Valerius will be in charge of the infantry and Prefect Lucius Domitius will command the double strength ala of Numidian cavalry. The infantry will be transported by the imperial fleet of the Danube while the cavalry will use the Via Militaris. I will be travelling with you, Lucius. I have sent orders ahead and we will be joined by other vexillations on our way to Moesia."

Immediately after being dismissed, I set off to find the Numidians.

I had commanded thousands of barbarian cavalry during my time with the Huns. Obviously this was not known to the tribune who commanded the cavalry.

Tribune Adherbal eyed me warily as I neared the area where they were performing training exercises close to the camp. I was riding Simsek, my favourite Hunnic horse. The tribune approached me and saluted. I returned his salute and handed him his written orders. While he was reading, I studied him and his mount. The Berber horse was about the same size as Simsek and appeared hardy. Adherbal had the look of a desert nomad, with shoulder-length curly black locks and olive skin. His eyes were dark and he was sinewy, but muscular.

The tribune looked up, having studied his orders, and said: "It is good to have you back in the legion, Prefect. You had quite a reputation when you were a centurion."

"Thank you Tribune. You honour me", I said, and inclined my head.

"Be ready to ride at first light, day after tomorrow", I said. "Make sure that you have as many javelins as your men are able to carry. We do not know what to expect. I have made the arrangements with the quartermaster."

Before he could answer, I turned my horse and headed back to camp.

Cai arrived not long after I had returned to my quarters. He travelled with a cart and a guard of four Roxolani. Not that Cai needed the protection.

The cart was necessary to transport the many amphorae of wine I brought all the way from Aquileia. Cai also brought my spare armour, weapons and the few items of clothing required by a soldier. Segelinde, my bride, or rather Ulpia Severina as she had been renamed, insisted that Cai take along the golden armour that I had stripped off the Heruli king.

7

After the guards assisted with the unloading, I sent them home to relay the news that I had been sent away on campaign. Cai did not seem surprised at all when I told him.

"Lucius of the Da Qin, I said storm is gathering. What you expect?" he said.

Again, he was right of course, and I just nodded.

"Good, very good, Lucius. To realise that you mostly wrong, big step towards enlightenment."

"I have present for you, Lucius of the Da Qin", Cai continued, producing a magnificent bearskin cloak. The hide was perfectly worked, with the edges embroidered and stitched.

"Bradakos gave to me. He said to tell you it was the bear you killed when hunt together and gift from gods."

I smiled when I recalled the day that I killed the bear and saved the life of my mentor, who later became the king of the Roxolani.

Cai poured us each a cup of wine and produced smoked fowl, dates, olives and cheese which he had brought from the farm.

"I bring three Hun horse. Spare for each of us. You eat, I pack. I better at pack than you, Lucius of the Da Qin."

"Cai of the Han, if I caught glimpses of the future like you do, I would also know what to take with."

Cai worked while I devoured the food that he had laid out for me. I noticed from the corner of my eye that he packed the golden armour that Segelinde had given me.

"Is that necessary?" I asked.

"I recall you promise wife that you take", Cai replied. He proceeded to neatly stow it in my pack. Wisely, I kept quiet.

Chapter 2 – Via Militaris

Tullus Menophilus could have easily commandeered a galley to transport him to our destination at Durostorum. He chose to do his own dirty work and travelled along the Via Militaris, stopping at the fortresses along the way to meet with the legates in person.

His orders, sanctioned by the emperors, of course, were sent ahead to allow the vexillations to be ready to depart upon our arrival.

Although Menophilus invited me to join his retinue, I requested to travel with the Numidians. I was not afforded the luxury of time to train with them, so I did the next best thing and spent my time observing them and talking to Adherbal.

The African auxiliaries wore no body armour. They had no protection apart from a small leather shield carried in the left hand. When fighting mounted they used short, light javelins, of which they carried a number.

They had neither saddle nor bit, but steered the horse with a simple collar and a short stick - riding into battle with two mounts and jumping onto a fresh horse without slowing down.

They were excellent riders and their horses possessed markedly better endurance than the Roman horses.

When fighting on foot, they used hunting bows and slings.

None of this helped to dispel the growing feeling of dread I experienced. We were on our way to engage the Carpiani, who, like the Roxolani, employed light and heavy cavalry. What I would not give to have led a band of auxiliary Hun cavalry.

I shared my thoughts with Cai on the third evening. I filled his cup to the brim with an excellent red and said: "Cai, I am concerned that the Numidians will be ineffective against the Carpiani. I need archers and I need men with armour. My horsemen possess neither."

Cai drank deeply. "General in army, like sculptor", he replied. "Good artist create work of art even with blunt tool. Sculptor without skill creates nothing, even with best tools. Numidians maybe not best tools. I agree."

He drank again, savouring the wine, and continued. "Good general find way to use tools. Bad general lose war even when command Huns. Secret is to know strength and weakness of enemy. Bigger secret is to know self."

As always, Cai was right.

I spent the days on the road well. I worked out how I could defeat the Carpiani by using my Numidians. The only way we could neutralise the heavy cavalry was to tire them. Engaging them would be suicide. The light horse archers of the enemy was a different prospect altogether. One that I knew I had to find a solution to.

At Singidunum we were joined by three cohorts of legionary infantry and an ala of Germanic medium cavalry. The VII Claudia at Viminacium provided us with a double strength ala of heavy Armenian cavalry in addition to three cohorts of infantry.

Ten days after we departed from Sirmium, we arrived at the legionary fortress of the I Italica at Novae. Our forces were bolstered with three cohorts of infantry and a regiment of five hundred well-armoured Syrian archers.

Hostilius and his men had arrived two days earlier and set up camp outside the walls of the fortress.

"About bloody time. Ever tried sitting on your arse for ten days?" was all he uttered when I met up with our scowling Primus Pilus.

Come morning, we marched for Durostorum. Our army was now a force to be reckoned with - five-and-a-half-thousand veteran heavy infantry supported by auxiliary archers, as well as cavalry.

The march to Durostorum took six days. Governor Menophilus was in command of the army and he tasked me to scout for any signs of the enemy. My Numidians were ideal outriders. I insisted to scout in the direction of the advance as well as both wings. To be certain, I instructed fifty of my men to trail the army by two miles. The Carpiani were horsemen and extremely mobile. It would not do to be surprised.

I spent most of my time with the advance scouts, accompanied by Adherbal.

A day away from Durostorum we encountered the first outriders of the enemy. We were scouting along a dry riverbed flanked by shrubby trees, when one of our own approached on a lathered horse. He came to a halt and reported to Adherbal in Numidian, gesturing over his shoulder while he spoke. I could not understand his words, but based on the scout's body language, I took three arrows into my draw hand.

The Numidian commander dismissed the rider with a wave of his hand. "Twelve light Carpiani horsemen are moving in our direction", he said. "Must be a scouting patrol of the enemy."

Our party consisted of a full turma of thirty-two riders, and I pointed to five men who were standing close by. "You stay, the rest of you, to the trees. Now!" I commanded. "Charge the enemy in the flank when they pass your position." Adherbal repeated my commands in Numidian and within heartbeats there were only seven of us left to be seen in the open.

Before we could do more, the enemy came into view two hundred paces away. They noticed us immediately and spurred their horses to a gallop.

We fled with the Carpiani in pursuit. My Hunnic bow was superior by far, and two of my needle point arrows struck the lead riders, sending them tumbling from their horses. As the enemy passed our original position, the Numidians burst from cover, casting their light javelins into the flank of the Carpiani. The barbarians were outnumbered two to one and in close combat, they had no chance. The enemy fell, pierced by the short javelins. None were left alive.

The men looted the dead and claimed the uninjured horses. Adherbal joined them and soon appeared with two arrows which he cut from the corpses of my victims. He handed it to me and I nodded in appreciation as I took it from his bloodstained hand.

He noticed my gaze linger. "It is not easy to retrieve an arrow when it has to be taken from a skull", he explained. "It requires a good knife, but an axe is better."

He paused, and eyed me warily. "I have served under Roman prefects for many years", he added. "You, sir, are no Roman."

I left ten men under the command of Adherbal and hurried back to report to the governor.

"We have engaged scouts of the Carpiani", I said. "We slew them, but soon the others will become suspicious."

"It matters not", replied the governor. "Our destination is the legionary fort at Durostorum. We will construct a fortified camp outside the fort, but we will effectively join the veterans from the XI Claudia. Once we have combined our forces, we will seek out the enemy. I need the Numidians to keep me informed of their movements."

That evening the legion built a marching camp for the first time on the campaign. Although we were in Roman controlled Moesia Inferior, a barbarian horde was roaming about the province unchecked. The camp, which was large enough for the whole of the army, was built by the legionaries while the auxiliary regiments guarded against a surprise attack.

I took the opportunity to seek out my old comrades who I had not seen since my return from exile.

They were seated around a cooking fire and they all came to attention. I waved away the formalities and took a seat beside them.

"I have not seen you since the Thracian chased me away. If not for you, I would have been on the other side of the river", I said.

"You have saved us all more than once, Umbra", Pumilio said. "We still owe you many lives, don't we? Not long ago you were still one of us. Now you are a prefect and the rumour is you are the reason that the Thracian's head was put on a spear. If he had asked me for advice, I would have told him to not cross swords with you. Umbra, the gods love you. It's one thing fighting against a man. It's a whole different story going up against the will of the gods."

"The poor bloody Carpiani would run home if they knew you were on your way", Ursa added.

Silentus just nodded and drank from his cup.

I reached under my tunic and produced a large skin of wine and filled each of their cups.

Ursa smacked his lips. "Seems to me that the gods give you some of their wine as well."

I grinned. "In addition, you also rescued Marcus, who is now the tribune laticlavius. You have made a powerful ally, my friends. He will not forget."

Chapter 3 – Plan

I have said this before. Romans tend to look down on barbarians and confuse their lack of education with stupidity. I learned at an early age not to fall into this trap.

We were still thirty miles from Durostorum. I left camp a third of a watch before sunrise leading five turmae of Numidians. We divided into groups with the aim of thoroughly scouting the road to our destination. Barely four miles outside camp we stumbled upon a lone horseman. Initially it seemed as if he wished to skirt our position, but when he was close enough to identify us as Roman auxiliaries, he approached, reining in his lathered horse.

The rider's clothing identified him as a Roman decurion.

"Prefect", he said, and saluted, "I am attached to the XI Claudia. Yesterday, late afternoon, Durostorum was besieged by a significant force of invading barbarians. We estimate ten thousand infantry and eight thousand mixed cavalry."

I realised then that the Goths had joined the Carpiani.

I left the turmae of Numidians to continue their mission to establish the exact movements of the enemy. I ordered them not to engage, but to hide or retreat should they come into contact with advance scouts of the enemy.

I rode back with the decurion to report to Menophilus.

"You are dismissed, Decurion, leave us", the governor said, and poured me a silver goblet of red wine.

"I would hear your opinion, Prefect", he said.

"It would be almost impossible to defeat the barbarians in a pitched battle, Governor", I said. "We should also not underestimate the Gothic infantry. We are outnumbered. Two to one is not favourable odds. On this flat terrain, our outnumbered cavalry will be crushed by the horse archers and heavy cavalry of the Carpiani. Once our cavalry has been annihilated, the barbarian horse will join their infantry. Together they are more than a match for the legions. Our only option is to separate their cavalry from their infantry. If we link up with the infantry of the XI Claudia, we could defeat them in turn, on ground of our choosing."

The governor nodded his agreement.

"May I question the decurion further?" I asked.

Moments later the cavalry officer returned and came to attention.

"Were there any wagons and baggage accompanying the enemy?" I queried. "Did you see only warriors, or did you notice women and children?"

"The enemy could be seen clearly from the walls, Prefect", the decurion said. "There was no baggage apart from livestock that they had looted."

"What is the news from the rest of the Province?" I asked.

"Looting, killing and destruction of farms, Prefect", he said. "Although most of the citizens fled to the forts or large, walled towns and cities where we have garrisons. The barbarians are not skilled at taking garrisoned, walled settlements. We heard that the enemy baggage train is amassing in the region of Histria."

"What about the legions based at the forts along the limes?" I asked.

"The V Macedonica lost two cohorts when the limes were breached", he said. "They are under-strength and cannot leave the fort for fear of being caught in the open by the Carpiani cavalry."

"One more question, decurion", I said. "Are you familiar with the rest of Moesia Inferior?"

"Yes, sir", he replied confidently.

"Good. Make sure you are well rested. I may have need of you soon. Dismissed."

I waited until the decurion was out of earshot. "Governor, there are a couple of reasons for the raid into Roman territory",

I explained. "The one thing that the barbarians do not covet, not yet anyway, is to settle in our lands. They raid for loot, and to provide their young warriors with the opportunity to fight and grow strong. They will soon be crossing the border back to their lands with wagons heavily laden with loot. The barbarian army that is camped close by has been sent to stop us from taking back the spoils of war. If they fear that we will attack their women and loot, most of their cavalry will leave to protect their wagons."

Tullus Menophilus smiled. "Tell me more", he said.

I continued to explain my plan. "The Germani and Armenian cavalry will not be able to outrun the horses of the Carpiani, but the Numidians will. They are sinewy men who fight without armour, and their horses are hardy. The enemy will never keep up with us."

I drank deeply from my goblet while Arash whispered into my ear.

"We get the Armenians and Germani to join us, as a ruse", I said. "They strip their armour and create the impression that we number in the thousands. When the Carpiani gives chase they split off from my Numidians and circle back to the army. We then ride to Histria where the barbarian baggage train is amassing. The Carpiani will send most of their horsemen in pursuit. The absence of the barbarian cavalry will allow

20

Hostilius's boys to join up with the XI Claudia, and take the Gothic infantry head-on. The Germani and Armenian cavalry can be used to strike the Gothic infantry in the flank. My Numidians and I will find refuge in Histria."

"I have no better plan", Menophilus said. "Let us make the necessary arrangements, Prefect."

I spent the next watch with Menophilus and unit commanders to devise our strategy, while three turmae of my Numidians scouted the exact position of the enemy.

As the first light of the false dawn illuminated the land, two-and-a-half-thousand riders and five thousand horses trotted from the camp. The Armenians and Germans were not happy with the arrangements. I couldn't really blame them for they must have felt vulnerable without armour. Although I argued against it, they refused to leave their swords behind. I eventually relented.

We knew the exact position of the enemy camp and rode slowly until we came close. We then changed mounts and skirted the camp at a distance of five hundred paces. Five thousand horses ridden at a gallop is akin to an earthquake and would be noticed.

I slowed the pace of the Numidians, to act as a screen for the Germani and Armenian cavalry to circle back towards the Roman camp on the route that we had planned. They would not gallop back, but once they were out of sight, they would walk their horses to make sure that they were invisible to the enemy.

We were on our way to a Roman fort on the Danube, called Carsium, which was ninety miles from Durostorum. Carsium guarded a shallow section in the Danube which was fordable. The decurion from Durostorum who guided us explained that the road between Histria and Carsium was well-used as a trade route. This ford across the Danube linked the barbarian lands with the port of Histria. I was sure that the Carpiani knew this road well and would use it to take their loot back home.

At first I was concerned that the Carpiani would not follow, but before long an immense dust cloud rose behind us. We travelled along the Roman road. It was cleared and levelled fifty paces on either side, so we had at least a hundred paces of width to utilise.

We had to be careful not to outrun the slower Carpiani. I allowed them to approach to within a mile and then adjusted our pace to ensure that they did not close with us. To keep up the ruse, I slowed down from time to time to allow them to gain on us.

When they believed that we were within their grasp, they spurred their horses with the excitement of the chase. I knew from experience that their actions would be immensely tiring for the horses. Only when I could feel their anticipation of the imminent catch did we increase our pace.

I found that Simsek was hardier than the horses of the Numidians. I rode with armour, albeit the lighter Scythian version, but I had to rein him in most of the time.

We had just changed horses again when I noticed Adherbal riding at my side. He pointed to Simsek. "Where you find this horse?" he asked.

"My horses were bred by the man-demons beyond the lands of the Scythians and the Goths. No other horses are able to keep up with them", I replied.

I could see the desire in his eyes.

"If we get back alive, I will give you a foal of Simsek's. You can train him yourself", I said.

Adherbal smiled the broadest smile I have ever seen.

Cai was riding next to me, also on a Hunnic horse. "Man from Africa love horse same as Gordas like scalp", he said.

Chapter 4 – Histria

The setting sun in the west ominously illuminated the smoke on the northern horizon. There was little doubt in my mind that Carsium had fallen. The barbarians were securing their route home.

A third of a watch earlier, my trailing scouts reported that our pursuers had given up the chase and they were setting up camp for the night. Since then we had been saving our horses. We made camp once we found a suitable spot, placing sufficient distance between us and the enemy.

The Roman decurion, who was named Laberius, joined us around the cooking fire.

"I do not think it would be wise to venture close to the border fort at Carsium", I said. "The smoke we saw came from there. I see the hand of the Goths in this. The horse people would not attack a fort."

Cai nodded. "The Goths are inventive and clever race. They learn from us."

He drank from his cup and continued. "Not unlike Romans. Short sword taken from Spaniards. Siege engines copied from Greeks."

I noticed that Adherbal was smiling, but Laberius had a frown etched on his face. Romans are proud people.

"And we will again gain the upper hand by learning from these barbarians", I added in support of Cai.

Laberius wanted to intervene but I stopped him with a raised palm.

"How many Roman horses do you see here today, Laberius?" I asked.

"None, sir", he answered.

"Learn from that", I said. "Do not be too proud. It is of no use to have cavalry when the cavalry is unable to get to where the war is taking place."

I could see that I had given him something to think about. He did not argue.

"Prefect, where do we ride tomorrow?" Adherbal asked.

"We will leave the road for a while and skirt Carsium", I said. "Then we will harry the wagons transporting the loot from Histria to the ford at Carsium. Once we have drawn the enemy to us, we will outrun them and find refuge within the fort at Histria."

They all nodded in agreement, except Cai, who was staring into the fire as if to find an answer from the gods.

The following morning a sentry woke us early. "The Carpiani are stirring in their camp, sir", he reported to Adherbal.

"Spread the word", I said. "Get ready, we will ride soon. Eat in the saddle."

Adherbal left to organize the men. I turned around to mount, but Cai was standing there, barring my way with a leather bag slung over his shoulder.

"Today you wear armour Segelinde gave you. Good husband not argue with wisdom of woman", he commanded.

I scowled.

"We may meet Goths today. Wife is Goth. Listen", he countered.

I nodded reluctantly. He assisted me to take off and stash my mail armour and don the golden armour of the Heruli.

Adherbal was back soon. He stared at me in surprise. "You look like the god of war today, sir."

"I took it from a giant Goth who had no need of it", I said, and mounted.

Our detour took us to the Roman road leading to Histria. When the sun rose, it was clear that the Carpiani had not given up the chase. A giant dust cloud rose behind us.

We had travelled less than five miles when we came across the first of the wagon caravans carrying the loot of the barbarians. The horsemen guarding the wagons fled into the countryside as soon as they identified us as Roman auxiliaries. The Numidians did not pursue, but set fire to the wagons. I could see by the pained expressions on their faces that it was a difficult order to obey. It was necessary, though, as we would be unable to outrun the enemy with horses burdened with loot.

We destroyed two more caravans in the same manner. Histria was only ten miles away and the Carpiani horsemen were still following us - my plan seemed to work exactly as I had anticipated. That is, until we came across the column of Roman infantry marching in our direction.

The centurion saluted. "Centurion Flaminius, second cohort, Legio V Macedonica. Our cohort garrisoned the fort at Histria, sir."

I anticipated bad news but had to hear it. "Report, centurion", I said.

"The fort was attacked during the night", Flaminius replied. "We were well prepared for an attack, but the barbarians did not come from the land. It has never happened before. They came in boats from the Dark Sea, eliminated our sentries on the walls, and opened the sea gate. Our first centurion was killed in the fight. The men that attacked us were not

27

Carpiani. They were giants armed with spears, swords and war axes. They wore armour and carried round shields. I have never seen their like. We escaped in the confusion."

"You did the right thing by saving these people", I said.

I looked behind him and noticed a group of fifty legionaries and a hundred and fifty civilians. Most of the soldiers were wounded, including the centurion. He was no coward.

"Is there a fort nearby that would still stand?" I asked.

"Argamum is less than thirty miles from here", he replied. "It sits upon the top of a cliff and has high walls. It will still stand."

"Adherbal, I will have a hundred of your men escort these survivors to Argamum. They are to mount double on the spare horses. The enemy is at least still eight miles distant. We will join you later."

Adherbal trotted back to us as the beleaguered group disappeared into the fields.

"Now we ride to Histria", I said. "We need to learn more about this new threat."

In my heart, I knew already. The masters of the runes had shown themselves to Rome for the first time. The Heruli had come.

A third of a watch had passed when we approached the fort at Histria. The gates were open, and I could see many sentries on the walls. These men were no fools. They were alert even though the chance of an attack was small. As soon as we were identified, hundreds of warriors streamed through the gate and lined up for battle outside the fort. I called a halt at least two hundred paces from the enemy and eyed the dust cloud of the Carpiani that was still visible behind us.

"They will be here in two parts of a watch", Adherbal said.

I nodded in agreement. "Our only way of escape is towards Argamum", I said. "We will not be able to retake Histria. There are at least four thousand warriors drawn up against us."

We walked our horses forward, planning to release a deadly volley of javelins and then retreat out of range of their heavy spears. As we initiated our approach, five riders detached from the Heruli, riding empty-handed, with their open palms held out to the side, facing upwards.

"Disengage", I shouted to the standard bearer close to me, who gave the necessary signal. The Numidians halted. We were one hundred and fifty paces from the enemy.

I signalled to Cai, Adherbal, and two of his best men to follow me as I rode to meet the Heruli.

Ten paces away, I dismounted and signalled for the rest to follow. We approached on foot. It would show them that we did not fear them, and it would also show respect.

I had spent many months in Segelinde's company, during which time she taught me the Gothic tongue. I could understand it well, although I still found some of their words difficult to pronounce.

What happened next took me by surprise.

The leader of the Heruli was a huge man whose arms bulged with muscles. He wore scale armour which extended to his knees. Gold and silver bands decorated his upper arms, testament to his skill as a warrior. His beard and hair was blonde and unruly, but his arms and armour were well-kept.

He went down on one knee and the rest of the parley group followed his example. He bowed his head. "I am named Red Wolf, Erilar of the Heruli", the giant said. "We will not fight you, lord. You wear the sacred rune armour of Teiwaz. Our magic will be useless against you. I was there when you defeated Hygelac the White. No man could ever defeat him although many tried. I witnessed how you killed him - like he was a child playing with a sword. We know that you are the messenger of the war god."

He motioned to his men and they parted, creating a gap at least a hundred paces wide.

I clasped Red Wolf's arm. "I need you to lay your hand on my armour and swear that my men and I will be safe", I said. "Do not fear, you will not be struck down by Teiwaz."

This man was the bravest of the Heruli. A fierce barbarian who had slain hundreds. Yet I could see the fear in his eyes as he laid his hand on my chest. Each of the golden scales were inscribed with a magic rune. "I swear that you, lord, and all your men, will be safe", he said. "We will defend you with our lives."

I nodded in acceptance of his oath.

Red Wolf turned around and yelled to his men in a booming voice: "Teiwaz favours us through his messenger. I have touched the armour of the god and he allowed me to live."

I entered the gap created by the warriors, followed by the Numidians. The Heruli bowed their heads and banged their spear shafts on their shields. In the distance, above the water of the Dark Sea, I could see a storm building, and as the Heruli closed their ranks behind us, lightning illuminated the sky.

The war leader of the Heruli thrust his spear in the air. "Teiwaz approves of our actions", he boomed. "The war god will strengthen our magic."

Again, shouts and chants emanated from the ranks of the barbarian warriors.

Cai turned to face me. "You see, much wisdom in listen to wife."

Chapter 5 – Wolf warriors

We entered Histria. None of the original inhabitants were left alive. The streets were littered with bodies.

"Close the gates, man the walls and burn all the bodies", I instructed Red Wolf. "Then we will talk."

He inclined his head as he went about seeing to my orders.

Segelinde had explained to me that in the culture of the Heruli, the strongest leads. The tale of my fight with Hygelac had elevated me to a god-like status. They would obey me - none would dare to gainsay my orders.

With difficulty I found a place for the Numidians to spend the night. It must have been the area originally occupied by the market. There was enough space for the men and the horses.

Adherbal was decidedly nervous. I could not blame him.

"We are in the den of the wolf, Prefect!"

"Yes, you are correct", I said. "Walk with me."

I led him to the ramparts. The barbarian horde of the Carpiani surrounded us on three sides - thousands upon thousands.

Adherbal exhaled slowly. "Maybe it will be safer in the den of the wolf after all", he sighed.

I left him in search of Red Wolf, or rather Rodoulphos. I found him in the open, sitting next to a fire with his sub-commanders. A slaughtered sheep was grilling above the roaring fire, tended to by a young warrior.

He handed me a horn of ale and I sat down next to him. "You have closed the gates to the Carpiani, I see. Are they not your allies?" I asked.

Rodoulphos grinned. "We took advantage of the turmoil in the Empire and the invasion of the Carpiani, but I have given them no oath. And", he added, "they have not filled my purse with gold. So no, they are not our allies today."

I nodded, as I understood the culture of the Sea of Grass.

"Rodoulphos, I see that the clouds hide the light of Mani", I said. "We will visit the camp of the Carpiani, leaving the first watch after midnight."

The big man smiled broadly, revealing wolf-like teeth, each filed to a point. "Lord Eochar, you look like a Roman, but you think like a Heruli." He handed me a leather bag of charcoal, ground to fine powder. "You will need this", he added.

We spent at least a third of a watch discussing tactics. I shared in the looted red wine and delicious stolen mutton, then walked back to my men.

I relayed the story to Cai and he nodded in agreement. "To do unexpected is to walk path to victory."

I stripped off all my armour, retaining my tunic, a dark cloak and boots. Cai assisted me to blacken every exposed part of my body with the charcoal, until only the whites of my eyes were discernible in the low light.

We exited the city at the sea gate and boarded the longboats. Fifty men to a boat. Ten of them silently rowed into the Dark Sea. We turned towards the land when we were a mile out and beached half a mile to the south of the Carpiani camp. They would never expect an attack from the rear, as all their sentries were placed between the walls of Histria and the camp.

I had my jian and gladius strapped to my belt. A shield would be too cumbersome. All my tutors had insisted that I become accustomed to wielding weapons with both hands. Using two swords would not be problematic.

Most of the Heruli had wolfskins draped over their shoulders to better their camouflage. The scene was akin to a troop of five hundred two-legged wolves descending onto the unsuspecting Carpiani. These men knew their business, they made no sound to give us away to the enemy.

The wolves spread out between the sleeping men, working in pairs as planned. At the signal of Rodoulphos the men howled like wolves. Although I was a part of the wolf pack, I could still feel the hairs raising at the back of my neck. It was a sign for the killing to start.

The aim was not to kill thousands, but if each of the Heruli could take down at least two men and disappear into the night, we would have dealt them a serious blow.

I was paired with Rudoulphos and we stood back to back. Around us, confused men rose from their sleep. In quick succession, I put down three men with accurate thrusts to the neck. A fourth managed to get his hand on a sword. I blocked his blow with my gladius and dispatched him with a rising cut, nearly severing his arm.

My partner tapped me on the shoulder and we retraced our steps towards the edge of the camp, cutting down men who stood in our way.

When we were clear, we turned around and ran back to the ships silently.

Behind us we could hear shouts and screams as the Carpiani killed each other in the confusion. We were out of range when the first of the arrows landed in our wake.

The Heruli war leader grinned his wolf-like grin. "Trick is not to get carried away", he said.

Soon we were back on board and rowing out to sea.

We lost no warriors in the attack. These were the best of the Heruli - the shape-shifting masters of the runes. On the morrow, the Carpiani would fail to find any bodies of attackers and they would be filled with fear of the demons that come in the night.

The following morning at first light, Adherbal woke me.

"Prefect. You would want to see this", he said.

I have had precious little sleep, but followed him to the walls.

The Carpiani warriors were leaving. They would escort their loot across the border rather than risk another night beneath the walls of a city infested with shape-shifters that cannot be slain.

Rodoulphos appeared at my side. "The Heruli will return home", he said. "We have much loot, but even better than that, we have many tales to tell during the winter. I have raided side by side with the chosen of Teiwaz. Never before had we lost none during a night raid. Your magic is strong, Lord Eochar."

* * *

I placed my empty goblet of wine on the table of Governor Tullus Menophilus and leaned back on the comfortable couch in his office in Durostorum.

"If I had not been with you on the walls of Aquileia, I would have doubted your story, Prefect", he said.

He refilled my goblet. "Two days after the barbarian cavalry left to pursue you, we tried to engage with the Gothic infantry", he said, "but when morning came, we discovered that they had abandoned their position during the night."

The governor sighed. "Again the Carpiani and their allies have taken advantage of the internal problems of Rome. That is ever the case."

We clasped arms and parted ways.

That was the last time I would see Tullus Menophilus, hero of Aquileia.

Chapter 6 – Meeting (November 239 AD)

Hostilius gestured with his open hands. "I can't even remember when last we had a good fight", he said. "Legionaries are not made to sit around doing nothing. Soon they will be fighting each other."

"We did campaign against the Carpiani last year", I said.

"Yes, I recall", he added with a sarcastic scowl. "We were forced to travel halfway around the Empire. And what did we accomplish? Nothing! I didn't even get to unsheathe my gladius. They could have sent you on your own. You were the one who put the fear of the gods into the barbarians when they ran back across the border."

Cai walked through the door, accompanied by Hostilius's clerk.

He bowed respectfully to the centurion and then to me.

"Prefect, I receive message, your presence required on farm", Cai said.

I went cold inside. Although Nik was still in good health he was not getting any younger and I knew that I would inevitably be receiving bad news.

"Well, then you had better get going", Hostilius said. "The ride will take at least two thirds of a watch and it is getting late."

Hostilius had long known that Cai was no ordinary servant. I had taken the Primus Pilus into my confidence and had told him the story of how my path had crossed with the man from the land of Serica.

Cai turned to Hostilius. "Message says you to go as well, Centurion. Must be important. Message brought by clerk of legate."

He handed a scroll to Hostilius, containing the written orders from the commander of the legion.

Hostilius raised his eyebrows and my concern over my father's health disappeared. This was official business.

Two-thirds of a watch later we rode up to my villa on the farm outside Sirmium.

Nik was waiting for us outside the gates, his hands folded behind his back. Segelinde was not at the farm, as she was at our villa in Sirmium which we had purchased months before. We did however visit the farm regularly.

We dismounted and the guards led the horses away. Nik was all business. "Follow me", he said.

Outside our front door stood four of the biggest men I had ever laid eyes on. They wore barbarian clothes and their arms and faces carried multiple scars. Nik turned to us and said: "Leave your weapons here." It was a strange request, but I sensed Nik's serious mood and made eye contact with Hostilius, giving him an imperceptible nod. Cai, as small as he was, could easily kill with his bare hands, but these men did not afford him a second glance.

We entered and Nik motioned for me to wait and led Cai and Hostilius into the study.

Nik emerged a couple of heartbeats later. I followed him to the dining room, where another two guards barred the door. My father nodded and they let me enter after a quick search for concealed weapons.

Inside the room on the couches sat two men and a boy of no more than fifteen summers.

I recognised senator Rutilius Crispinus, but the other two were not familiar.

Crispinus immediately rose and embraced me. "It is good to find you well, Lucius", he said, and steered me towards the boy with his arm around my shoulders.

The boy stood, smiled sincerely, and clasped my arm.

"Lucius, I want you to meet the emperor", Crispinus said. For a moment I did not know what to do and then I went down on one knee and inclined my head.

Gordianus III smiled again. "Lucius Domitius, please rise. Senator Crispinus told me that you saved us all on the walls of Aquileia. It is good to meet you", he said.

While I was recovering from the shock, I clasped arms with the third man, who was a few years younger than the senator, and appeared to be in his late forties. "Well met, Lucius", the stranger said.

"Gaius Timesitheus is a friend of mine", Crispinus explained. "I am serving as the governor of Lugdunensis and Gaius is the procurator."

"Well met, sir", was the only thing I could think of to say.

The boy emperor retook his seat, followed by the rest of the guests, and Crispinus gestured for me to join my father on the couch opposite him and Timesitheus.

He motioned towards Gordian. "The senate is assisting the emperor following the untimely death of his joint emperors, Pupienus and Balbinus and …"

Gordian interrupted him mid-sentence. "What the senator is trying to say, Lucius, is that I am too young to rule. They have asked him and Gaius to assist me. Please carry on senator."

Crispinus grinned. "That is one of the reasons the emperor is here today", he conceded. "To watch and learn. Officially he is in camp, on his way to visit the Danubian legions."

He continued, now with a serious expression. "Let me get to why we are here today. There is trouble in the eastern provinces. For years, the Parthians fought the internal uprising of the Persian resurgence under Ardashir. He eventually reached his goal and became the dominant power among the Parthian lords six years ago. Ardashir immediately attacked the Roman border fort at Nisibis, garrisoned by the Legio III Parthica, but we sent them packing. Alexander Severus held victory celebrations back home in Rome."

I nodded, Nik having always kept me up to date with happenings around the Empire.

"Then all went quiet while the king of kings was bringing the last of the Parthian opposition to heel. Until recently, that is."

Crispinus leaned forward conspiratorially. "Shapur, the son of Ardashir, attacked the forts at Nisibis and Harran a few weeks ago. A number of survivors escaped, the rest were slaughtered or taken as slaves. The Sasanians constructed siege engines and battered down the walls. This is not something the Parthians were capable of."

He frowned then. "For some time now we thought that we were dealing with the same foe, just a different name, but we were wrong. Parthia was content to defend its borders. Ardashir and Shapur have a desire to revive the Persian Empire of old. Like Darius and Xerxes they wish to expand their domain. They do not fight as the Parthians did. We have underestimated them at our peril."

Timesitheus picked up the thread. "The problem is that we do not know what we are dealing with. Rome needs to respond and do it quickly, but we lack reliable information."

"This is where you come into the picture", Crispinus said. "We need you and your man from Serica to scout the lay of the land. We have spies, but none who understands war. None who is able to assess the quality of the enemy troops. The mission we have in mind requires special skills."

Silence descended on the meeting as we digested the information. "What exactly do you have in mind for my son and his companions?" Nik asked.

Crispinus answered directly. "They will travel through the lands of the Scythians and continue past the Ural River, skirt the eastern border of the Sea of Islands, and join the Silk Road at Maracanda. We will supply them with silk and spices as they will pose as travellers from the land of Serica, approaching Persia from the east."

It was Nik's turn to frown. "I have heard of that road. They would have to travel through the lands of the Kangju and the

Kushans. It will be dangerous. Some would say that it is impossible."

Crispinus glanced in my direction. "We require that Primus Pilus Hostilius Proculus travel with you, Lucius. We value the opinion that a man with his experience will add to your report."

Before Nik could object I said: "I will do this, but only if Cai agrees out of his own free will. He is a free man from the land of Serica and the choice is his to make. Hostilius, like me, is a soldier and we will obey."

Crispinus held up an open palm. "No, this is different. Rome already owes you a great debt. This mission will not be forced on you. Should you wish to decline, no word will be mentioned about this ever again."

Hostilius and Cai were summoned.

The Primus Pilus listened to Timesitheus's request stone-faced. "I understand and I will obey", he said and saluted.

Cai volunteered to join the expedition even before he was asked to go. "Wise general of Han said that to be victorious in battle, enemy must be studied. This wise. I go to make sure you remain alive."

When Cai and Hostilius were dismissed, I smiled and asked: "How many bolts of silk would we need to transport to make the ruse believable?"

Crispinus's eyes narrowed. "Well, at least seven hundred bolts of silk would be my estimate."

I did the arithmetic in my mind. "Would it be unreasonable to ask whether we could retain the proceeds of the sale of the material?"

The young Gordian laughed out loud. "You are truly a Roman, Lucius Domitius. And yes, you may keep the proceeds, but even better than that, you would gain the gratitude of the emperor."

Chapter 7 – Logistics

Hostilius, having earlier agreed to the request of the emperor, was philosophic after the fact.

"That's what they tell you, Domitius. We never really had a choice, but by offering us a choice, they get us to buy into the whole idea, giving us a feeling of ownership."

I was bowled over by the deep response of my brutish Primus Pilus. As always, Cai provided the retort.

"For barbarian, you are closer to Dao than it appears."

Hostilius scowled.

In any event, our imperial guests had departed and we spent an enjoyable evening with Nik and Felix. We spoke about the coming mission.

"It will take time to arrange all", Nik said. "Timesitheus will return in the spring with the packhorses and the goods."

He drank deeply from his goblet. "You need someone who speaks the tongue of the Persians", my father added.

Then Felix raised an even more pressing issue. "So Umbra, how are you going to break this news to Segelinde?"

I replied truthfully. "That is a very good question."

* * *

Two days later I stood in the atrium of my villa in Sirmium, facing an angry Segelinde. She placed her hands on her hips and looked at me defiantly.

"Segelinde, I will have none of it", I said. "My decision is final. You will not travel with us."

I was losing the fight and in desperate need of support. "Ask Cai how dangerous it will be, even if you only travel with us until we reach the lands of the Goths." I looked over my shoulder for support. Cai wore his face of stone. I scowled.

I narrowed my eyes at Segelinde. "Did you arrange this with Cai?" I asked. "Are you that devious?"

Cai answered on behalf of my wife. "Lucius of the Da Qin, you are closer to Dao than it appears."

I soon realised that my wife would travel with us, no matter what I said. She would visit with her family in the lands of the Thervingi Goths. Her excitement about the coming journey was infectious and I realised that I had been wrong to be overly protective.

With Segelinde content, I could focus on addressing the next problem, which was finding a man I could trust who happened to speak Persian.

I sat in my office, studying the list of cavalrymen of eastern origin provided to me by Marcus. One name seemed familiar, a duplicarius called Vibius Marcellinus. I was curious and I had the junior officer summoned to my quarters.

The cavalry was involved in training manoeuvres and I was forced to keep my curiosity in check until the second watch of the afternoon. There was a knock on the door and Cai stepped in, followed by a familiar face.

The officer saluted. I returned his salute. "At ease", I said.

I clasped his arm. "Vibius, how are you keeping?" I asked. "I haven't laid eyes on you since we had joined the legion."

I could see that he did not fully trust my familiarity. "I have been doing well, Prefect", he answered cautiously. "The heavy losses the cavalry sustained when we were ambushed by the Yazyges three years ago opened up opportunities."

"I remember well, Vibius. That same attack gave me the chance to become a centurion", I replied.

I sighed, poured two cups of my best red wine and handed one to Vibius.

I was never one for beating around the bush. "Vibius, I spent time with you when we enrolled into the legion, yet it was only for a couple of weeks. But we became friends, although after that our paths separated. Life is life."

He nodded and sipped on the wine, still suspicious.

"Before I continue, let me ask you one question. Are you able to speak the tongue of the Persians?"

"I grew up in Palmyra in the province Syria Palaestina. My father was a Roman functionary. He and my mother were too involved with their social calendar to look after children. My sister and I were raised by a Parthian slave woman from Gorgan, near the Hyrcanian Sea. Barsini was her name", Vibius explained.

I could see that he was recalling happy memories from his childhood and I allowed him the time.

Snapping back to the present he said: "The answer is yes, Lucius. I can speak it better than a Parthian."

I gestured for him to take a seat and refilled our cups. I sat down as well. "I have a proposal for you, Vibius", I said.

We spoke for a full watch, mostly because we enjoyed the conversation, but also to enable me to provide Vibius with enough information to make an informed decision. He agreed to join us, although he understood that the risks were a great many, and the reward uncertain.

The three winter months were unusually cold but the time passed quickly due to the preparations. Early in the month of the war god Mars our small group rode out to the farm. Timesitheus had arrived.

Chapter 8 – Crossing the Danube (March 240 AD)

Gaius Timesitheus possessed an incredible capacity for attention to detail and it soon became evident why he had been tasked with the arrangements.

He looked up from the map spread out on the table in the study, pressing his stylus onto a marked location. "Do not be fooled. Ardashir has many spies in the lands of Rome", he said. "Silk does not travel from west to east within the borders of the Empire. It will arouse suspicion. You will travel east to the fort at Novae. That is where you will cross the river and meet up with the horse caravan that will arrive a day in advance."

He drank some wine to wet his throat. "By the way, Lucius, where do you get this wine?", he asked. "I can't even get this in Gaul!"

I smiled. "My father knows things about people and they give it to him to keep quiet", I explained.

He grinned at what he thought was an obvious jest.

"I will ensure that a batch of amphorae travel with you when you leave, sir", I said.

Timesitheus inclined his head, accepting my offer.

"I will travel to Novae with an advance party, leaving in three days, on the eighth day of March", he added. "You will leave on the tenth day and arrive at Novae on the twenty-first day of March. Make sure you pace yourself." He handed Hostilius an itinerary with the route of each day indicated. The centurion nodded, accepting the scroll. "On the afternoon of the twenty-first, you must rest five miles outside of Novae. I will meet you there and ensure that you cross the river and join the caravan. Three turmae of praetorian cavalry will escort you for the first two days of your trip into the barbarian lands. From then on you are on your own."

"I am aware that you have strange alliances with the Scythians, Sarmatians and even the Goths", he said, and held up his open palm to discourage any response. "Which we approve of, as we know your true loyalty lies with the Empire. It is also the reason why you were chosen for the mission. For anyone else, this would be impossible."

We departed on the tenth day of March. Timesitheus gave me command of the mission. Not because I held the highest rank, but due to my knowledge of the Sea of Grass. He handed me written orders that carried the seal of the emperor.

I insisted that Hostilius shave his head and grow a beard. Vibius would grow his hair and a beard, but I would remain clean-shaven. To fit in with the eastern way, of course.

Hostilius agreed, reluctantly.

We all rode Hunnic horses, so to achieve the required distance was easy. My wife rode with us and all enjoyed her company. Even Hostilius scowled less.

"Centurion, it is a pity you are not allowed to grow a beard in the legions. It suits you", Segelinde said.

From then on, I knew the next challenge would be to get him to shave the beard when we returned. If we returned.

We enjoyed the journey and stayed over in some or other inn every night. Timesitheus had booked the accommodation in advance. On the twenty-first day of March we rested next to the road, five miles from Novae. Timesitheus arrived within a third of a watch, escorted by five praetorians.

"Right on time, Prefect. Let's get going", was all he said.

Timesitheus and his entourage cautiously skirted Novae, left the road, and walked their horses into the dense shrubs that bordered the river. We followed close behind.

"Now we wait for the cover of darkness", he said.

Once the darkness was thick around us, one of his men who had been watching, appeared. "They are here", he whispered.

We walked our horses to the river's edge where a large military barge lay anchored against the bank. The barge was seventy feet long and ten feet wide. It resembled a floating bridge and was built to be easily accessible to horses and wagons. As a result, it did not prove difficult to get the horses aboard.

Soon we were silently gliding across the mighty Danube.

As we approached the eastern bank, Timesitheus clasped my arm. "May the gods keep you safe and guide you, Prefect Lucius Domitius", he whispered.

I nodded.

We walked the horses through the shallows and ascended the far bank with the cavalrymen leading the way. As always, Timisitheus planned ahead and they had prepared a camp with tents and enough cold fare of quality. We enjoyed the cheese, olives and smoked pork, all swallowed down with excellent red wine.

Exhausted, we retired for the night.

Early the next morning we were three miles into the hinterland when it became light enough to travel at a faster pace than walking. Within less than a mile, the trooper leading our party held up a hand and whistled three times. He led us off the greenway to a clearing where the turmae of cavalry were waiting with the caravan of silk and horses.

Hostilius reined in next to me as a haughty officer walked his horse towards our group and saluted. "I am Tribune Gaius Julius Priscus, attached to the Praetorian Guard. I am leading your escort, the three turmae of cavalry", he said.

We returned his salute and introduced ourselves. "I am the one leading the convoy", I said. "During the time that you escort us, I will command, by order of the emperor." Strangely he did not acknowledge my statement, but I brushed it off as we would only have to endure him for two days.

I felt at ease, as we had crossed into the tribal lands of my people, the Roxolani. I did not expect to come across any of their patrols as they were at peace with Rome and no invasion would come from the south.

I approached Priscus. "Do you have outriders patrolling the area?" I asked to be sure.

"Yes, two ahead, two behind us and two on each flank", he said. He obviously knew his business.

I nodded and fell back to talk to Segelinde and Cai. Hostilius was riding next to Vibius who was teaching him to say 'where may I find a tavern with decent women and cheap wine' in Persian.

The lush vegetation so typical of the Danube region was growing sparser. From time to time we passed through clearings and valleys devoid of anything but the typical grass of the plains.

We were trotting through a treeless valley when Simsek's ears pricked up. I immediately called a halt, strung my Hunnic bow and hung it across my back. From a distance I saw the advance scouts galloping hard in our direction. I walked my horse and reined in next to Priscus. The scouts and their horses were breathing heavily. "Sixty nomads up front, sir. It looks like Carpiani. Huge bloody horses, armoured like their riders, with scale and chain." Most of the troopers, as well as all in our party, heard the words uttered by the scout.

The Roman cavalry would be slaughtered by the heavy horse of the Carpiani. We could not outrun them as we were laboured with the packhorses carrying the bolts of silk and bundles of spices.

I made the decision and commanded Priscus: "Tell your men to dismount and report to me."

He looked at me the way one would look at a child speaking out of turn in the company of adults. "I have been fighting barbarians while you were still nursed by your mother, boy", he hissed. "If we dismount we are as good as dead."

It was clear that Priscus regarded me with contempt and that he would get us all killed. He had not donned his helmet yet, so I motioned for him to come closer, as if to whisper something to him. As he complied, I struck him on the temple with the pommel of my dagger. He slid from his horse, but I steadied him and gestured to a trooper to take him away.

His men gaped at me with shock and I boomed in my best centurion voice: "Is there anyone else who wish to gainsay the direct orders of the emperor?" I waited a couple of heartbeats and repeated the offer, but could find no volunteers. Not obeying orders by your superior officer is punishable by death, especially when you have no rank.

"Get them to dismount", I said to Hostilius who had appeared next to me. I pointed to a small hill a hundred paces distant. "We will form a half-circle, with our backs against that rocky copse. Hobble the horses and get them behind us. Primus Pilus, we require a wall of shields with spears protruding between them. If we cannot get this right, we die."

Hostilius did not get to be a primus pilus for nothing. Within heartbeats all had moved to the hill and the horses were hobbled. He was correcting the line and pushing the cavalry shields into the correct position.

"If all this goes wrong, you stay with Cai and ride to safety", I said to Segelinde. "Either to the river or to the Roxolani. The Carpiani will never catch the Hunnic horses."

"No need be concerned, Lucius of the Da Qin. No evil will befall her", Cai replied.

I nodded and retrieved three quivers and both bows.

We had hardly formed up when the earth began to tremble and the enemy appeared over the crest of the hill. I could see that they were surprised at our tactics. No horse can be made to run into a solid wall, and the riders were aware that they could not simply bowl us over. Neither could they outflank us, as the rock-strewn ground next to the copse created a natural barrier against riders. They walked their horses slowly down the hill until they were a hundred paces from us.

I had time to study them. The riders were protected by scale and chain and wore conical helmets with nose guards, the rest of their faces were covered with chain as were all the vulnerable parts of their horses. They carried spears, at least ten feet long, with thick wooden shafts. These weapons were too heavy to handle single-handed, so no shield could be carried. Multi-coloured feathers adorned the shafts, fastened just below the heavy iron spear tips. The wings of the spear tips were turned back on themselves to prevent the spear getting stuck in an enemy. They had no bows, but I noticed hand axes and maces tied to their saddles, as well as longswords at their sides.

We outnumbered them, but if it came to hand-to-hand combat, many Romans would die trying to put down one of these iron-clad monsters.

All my arrows were armour-piercing and at a hundred paces, I decided to risk a shot.

I identified the leaders as the two men talking and pointing in our direction. I prayed for Arash to guide my arrow as I drew back the mighty composite bow to its full extent. As the arrow left the string I knew that it would fly true and a heartbeat later one of the Carpiani tumbled backwards from his saddle, as if struck by a war hammer. An arrow protruded from the eyehole of his helmet.

The Carpiani charged. It was a reaction to my arrow rather than a sound tactical decision. Nonetheless, they rode boot to boot in a near straight line. I was unable get a clear shot at the other leader, but managed to topple four riders before they reached our shield wall. Most of my arrows were wasted and just deflected off the thick armour.

I never really understood their plan, or if they even had one. They charged, but then had to slow down their horses before they impacted our line. It ended up as a spear jostling contest. I imagine that they had hoped for a gap to appear in our line. That would have provided them with the opportunity to break through and lay into us with their maces and axes.

With Hostilius in command, our line held.

At a range of ten paces, my needle point arrows could pierce nearly any armour. After losing ten men to spears and arrows, the Carpiani disengaged and retreated a hundred and fifty paces to regroup. Four of the Roman cavalrymen lay dead, pierced by the long lances which found small gaps between shields.

"These men are attacking us because they think we were are Romans", I said to Hostilius. "I will go speak with them."

I mounted Simsek and walked forward forty paces. I wore my Scythian scale armour of hooves and my ornate Scythian helmet.

Less than ten heartbeats passed when the surviving leader detached from the group. He walked his horse and stopped ten paces from me. I could see why he was their leader. He was a bear of a man, his muscles visible under his thick chain armour.

He spat in my direction and hissed in broken Latin. "What do you want, Roman?" he asked. "Is it not enough that you reneged on the payment that was due to us? Now you invade the land of the Scythian. You will die here today. That is the wish of Arash, the god of war and fire."

I replied in Latin, speaking slowly so that he could follow me. "Who are you to know the wishes of Arash?"

He did not answer my question. "Who are you, Roman pig?" he sneered.

I removed my helmet and replied in the language of the Sea of Grass. "My name is Eochar, nephew to King Apsikal and sword brother to King Bradakos of the Roxolani. I am a prince of the Royal Scythians. Do you dare to attack me in my own lands? Unprovoked? Do you challenge the might of the Hunnic alliance that you are surely aware of? Do you wish to be the cause of the annihilation of your people?"

He immediately removed his helmet and I saw that his complexion was ashen, realising the terrible position he had just placed himself in.

He dismounted and kneeled in front of my horse with both hands in the dust.

"I am called Thiaper, lord. I am a junior cavalry commander of the Carpiani. I have heard your name whispered on the steppes. You are the one who speaks to the god of war and fire, the one favoured by Arash the destroyer."

I decided to push this a bit further. "Do you wish to test the will of the gods and face me in single combat?"

I did not believe it possible, but he turned even paler. "Lord, no man can defeat you. If you choose to take my life, it is yours, but only a fool would anger Arash and spend eternity wandering the shadows."

I did not reply for at least a hundred heartbeats. I could see the sweat forming on his bowed head and dripping to the ground via his nose, even though the day was bitterly cold.

"You will escort us to the summer camp of the Roxolani to ensure that none of this foolishness is repeated. There you will apologise to the king and send him a hundred horses on your return to your lands."

Chapter 9 – Thiaper

I dismounted and extended my hand to raise Thiaper to his feet. "Rest easy, Thiaper of the Carpiani. All will be well. Arash has brought you across my path."

That seemed to settle him and the colour returned to his face. "Bury your dead with honour. Be here tomorrow at first light." He nodded. I had spoken.

Slowly I turned my horse and made my way back to where the Roman shield wall was still intact.

I glanced over my shoulder and I could see the Carpiani collecting their dead.

"Stand down, at ease", I said, addressing the Roman soldiers.

I dismounted and walked to where Segelinde was standing next to Cai. Before I could speak he nodded. "Best way to make war is not fight."

She embraced me. "There will be no more fighting today", I said.

I heard a commotion and walked over to where the cavalrymen were bunching. Priscus had regained consciousness and a decurion was reviving him with water.

I knew that to confront Priscus would not end well. For him, that is. Although I never shied away from conflict, I avoided it where possible.

I took one of the decurions by the arm. "Follow me, Decurion", I said.

When we were out of earshot I said: "Tribune Priscus is in no state to lead. He is injured. I am placing you in command."

"Yes, Prefect, I understand and I will obey", he said, and saluted.

"Here are your orders", I said. "You will mount immediately, turn your three turmae around and report to Timesitheus. Your mission is concluded. In my report, I will state that Priscus was wounded in an attempt to save us. I do not wish to cause trouble."

He nodded.

"Do it, and leave immediately", I said, and dismissed him.

The decurion was true to his word and shortly we were on our own, save for the forty packhorses loaded with silk.

We did not light a fire, but feasted on the cold fare. Hostilius used his dagger to menacingly stir honey into his wine. He possessed the talent to turn a basic activity like stirring wine into a brooding, intimidating affair.

He took a deep swallow. "You seem to trust these Carpiani, Domitius", he growled. "They have been Roman allies for many years, but recently they have turned against us and started raiding into Moesia Inferior, which you are well aware of. Things like that worry me, how quickly they turn against their allies." He added more honey and stirred again. "That is why I am reluctant to trust them."

I nodded, took a swallow from my cup, and kept quiet for a while, allowing the wine to warm me from the inside. "You are not wrong, Primus Pilus", I said. "The tribes of the steppes are easy to anger and slow to forgive. They have a culture and religion based on war and conflict. I will speak with their commander, Thiaper, on the morrow. Then I will seek to understand."

We lit no fires, and huddled together in the tents, wrapped in thick furs. All of us, except Segelinde, would take turns to watch during the night.

I had drawn the last watch before sunrise. At the appointed hour, I reluctantly left the comfort of the warm furs and donned my Scythian scale armour. I took my bear cloak and draped it over my shoulders as I left the tent. It felt good to be back in the lands of the Scythians and I realised that I was looking forward to riding with the Carpiani. They were not that different from my own people, the Roxolani.

I had to walk around to warm my limbs so I went to check on the horses and their precious cargo which was stacked next to the tents. Every horse carried fifty pounds of silk, which equated to about sixteen bolts. That translated to two thousand pounds of silk and six hundred and forty bolts in total. Silk was worth a third of its weight in gold, meaning we carried the equivalent of six hundred pounds of gold. To put it differently, nearly fifty thousand gold aurei worth of silk. We would be a tempting target.

I did not tell Vibius and Hostilius that we would keep the proceeds of the silk. I carried that weight alone, but they would each receive a quarter of whatever we retained.

I was still deep in thought when the Carpiani arrived. They rode smaller steppe horses and their young apprentices led their warhorses.

They dismounted fifty paces from our camp and Thiaper approached on his own.

I appeared from the shadows and the Scythian's hand went to his sword, which was a reflex reaction.

"Peace, commander", I said, and showed him my open palms.

He smiled. "My apologies, lord, but you know that no Scythian trusts the darkness", he said. "It is the time when the shades wander the Sea of Grass."

While the rest of our party readied to leave, Thiaper and his men assisted with loading the silk onto the packhorses. As they had an intimate knowledge of horses, like all Scythians, the bolts were expertly fastened with the weight spread around.

Thiaper studied the horses. "The Romans must have magnificent horses in their lands", he said.

"Why do you say that, Thiaper?" I asked.

He looked at me as if the answer was obvious. "These packhorses are splendid animals", he replied. "They would be good for riding as well."

I grinned. "They are not packhorses, Thiaper. My plan is to exchange them for the horses of the steppes. I cannot trade packhorses for steppe horses. I needed good horseflesh to trade with."

He grinned like a wolf. "I would trade forty of my apprentices' horses for these animals."

"I will think on it", I said.

We could not travel at speed with the pack animals, but we did manage a trot in between rests. Hostilius was not used to travelling on a horse and I could see that he struggled. He would never complain.

It was early spring and the Sea of Grass was teeming with new life after the cold of winter. The day was cloudless and beautiful and I found the ride relaxing and enjoyable. We were in friendly territory and protected by heavily armed men.

I sped up my horse until I drew level with Thiaper. We talked about many things and I found that I liked him. He was of an age with me, and also born of mixed tribes. His father had been a Dacian, killed in battle with Rome when Thiaper was a boy. His mother was of noble blood of the Carpiani and he was raised as such by her family. I told him about my travels and he found the Huns fascinating. He had heard of them, yet never met one.

A comment he had made earlier when we met stuck in my mind, and I decided to ask him about it. "Thiaper, you mentioned that Rome owed the Carpiani gold. Are you willing to share the tale with me?"

"As long as the Roman blood in you will not take offence, lord", he said.

I nodded and he continued. "For many, many years, my people have been allied with Rome. We protected our borders against foreign tribes and so shielded the borders of the Empire. In turn, we traded with Rome and we flourished. We were allowed to buy iron and mail which, as you know, are not so easy to get hold of on the steppes. The Goths appeared on the scene and the Carpiani heard that they were paid many talents of gold for peace. An envoy was sent to the governor of Moesia Inferior. It was the first term of the man called Menophilus. Noblemen and warriors were sent to ask Menophilus whether Rome would honour the Carpiani with a payment of gold as well."

He looked at me as he interrupted himself. "Lord, you might be of Roman blood, but I am not blind to see that you are a Scythian in your heart. You know our way. It is the way of honour. It is the direct way. It is not the way of lies and deceit."

I nodded and he continued, content that I understood. "This man, Menophilus, treated the men badly. He made them wait for ten days before he granted them an audience. When it finally happened, he had his commanders present but mostly ignored the men of our delegation. They asked him about the gold and he said that the emperor will give gold to whom he chooses, but that he would give them an answer when four moons had passed. When the time came and the men returned, he again treated them with contempt and told them to come back in another three moons. Reluctantly they returned and he told them that there would be no gold, but if they so choose, they could throw themselves at the feet of the emperor, and then maybe he would give them gold out of pity."

I believed the tale. Many Romans thought the barbarians to be stupid because they were unable to read and write. They viewed them as children due to their reluctance to deceive. Menophilus made a grave error in his handling of the situation. He had insulted the honour of these men.

"Why did they not attack immediately?" I asked.

"They bided their time", he said. "When we were told of the Romans fighting amongst themselves, we mobilised and raided their lands. The Goths joined us when they heard of the death of the Thracian. They said that they had given the emperor an oath not to attack, but that the oath died with the emperor."

"You are correct, the Goths do not give oaths to an Empire. They give oaths to men. It is their way", I confirmed.

"In Rome it is expected of the nobles to deceive", I explained. "That is their way. I am not fond of it, and I now understand why you invaded the land."

More would come to light later on. Sadly, it did not end well for Menophilus.

Chapter 10 – Vandali

After two days in the saddle, we were intercepted by a Roxolani patrol.

The Carpiani was not enemies of my people, but the fifty horse archers' approach made them close ranks and form a defensive line. I pushed my horse through the ranks and rode ahead to meet the riders. I could see that they had their bows at the ready, so I held my hands at my side, palms open.

A single rider detached from the group and soon a smiling Elmanos clasped my arm. "It is always good to see you, lord", he said.

"And you, Elmanos", I replied.

Before the sun had set, Cai, Segelinde and I were seated in the tent of the king, my friend and mentor.

We shared our wine and our story with him.

"I have brought you three amphorae so you can think of us while we are in the land of Persia", I said.

Bradakos drank deeply, savouring the excellent vintage. "Then I will think of you often, Eochar", he said, and refilled his cup.

I had told him about my encounter with Thiaper. "I have another suggestion for you Eochar. I have been planning a little adventure of my own", the king said. He touched Segelinde on the shoulder. "My daughter could stay here for a few days while we show your Roman friends the countryside."

I grinned, knowing that the last thing in the world Bradakos would enjoy is a relaxed tour of the countryside. "So, who will we be fighting?" I asked.

"They speak of themselves as the Shining Wanderers, but your people call them the Vandali. It seems to me that the whole world is moving someplace. The Vandali is encroaching on our territory and have overrun the Costoboci to the northwest. We do not desire to fight them, but we need to show them that it would be a mistake to cross swords with the Roxolani."

"Have Gordas and his men returned from their war in the east?" I asked.

Bradakos grinned like a wolf and I knew what the answer was.

"If Gordas and his men are with you, Bradakos, I will not stay away for all the gold in the world", I said, and grinned.

The king suggested to forgive Thiaper the hundred horses if he agreed to accompany us. We would also travel closer to his home which would suit him.

Segelinde was grateful to have a few days of rest, but Vibius and Hostilius insisted on joining us. Cai agreed to stay in camp with my wife.

The king chose to take four hundred heavy cavalry on the excursion.

The next morning was overcast and the pre-dawn light provided little illumination. We were busy adjusting our saddles by the light of fires when I felt the earth vibrate, followed by the bone-chilling howls of human wolves. The Huns had arrived.

Hostilius gave me a sideways glance and grinned. "It seems we will be meeting your old friends soon enough."

His grin vanished as soon as they appeared from the gloomy surrounds. With the grace of a cat Gordas jumped from his horse, throwing the reins to an underling. His scarred and tattooed face broke into a smile and he embraced me like he would a brother.

"The gods favour us. Arash has sent his messenger!" the Hun said.

He placed his hand on my beardless cheek. "It is good that you are rid of the hair in your face. All that is left to do is add the marks of the warrior."

"It is good to see you too, Gordas", I said. "For now, I will leave my face as it is."

He frowned. "It is a pity, you could have been handsome." He proceeded to laugh at his own attempt at humour, somehow emphasizing the deformation of his skull as the swirling tattoos on his elongated forehead came to life in the flickering light.

Gordas ignored Vibius and Hostilius and jumped back onto his horse. "We will feast together tonight, Eochar. I would hear your tales."

I nodded and he turned his horse and rode off at breakneck speed, howling of course.

"I'll be damned", Hostilius said. "By all the gods alive, was that even a man? At least it seems to be fond of you, Domitius, which means it won't try to kill us."

"Let me give you some advice Primus Pilus. Don't put your hand on your sword again while you are in their company", I said.

Hostilius lifted his hand from where it had been resting on the hilt of his gladius. "Thanks for the tip, next time tell me in advance", he said and scowled.

Vibius stared reflectively at the dust that still hung in the air after Gordas had ridden away. "Barsini, the Persian slave woman who raised me, shared a tale with me from her childhood. She told me that to the north of Gorgan, on the steppes, there dwells a great evil. Demons, part man part horse, roam the land. No one would venture north for fear of meeting them. In days long past, the evil spilled into the land of Gorgan, killing and plundering. The Parthian king of kings fought against the demon invasion, but they could not be defeated as they would just disappear into the night to appear again and strike elsewhere. Eventually he ordered that a wall be built, a wall that no horseman could surmount. The Great Wall of Gorgan took ten years to build and spans more than a hundred miles. The wall is thirty feet wide and ten feet high. It connects the Hyrcanian Ocean to the west with the mountains to the east – thirty thousand soldiers is said to man the battlements."

He took a swallow from his waterskin. "I have never laid eyes on this wall. The locals call it the Red Snake or the Wolf Wall. I wrote it off as a story, a myth. Now I understand the need of such a thing."

He pointed in the direction that Gordas had taken, shaking his head in disbelief. "They must be the demons, the wolfmen Barsini spoke of."

I slapped him on the back. "At least the demons are on our side."

We rode at the fastest pace the warhorses could manage. Although they were huge, muscular and extremely fast over short distances, they did not possess the endurance of the smaller steppe horses, not even mentioning the Hunnic horses which never seemed to tire.

Gordas invited Bradakos and us, which included Hostilius and Vibius, to feast with the Huns that evening. Bradakos and I looked forward to it, but I could see that my two Roman friends were not that eager to join us.

"If you come along I will ask that they cook the food and not eat it raw as is their way", I jested.

In any event, as the sun set, and having made camp earlier, we found our way to the cooking fires of Gordas. His scouts had hunted a variety of game and wild fowl during the day. We were welcomed by the mouth-watering aroma of roasting pheasant and deer.

I produced an amphora of wine which I had packed for the occasion.

All of us sat cross-legged on old furs around the fire. I relayed what had happened to us since I last saw Gordas nearly five years before. My Hun friend greatly enjoyed the part where I had fought Hygelac the Heruli.

"I am disappointed that you did not bring us the golden armour with the magic markings", Gordas said. "I would see it next time we meet." I nodded, knowing the value the Huns placed on anything martial.

For a barbarian, Gordas went out of his way to make the evening enjoyable for Hostilius and Vibius. He retold the story, for their benefit, of how he had been saved from the Xiong-nu shaman. True to their culture, he re-enacted the story by mimicking my actions during the rescue, which was hugely exaggerated, of course. As all was told in the Hun tongue, I translated the key elements. We all drank more than we should have, but in the end it was a fine evening.

We were walking back to our tent when Hostilius said: "It was not unlike spending an evening with the boys back home. The only difference is that the food was better and the wine much better." We all laughed, but what he said was truthful.

As was the custom on the steppes, the following morning we struck camp at first light while it was still bitterly cold.

Vibius rubbed his hands together. "This place is colder now than Pannonia in the middle of winter."

I nodded. "Wait until you get to where the Huns live", I said.

We broke our fast with the leftovers from the previous evening and soon we were on our way. As we travelled north, the plains became interspersed with copses covered with small trees. As always the Huns scouted far and wide. By the first watch of the afternoon we noticed two Hun scouts approaching at full gallop. I was riding with Gordas and Bradakos when a scout reined in beside him.

"General, there is a band of riders raiding the countryside", the scout said, and spat in the dust. "They look like Goths, but they ride horses. They wear boiled leather armour and they use stabbing spears. They killed people in a small tented settlement and took the livestock. There are at least four hundred riders. It is not far from here." From his explanation it seemed that all this had taken place eight miles away, to the northeast.

Bradakos decided to send Gordas and his five hundred Huns to deal with the threat.

"Go ahead, Eochar, go with them", Bradakos said.

I smiled and followed Gordas, allowing Simsek to open his legs. We travelled at full gallop, first laying eyes on the enemy around the remains of the tented village about two miles in the distance. The Huns had sighted their prey. They howled, yelled with excitement and strung their bows.

The raiders were slow to notice us. They mounted and milled around, uncertain of how to proceed. It was then that I felt Arash whisper to me and I looked behind me towards the distant hills from where we came. My eye caught the faintest glint - the sun reflecting off metal.

I pulled my horse in next to Gordas. "We have to turn around", I shouted.

He looked at me as if I had taken leave of my senses, but then I added: "Arash wills it so."

Within heartbeats we were racing back in the direction from which we came.

"We were drawn away, Gordas", I shouted above the pounding of the hooves. "The Vandali is attacking the king. We must kill the cavalry first, then we will turn our attention on any infantry."

He nodded and passed on the commands to his men. The horses of the Huns were endowed with never-ending endurance, which was probably what saved the lives of our friends.

We raced around the base of a forested copse and I took in the scene. The five hundred Roxolani warriors and their apprentices were surrounded by three thousand Vandali. My people had been caught unawares and were not afforded the opportunity to don their armour or mount their enormous warhorses. Most of the Vandali army consisted of infantry, but at least five hundred were mounted. We could not release arrows indiscriminately as we would risk killing our own.

We approached the enemy at impossible speed, racing along their line, releasing arrow after arrow at thirty paces. At that distance, every arrow was either fatal, or inflicted a serious wound. The armour worn by the enemy did not protect them against the incredible power of the composite Hunnic bows. The warriors in the rear ranks of the enemy turned to face the new threat, their shields providing some protection against the arrows.

We came around for a second time, pouring arrows into the rear ranks of the Vandali. At Gordas's signal the Hun horde swerved to their right and then the wolves were amongst the sheep. The Huns used the lassos tied to their saddle horns to rip shields from enemy hands. Some warriors were dragged behind horses, while the Hun riders, seemingly unaware, still lay into the enemy with hand axes, swords and broad-headed stabbing spears.

I frantically pulled back on the reins, trying to locate the king. To my right, I noticed an area where the fighting seemed to be the fiercest. I turned Simsek's head and rode to save my friends. I caught a glimpse of Gordas following close behind, wearing a wolf-like grin.

"Eochar, unleash Arash's fury", Gordas shouted while swinging his axe above his head. Huns.

I had an arrow nocked and four in my draw hand. I opened a path before us as I sped towards where Hostilius and Bradakos were fighting for their lives. I pulled on Simsek's reins and as he skidded to a halt, I released the last of my arrows at the warrior facing me. The armour-piercing arrow went through his helmet and half of it disappeared into his skull.

In a heartbeat I jumped from the saddle, sword in hand. And the Vandali died. One came at me with his spear drawn back, ready to pierce my chest. I moved to the right as he lunged, allowing the spearhead to scrape along my scale armour. I severed his arm at the elbow. The next warrior was in front of me, a huge, bearded monster with a long-shafted battle-axe held high, ready to strike. His massive strength allowed him to wield the weapon with one hand. An inch of my blade entered his eye as my sword moved with the speed of lightning, scraping the rim of his shield as he tried in vain to deflect the blow. His body fell twitching at my feet. I stepped over him and took the head of an over-eager young warrior. The one who came at me from the left lost half his foot before Gordas struck him in the face with his hand axe.

The Vandali realised that no single warrior could overpower me, so eventually three of them turned to face me. A dark-haired man, thick-limbed with small pig-like eyes, brandishing a longsword, ran at me from the front while the others approached me from the left and the right. One swung his broad-headed axe from side to side like a scythe while the other carried a stabbing spear held at the ready in an overhand grip. Without thinking I attacked the man with the sword. Deflecting his strike, I opened his throat with the razor-like edge of my blade as I passed him. I turned, severed the shaft of the descending axe and cut deep into the man's thigh. The third warrior's spear struck me mid-turn and deflected off the hoof scales of my armour, but still scored a bloody line along my side as it ripped scales from the wire. He drew back to finish the job but Gordas's sword bit deep into his shoulder.

I was covered with gore, and blood dripped from my armour. The next man's eyes met mine briefly, but then he looked to the side and I knew he would not face me. He dropped his sword to run, but the Huns were now with me in numbers and no one could stand before us. I dispatched the last of the enemy to find Bradakos and Hostilius shoulder to shoulder, leaning on their swords. Vibius was standing behind them, stemming the blood from a cut to his upper arm.

Gordas and his men were looting the dead, taking scalps, heads and forearms.

Hostilius crouched down, leaning on his sword. "Domitius, these Huns are truly demons. Never have I seen or even heard of anything like this", he sighed. "But, by the gods, man, you are even scarier."

Chapter 11 – Recovery

The Roxolani lost many warriors, the Huns only a few, but the Vandali army was annihilated. It later came to light that we fought against a Vandali tribe called the Hasdingi. Following the battle, they summarily changed the direction of their migration and headed west. The Huns tend to have that effect on their enemies.

In any event, we celebrated our victory with the compulsory feast. Hostilius and Bradakos had grown close in the aftermath of the fight.

"For a barbarian king, he surely knows how to fight. He must have slain twenty of the Goth bastards", Hostilius said.

"They were Vandali, Primus Pilus", I replied.

"Don't matter to me who they were, bloody Goth bastards. They all look the same to me", he said as he raised his cup again and toasted Bradakos who was sitting at his left. Hostilius was seated on the king's right hand side, the position of honour.

Bradakos leaned forward to speak to me. "I know it was you and the Huns who saved the day, Eochar, but the centurion fought by my side." Bradakos's eyes narrowed and he said:

"Cai hasn't been training him, eh? I remember clearly he said the gods wanted him to train only you."

"No brother, but the Romans are good fighters and this man is one of their best", I said.

Again, Bradakos toasted Hostilius, who basked in the glory. "I think I am beginning to understand why you stayed with the Roxolani for so long", the Primus Pilus said.

I spent most of the evening talking to Vibius, who sat at my right. He was a bit shaken, but I had our injuries seen to by the Huns who were experts at treating wounds.

The mood was merry and soon Hostilius joined the Roxolani and Huns in singing songs, the words of which he could not understand, of course. I used the opportunity to speak with the king.

"Bradakos, we will have to leave soon, heading for the lands of the Huns. Is it possible to arrange an escort?" I asked.

"I would not have you leave our lands without an escort, Eochar", the king answered. "Gordas has already approached me, and volunteered. After today, he is rich with loot and keen to take some back to his people. He suggested to me that he takes thirty of his best men along."

Bradakos drank from his cup. "It has all been arranged", he said. "Do not worry overmuch."

I leaned in closer. "I would like to talk to you about the Carpiani." I shared my ideas with him and he nodded in agreement.

Thiaper and his men had acquitted themselves well in the fighting as they were the only ones who had been wearing armour when the Vandali sprung their trap. If not for them, the Roxolani casualties would have been much higher.

Bradakos waved Thiaper to our side and gestured for him to sit with us.

The young Carpiani bowed low and joined us on the furs.

"Thiaper, you have honoured the name of your people today", Bradakos said.

Thiaper inclined his head again. "It is the duty of a warrior, lord", he said.

"Nonetheless", Bradakos said, "we have taken four hundred horses from the enemy. One hundred of those horses are yours."

He would not interrupt the king until he was done. Bradakos took another deep swallow of Crispinus's wine.

"Lord Eochar has also agreed to trade his Roman horses for the horses of your apprentices", the king added.

All went quiet until Thiaper was sure the king was done speaking. "My lords, I thank you. I will be returning to my home a rich man. You have granted me a fortune."

Later on, Vibius and I dragged a singing Hostilius to his tent.

We rose early on the morrow, greeted by blue skies and pleasant weather.

I was adjusting the tack of my horse when Hostilius crawled out of the tent, holding a palm to his temple.

"The sweet stuff that you drank so much of last night is called mead", I explained.

Hostilius nodded his head groggily.

"You have to be careful with it", I added. "It will give you a killer headache if you drink too much."

He scowled. "You keep on giving me advice after the fact."

I motioned with my head towards his horse, which I had already saddled in anticipation of his condition. "I didn't wish to spoil your mood, you were singing songs about the Roxolani's victories over Roman armies."

He suddenly became serious. "Really? Was it really what the words meant?" Hostilius was fiercely loyal and he was shocked at his own conduct.

"I am sorry, Primus Pilus, it was a bad attempt at humour", I said.

He scowled.

To make amends I handed him a cup filled with a potion that Cai brewed especially for me. "Drink this", I said.

He reluctantly took the cup and drank the vile-tasting liquid. "If I didn't know you well, I would think that you are trying to poison me", Hostilius said, and handed the empty cup back to me.

Hostilius avoided me for the first watch of the morning as we made our way back to the summer camp of the Roxolani. I think he was angry with me for my ill-conceived attempt at humour, or maybe his mead-induced condition caused it.

In any event, during the second watch of the morning he came galloping up to where I was in conversation with Vibius.

"What was in the potion you gave me this morning?" the Primus Pilus asked.

"It is a potion that Cai mixes, centurion. He would never reveal it. His oath prohibits it", I answered.

"I see", he said, and frowned. "Well, I would have liked to prepare some for myself - not that I plan to ever overindulge again", he added.

"Why don't I just ask Cai to mix you a batch then you can use it when you need it", I offered.

"He would do that?" Hostilius asked.

"Certainly, if I asked him, he would", I said.

Hostilius rode towards the head of our column, whistling and smiling.

Chapter 12 – In-laws

I was confronted with a problem. It would be unwise to cross into the lands of the Bastarnae with the Huns in tow. The Bastarnae was allied with the Goths and the Huns was their enemy.

The only option left to me was to employ stealth. My wife and I would be accompanied by Hostilius. Segelinde had asked him to join us, maybe to try and address his misgivings regarding the Goths.

"She is such a nice girl, I couldn't say no to her", Hostilius confessed.

"I thought you disliked all 'the bloody Goths' to use your own words, Primus Pilus", I countered.

He scowled and turned away to inspect the tack of his horse, cursing under his breath.

In any event, Gordas provided the services of the same Hun scouts who had escorted us through the heavily forested lands of the Bastarnae some years earlier when I first met Segelinde.

Our scouts ranged far ahead, and although we conversed, we tried to keep it to a minimum. I rode twenty paces ahead of Segelinde and Hostilius, as I had been trained as a scout by the Huns.

The distance we had to travel was not great, but the forested terrain limited us to walking the horses.

There were occasions when our Huns appeared out of the gloom of the forest like wraiths and told us to halt, allowing a Bastarnae patrol to pass.

Three days after leaving the Roxolani tribal lands we forded the shallow river that bordered the lands of the Thervingi Goths.

The Huns still scouted to ensure our safety as we headed for the main settlement of the tribe. We did not wish to be discovered, since not all of the Goths would know Segelinde by sight.

Three days passed without incident when our Hun scouts informed us that we were within five miles of the Gothic fort. They would venture no closer, but wait for Hostilius and me to return.

We joined other travellers on the road leading up to the fort, trying not to attract unnecessary attention.

The gates of the settlement were open, with eight burly warriors guarding it. They scrutinized all who entered, asking the occasional question.

When we came close to the gate, Segelinde whispered: "The best is for me to announce myself. The only risk is if my family had fallen out of favour with the king." She spoke Latin for the benefit of Hostilius.

Segelinde directed her horse to the nearest guard and they exchanged words in the Gothic tongue. The guard yelled something to his fellows that I could not follow and at least another ten mailed guards left the parapet and raced for the gate.

Hostilius looked my way, worry etched on his face. "Domitius, is this good or bad?"

"I honestly don't know Primus Pilus", I said, and shrugged.

Then Segelinde turned towards us, smiling from ear to ear. "Things have certainly changed. It is not every day that the sister of the king arrives for a visit."

A contingent of guards escorted us to the hall of the king. No one queried the presence of Hostilius or me, although we were asked to hand over our weapons. They knew of the affection Kniva had for his sister. Only a fool would risk the wrath of the iudex of the Thervingi.

Segelinde entered the huge hall without delay, leaving the confused guards at the door.

A raging fire blazed in the hearth. Kniva sat at the table, absentmindedly tapping the flat of his dagger against the thick oak of the top, obviously deep in thought.

Kniva heard the approaching footsteps and shouted without looking up: "I commanded not to be disturbed!"

"Yes, but the new king needs to get an urgent lesson in manners", Segelinde responded.

He swung around, a heavy frown creasing his brow, but in an instant he was smiling like the Kniva I knew and he ran to embrace his sister. They held their embrace for a while, then Kniva looked up at me and said: "I knew that Eochar the giant slayer would not be far away." As he approached, I went down on one knee with Hostilius following suit.

He raised me by the hand and embraced me as well. "Welcome to the lands of the Thervingi, Prince Eochar of the Roxolani."

Hostilius was still kneeling awkwardly, not really knowing what decorum dictated.

The king sensed this, gripped his forearm in the way of the warrior and raised him.

Segelinde was standing next to her brother and said: "Centurion Hostilius assisted to protect me on the journey."

"A friend of my brother-in-law is a friend of mine", Kniva said and released Hostilius's hand, slapping him on the shoulder.

I turned to Hostilius. "Segelinde told him you hate Goths", I said. "He said he hates Romans as well."

I smiled, Hositlius eyed me suspiciously, and Segelinde scowled.

She walked over to Hostilius and linked her arm in his. "My brother is not the only one who needs manners", she said in Latin. "Come centurion, let me go introduce you to my parents."

Kniva detailed two of his guards to escort Hostilius and my wife. He also commanded them to return our weapons.

"We will join them later on when the women are done crying", Kniva said. He waved his hand and a servant appeared with two huge horns brimming with ale.

"Make preparations", he told the servant. "We will feast this night. Send word to my father and mother to attend me as soon as darkness falls. Make sure they are guarded."

The servant nodded and hurried away.

Kniva turned to me.

"First wet your throat. Then I would hear your tale from the time we last parted company", he said.

It was nearly dark when I had told him all, having emptied many horns of ale.

"I envy you, brother", he said. "You have more adventures in a couple of moons than many men have in a lifetime."

"It may be so, but it sounds much better when it is told as a tale", I replied. "Many times I felt as if the gods had abandoned me during my 'adventures'".

He laughed out loud and shook his head slowly. "You speak the truth, Eochar. You should hear the stories being told about your fight with Hygelac and how we killed his oathsworn afterwards."

"I would hear your story too, Kniva", I said.

"I will share my tale when we feast together as a family tonight. I will wait for Segelinde to hear it as well", he replied.

He stared at me then, in silence, clearly considering whether he should share something with me.

"There is something else", he said, and took a deep swallow from his horn, as if the ale could wash it away.

"If you were just passing through, I would not have told you this, but you are leaving your bride in our care. It could be many moons before you return."

I nodded, suddenly concerned for the safety of my wife.

"Four moons ago, my uncle led a war band to strike at the Venedi who dwells in the forest along our northern borders. They are a scheming race and encroach on us constantly."

He smiled and patted my shoulder. "With Hygelac gone, I had become Argunt's second in charge and battle by battle we grew closer. I don't think I was ever really his favourite, but he came to realise that I had a talent for winning wars. Sometimes I feel as if my actions are guided by Teiwaz. You would understand, Eochar. You are like me in that way."

Again, I nodded.

"In the ice forest of the north we fought a great battle against the Venedi. Although we were outnumbered, we prevailed in the end. Argunt and I were separated during the fight when I led a mounted charge at the enemy flank, which broke them eventually."

"On returning to the battlefield, I found that the iudex had fallen. An errant arrow had found his neck and he died with his sword still in his hand. A noble death."

"The kings of the Thervingi are chosen from the nobility. The warriors will however not follow a war leader who does not lead from the front, or if his bravery on the field of battle does not surpass that of his warriors."

"As many times before, I had turned the tide of the battle on that day. When the warriors learned of the demise of Argunt, they declared me the iudex of the Thervingi."

He wetted his throat with ale. "I do not tell you this to rise in your esteem, Eochar, but to sketch the background to a situation you need to understand."

"Kniva, make no mistake, I can see in your eyes that you are no fool or braggart and never have I met a man more deadly with a spear", I replied.

He smiled, and nodded in acceptance of my words. "When I was alone with his body and saying goodbye to the shade of my uncle, Teiwaz whispered to me to cut the arrow from the corpse's neck. It was a Thervingi hunting arrow."

He opened a small leather purse and placed an arrowhead on the table, with half a finger length of the bloodstained shaft still attached. "This is what I was looking at this morning when you arrived unexpectedly."

"I suspect the son of Argunt's sister, my cousin Werinbert. He was with my uncle the day that he was slain. He is next in line to be king and carries a hunting bow on his saddle. Werinbert the Cruel is the name that he is known by. He is a skilful warrior, one of the best. But he has a cruel streak. Gets it from his father's family," he said, and grinned like a boy.

Kniva was easy to like.

"And he still covets the throne?" I said. It was a statement, not a question.

"I fear that he will strike soon", Kniva answered. "He has many supporters among the warriors that are less than honourable. All he has to do is eliminate me, weave some tale, and he will be king. Should he succeed, who knows what he will do to my family?"

"Why do we not go there now and end this threat forever?" I asked.

Again he laughed and dismissed my suggestion with a wave of his hand. "You have been among the Romans too long, Eochar of the Roxolani."

Just then we heard the voices of our approaching guests. We both knew the subject was closed for discussion while we had company.

We sat on benches at the thick oak table, the hearth fire burning brightly next to us. Although I have always had Nik to look after me, I never experienced the joy of having a real family. Being with the family of Segelinde was the closest I had come.

She brought presents of silk and spices for Avagisa. I presented Kniva and Hildebald with a magnificent dagger each, which I had made to order by a master smith in Aquileia. And of course two amphorae of excellent red.

Kniva laid on an impressive feast on short notice. Beef, boar, deer, wild fowl and a selection of cheeses. He opened one of the amphorae and we enjoyed the wine with the food.

I drank sparingly. I knew from experience that the battle for control over a powerful tribe like the Thervingi could be bloody. I leaned over to Hostilius who was sitting across from me. "Better keep your hand on your sword Primus Pilus, there is another who wishes to be king of the Thervingi." Hostilius nodded, immediately grasping the seriousness of the threat.

Segelinde was overjoyed to be back with her family and I could see that they, in turn, could hardly contain their excitement to have their daughter back home for an extended visit. Soon I had forgotten about the troubles and we feasted and laughed together. Even though Hostilius could understand little of what was said, he clearly enjoyed the evening. He was asked to share tales of his time in the legions and Segelinde and I translated.

Chapter 13 – Family

Kniva held his horn aloft which prompted a servant to approach and fill it to the brim. He bowed respectfully while taking a step backwards.

I sat at Kniva's right hand side, the place reserved for the guest of honour.

As the servant righted himself, my eye caught the unmistakeable glint of metal from the periphery of my vision. I was still wearing my full armour, since I had no time to change.

My left hand shot out like lighting and the metal strips of my vambrace took the brunt of the killing blow meant for Kniva's neck. The tip of the dagger scored a line on my upper arm, but before the attacker could recover, the side of my open right hand struck him on the throat with such force that I could hear the bones break inside his neck. With compliments from Cai, of course.

I realised what was happening, and as I pulled my right hand back, I drew my sword and swung it in a horizontal sweep behind me as I turned. My instincts were rewarded with a howl of pain. The second attacker lay writhing on the floor, trying to keep his guts from spilling out - with little success.

We all stood at the ready with our swords in our hands, but no other attackers showed themselves. From outside the hall we heard the clash of blades. It would have been foolish to venture into the night. Kniva started towards the door, but I restrained him. "Either your oathsworn will protect us or we will make a stand inside. We will fight shoulder to shoulder, brother", I said.

He relented and nodded. The four of us formed a half circle around Segelinde and her mother. I could feel the hand of Arash on me. I breathed deeply to calm myself as we waited for the onslaught.

The clash of steel on steel died down. Heartbeats later a man walked through the main doorway of the hall on the far side, followed by twelve mailed warriors with swords drawn.

He rolled his huge shoulders and grinned.

"Let me introduce you to my cousin Werinbert", Kniva said, scowling.

Werinbert replied with a voice dripping with menace. "To rule the many tribes of the Thervingi, you need cunning, *little* cousin. You understand war craft, that I will grant you, *little* cousin, but of cunning you know nothing." He spat on the floor to emphasize his point.

He noticed the women standing defiantly behind us and for a moment he looked genuinely sad.

"It is a pity that you have dragged the women and the foreigners into this. Their demise was never part of my plan." He shrugged. "But no plan is ever perfect, is it?"

"I will give you a chance to submit", he added. "Lay down your weapons and you will have a clean death. A warrior's death. You know that it is impossible for you to prevail against twenty. And I have ten more men outside."

From the servant's door in the hall, another ten warriors entered. Blocking our only escape.

Cai always taught the value of patience and I could hear his words echo inside my mind. "Man who learns patience conquer all." But Arash was speaking to me, whispering into my ear. He wanted blood. The god knew no patience. And I yielded to him willingly.

I ran at Werinbert, which was the last thing that he expected. The big man aimed a straight thrust at my stomach. I did not block the blow but moved slightly to my right and pivoted on my left foot, his sword ripping scales from my armour. As I rotated, the razor edge of my blade gained enormous force and sliced down into his neck, severing his spine.

I drew my dagger with my left hand and blocked the overhead slash of the next in line with my jian, my dagger severing the main artery in the leg of my foe, as I struck low. Then the rage of Arash took me and I was amongst them. Like a wolf among the sheep. In the confined space of the hall, they could only face me one or two at a time. And they died. When the anger of the god subsided I stood among the corpses of thirteen men.

"You can stop now Domitius, there's no one left to kill", Hostilius shouted from across the hall.

My armour dripped with gore and blood. I noticed a warrior walking through the door, followed by more, but he paused as he took in the bloody apparition standing among the corpses of his friends and his lord. Then they ran. Only a fool would have entered.

Kniva, Hostilius and Hildebald were all excellent swordsmen, attested to by the corpses of slain warriors on the far side of the hall.

Kniva shrugged. "What happened to your plan of fighting shoulder to shoulder?"

Segelinde translated and Hostilius turned to her and said: "Tell your brother that Domitius is an only child. He never learned to share."

It goes without saying that the feast had come to an abrupt end. We escorted Hildebald and the women home and Hostilius and I returned with Kniva to sort out the mess.

Werinbert's men had barricaded the door of the oathsworn's warrior hall to keep them from interfering. Then they had overpowered the ten guards on duty - one by one.

They had already gathered the glowing embers to burn the hall with the warriors trapped inside. We opened the door and thirty relieved oathsworn exited the hall. With their assistance, Kniva quickly restored order and had the bodies removed. They would be thrown into the river as a reward for their treachery. Kniva walked over to the captain of his guard. Heartbeats later twenty mailed warriors trotted out of the compound of the king.

"Where are they off to?" I asked.

"I am ensuring that none of Werinbert's family will ever cause mischief again", Kniva explained.

I raised my eyebrows, but said nothing. Kniva had a good heart, but he was also practical and did not suffer treachery. Werinbert's family would not see the sun rise. Better safe than sorry, eh?

As soon as Kniva had all under control, we accompanied him to the compound of Hildebald.

Segelinde had arranged for a warm bath and I soaked away the blood and grime. Hostilius was afforded the same pleasure in the adjacent room. I later learned that they had to soak my armour in hot water as well.

When I left the bath I realised that I was bleeding from minor wounds which the hot water had opened again. My wife noticed and was soon sitting next to me on the bed, cleaning and bandaging the cuts.

"It is the first time I saw you fight", she said. "Except for the duel with Hygelac, of course, which was over before I could open my eyes."

She looked sad and asked: "Do you enjoy it? The killing."

I thought through her words, trying to give an honest answer. "No, I do not enjoy taking lives. Today the rage of Arash, or Teiwaz as your people call him, took hold of me. It was as if I just watched, like I was a spectator. I think mayhap the god helps me when the odds are too great for a mortal to overcome?"

She nodded. Content with my answer.

A sudden tiredness overcame me and as my head touched the bed, I was already asleep.

Chapter 14 – Oath

We woke up early and I was feeling my old self again, albeit a bit tender where I had been bruised in the fighting.

Uncharacteristically, the whole household was awake. Segelinde joined her mother, and Kniva gestured for Hostilius and me to join him.

We were served large chunks of fried smoked pork, fried eggs and soft cheese. All swallowed down with ale, of course.

Kniva's whole demeanour had changed. He was visibly relaxed.

"There is more news that I have not shared with you", he said, and started to chew on a particularly large piece of pork.

Hostilius ignored our jabbering, intent on consuming vast quantities of pork and eggs.

"Kniva, don't tell me you have another cousin you haven't introduced us to", I jested.

He grinned and shook his head. "No, brother. This is something completely different. My father has chosen a bride for me. She is the daughter of the Greuthungi King, Ostrogotha the Patient, son of the famous warrior Hisarnis, the Man of Iron. I have never met her, but she has seen nineteen summers so she is not much younger than I am. I could not leave here until our little family matter had been resolved. By the way, I am gifting you and my sister the treasure I have taken from Werinbert."

I opened my mouth to protest, but he waved it away. Kniva was a friend, but he was also the iudex of the mighty Thervingi, and in their lands, his word was law.

"The treasure is considerable, but I am still in your debt", he added.

I nodded.

He produced a purse, or rather a leather bag, bulging with coin. "This is for your friend. It is his share."

Hostilius stopped chewing when the bag was placed on the table. His mouth was still stuffed with pork. He swallowed the last of it and drank deeply from his ale horn.

"Primus Pilus, this is a little gesture from the king for your assistance during their family squabble last night", I explained.

He took the bag and peered inside.

"I have never seen this much gold", Hostilius said. "Tell him that I normally kill Goths for free."

"He says he appreciates your generosity", I translated. Hostilius and Kniva clasped arms.

"I am now ready to travel to the Greuthungi to meet my bride", Kniva continued. "Since you are on your way east, I was hoping that you would accompany me on the journey."

By now I knew the way of kings. The request was in actual fact an order.

"I would be honoured to join you", I replied, "but I do not know if my friends would be welcomed?"

"Friends?" he asked, suddenly confused.

"As I mentioned yesterday, we are on our way to the lands of the Kangju, even more distant than the most eastern tribes of the Huns. We travel with a caravan of valuable trade goods and we are protected by a war band of thirty Huns. They are awaiting us on the border between the Roxolani and the Bastarnae."

Kniva frowned. "I see the problem." But then he brightened and said: "But I am in no hurry. I will instruct my oathsworn to gather a mounted war band to escort us. We will cross through the lands of the Bastarnae to join your caravan. The Bastarnae is under our heel and will not dare to cause trouble. We leave at sunrise, overmorrow."

Kniva repeatedly invited Hostilius and me to join him on a hunt. I declined as I wanted to spend as much time as possible with Segelinde. Eventually Segelinde and I accompanied them, but we trailed far behind, preferring to enjoy a relaxed ride through the countryside. Hostilius possessed a hidden talent when it came to hunting. He emerged from the forest with two enormous wild boar that had fallen to his spear. Kniva only managed to kill a deer.

"Domitius, these Goths sure know how to hunt. For barbarians, that is. Have you ever seen Kniva cast a spear? He killed that deer with a throw of at least fifty paces", Hostilius rambled on, his blood still up after the excitement of the hunt.

I was never keen on killing animals for sport but I did not want to douse his excitement. "You seem to have done well, Primus Pilus", I said.

Hostilius nodded proudly. "I dismounted when those hairy bastards stormed out of the undergrowth. All those years skewering Goths with my pilum has paid off, eh?"

On the morrow we left before first light as we had said our goodbyes the previous evening. I was beset by a dark mood while we travelled through the lands of the Bastarnae. I slipped off on my own when we entered the forest, knowing that my guardians were watching. Soon the Hun scouts appeared as if out of thin air.

"We are being escorted to the caravan by the Goths. You may find your own way there", I said.

"The Goths are deceitful", the Hun scout grunted. "We will watch from the shadows, lord."

I nodded, turned Simsek around and joined the war band, riding at the back of the column.

Kniva and Hostilius had struck up a friendship of sorts even though they battled to communicate. I brooded while they talked and gestured interminably.

We safely traversed the tribal lands of the Bastarnae and on the evening of the third day, we were close to the camp where we had left the caravan many days past.

As soon as we crossed the river into the lands of the Roxolani, I relaxed for the first time in days. We struggled through the dense shrubs that bordered the river, and eventually emerged into a clearing.

The caravan was gone.

I looked at Hostilius, who was riding with Kniva, of course. The Primus Pilus was staring at the deserted campsite wearing much the same expression of desperation as I.

Simsek's ears pricked up, and I took my strung bow from the saddle, grabbing an arrow from my quiver only to see Cai emerging from the shrubs, whistling, with his horse in tow.

I approached hesitantly, not knowing what to expect.

"Too many insects this close to river", he said. "We move camp."

I scowled.

He grinned. "You think we leave without you?"

I ignored his words. "I am going ahead to the camp, Kniva", I said. "I will return soon."

Cai showed me to the camp and I went to speak with Gordas. After clasping arms, I explained the situation to him.

He nodded in understanding. "We will form the vanguard and ride a mile to the front. It is better that we do not mix with the Goths." He gathered his men and soon they rode away.

The area teemed with game. It was still early in the day, allowing Kniva and Hostilius to hunt again. Hostilius was becoming quite the hunter, returning with another fat wild boar which fell to his spear.

When darkness descended we found ourselves seated around the fire.

I was growing tired of the Gothic ale so I opened an amphora of red that I knew would go well with the boar that was slowly roasting over the open fire.

Cai and I sat with Kniva, Hostilius and Vibius.

"Eochar, I have not thanked you and Hostilius enough for coming to my aid." Kniva drew his sword and placed it on his lap with his hand on the blade. "If ever you need assistance, let me know, I will come to your aid. I give my oath, as Teiwaz is my witness."

I nodded and clasped his arm, as did Hostilius.

The oath of a king, with the war god as a witness, is not to be taken lightly. We sat in silence for a while, each preoccupied with their own thoughts.

Chapter 15 – The road east

For many days we rode north and east. We travelled close to where the Sea of Grass gave way to the never-ending forests of the north. The forest dwellers feared to be caught in the open by the nomads, while the nomads believed all that are evil lurked within the dark forest. Hence the area was sparsely populated, which suited us.

These grasslands were inhabited by small tribes of nomads who answered only to themselves. Most used to be part of greater coalitions like the fearsome Siraki or the bloodthirsty Navari. Of these once mighty peoples, only scattered tribes remained. They lived on in the markings of old Greek scrolls buried away in the pigeon holes of Nik's study.

Once or twice we noticed the ears of our horses prick up as they nervously turned away from the distant trees. I could feel the hairs raise on the back of my neck, making me wonder which dark god these tribes were invoking.

Needless to say, we never camped close to the trees. We set watches throughout the night. Most mornings sentries reported seeing shapes move in the dark. Not even the Huns caught any of them, which just served to reinforce the belief that these were no men, but evil spirits of the forest.

In any event, apart from the rumours and growing concerns regarding demons and the like, nothing bad actually happened. Within half a moon we were close to Kniva's destination.

As we had agreed earlier, we would not accompany Kniva into the lands of the Greuthungi. We would continue our journey with the Huns as our guides and protectors.

It was with mixed feelings that we said goodbye to Kniva and his war band. Although I was tied to him by marriage and liked him, there was a constant tension between the Huns and the Goths. Even Hostilius seemed sad to see the back of the Goths.

"Domitius, your brother-in-law is a proper warrior", Hostilius said, no doubt fond of his barbarian hunting partner. Then he added. "For a Goth, that is."

"Primus Pilus, it seems to me that you prefer to hunt with them rather than to kill them", I replied.

He scowled and rode ahead to speak with Cai.

The caravan forced us to travel slowly while the escort of Huns kept any prospective bandits at bay. We still travelled close to the forest and once or twice we were forced to enter the trees to hide from war bands of nomads who patrolled the Sea of Grass.

* * *

Two moons had passed when we finally forded the Volga River.

"It is good to be home, my friend", Gordas said with a broad smile. It was bitterly cold, but he seemed to relish it. "I have missed this, the crispness in the air. You only feel it in the lands of the Hun."

I pulled my bear skin cloak tighter around my shoulders. "Gordas, I think that you have lost your mind", I said in all honesty. He just smiled and slapped my shoulder, ignored the insult, and galloped away, howling with joy. Huns.

Gordas sent messengers to the king to announce our arrival. I did not expect a hostile reception, but I could not be sure. Although I had vowed never to return to the lands of the Huns, I was technically only passing through.

As soon as we entered the camp of the Huns, I was summoned to the tent of the king.

I bowed low, but the Hun king waved it away and gestured for me to join him next to the hearth fire in the centre of the tent. He clapped his hands and servants appeared carrying cups of warm milk with honey.

"It is good to see you, Eochar, although I did not expect you back", he said, frowning. "Gordas explained to me that you are only passing through."

He stared at me with a sudden coldness in his grey eyes. "You do understand that you have broken your vow."

This was not going well and I did not know what would come next. I nodded in acceptance of his words. A man who presented excuses for his actions was not well accepted in the culture of these people.

Octar did not become the high king of the Huns by being stupid. A hint of a smile spread across his scarred face.

"Do not be concerned, Eochar of the Roxolani", the king said. "You have not displeased me. On the contrary, you come as if you were sent here. I have spoken with Gordas and he believes that you are the messenger of Arash. So why would I believe any different?"

He took a deep swallow of the milk and I followed suit. The honeyed liquid warmed me from within.

"First, explain to me why you have come to my lands", Octar asked.

I spent a third of a watch detailing our mission to Octar. There was no use in lying. Trying to deceive the king could easily cost me my life, as I was on thin ice already.

117

He nodded, clearly in agreement with the mission. "It is good to understand the enemy. Storming in blindly only leads to disaster. The king of the Romans is cunning. I approve."

Again he clapped his hands but this time the servants did not bring milk. From a silver jug, they poured us each a goblet of mead.

"Bear with me, Eochar", Octar said. "It is important for you to understand what is afoot in the lands of the Hun."

"To the south lies the great Hyrcanian Ocean, and farther to the west, the Maeotis Swamp. In between these two great bodies of water, the vast lands are controlled by the mighty Alani. The Alani is much alike the Roxolani. Some even say that the Roxolani and the Alani were once one people."

"They are numerous and they are feared on the Sea of Grass. Many times have we clashed with them, but never has there been full-blown war. The Hun and the Alani endure each other. Mostly."

He emptied his goblet and held it out for a refill. "But change is in the air on the Sea of Grass. The Greuthungi Goths that dwell on the northern banks of the Dark Sea are encroaching on the Alani. They are cautious, though, and do not take them on in open battle. They pay the warriors of their neighbouring Alanian tribes to fight for them and then they bind the nobility to the Greuthungi by marriage. The Goths are slowly swallowing the western Alani. The Alani King has realised the danger and he is campaigning against the Greuthungi, but I fear it may already be too late."

"Also, the Greuthungi and the Thervingi are becoming closer allies. If ever they join, it will be difficult to withstand their combined might."

I did not inform Octar of the marriage between Kniva and the Greuthungi princess, but it showed me that his information was accurate.

"But there is more", Octar said. "This information will interest you."

He drank deeply to lubricate his throat and continued. "Between the lands of the Alani and Persia is a barrier. A mountain range that cannot be traversed - except in two places."

"The Gates of the Alani, or the Darial Gates, are halfway between the two great waters in the middle of the mountain range of the gods. In times of old, thousands of Alani poured through this gorge and devastated the lands of the king of kings. But a wall has been built by the Parthians. They feared the Alani so much that they did not even build a gate within the wall. It is closed for all time."

"Where the great mountain range joins the western bank of the Hyrcanian Ocean, there is a strip of land. The Persians call this the Gruzinian Guard, where many forts protect against invasion from the Alani."

"Alas, the king of kings of Parthia was defeated and the shahanshah, Ardashir the Unifier, now rules the vast lands of what once was Parthia. But you know all this."

I nodded. Rome was well informed.

Without being told, servants brought platters of meat and placed it on low tables next to us.

Octar took a joint of mutton from a silver plate and started tearing at the succulent meat, the juices dripping from his chin onto the furs.

"But there are things that you do not know", he said.

He tore at the meat again and wiped his mouth with the back of his hand. "The Persians' hold on power is tenuous at best. The old Parthian lords still rule the provinces on behalf of the king of kings. These lords are prone to dissent, although they are not united. So Ardashir devised a brilliant strategy."

He pointed at me with the half-eaten joint. "What would you do? If you were the shahanshah."

I finished chewing a mouthful of meat and swallowed it down with mead.

120

"I would start a war", I answered. "There is no better tool to build loyalty and to unite people under the same banner than war."

Octar laughed out loud. "I have made the right decision to banish you from this land. You are not only a killer, but you understand the ways of men."

He slapped me on the back and for a moment I thought I saw a glint of pride in his eyes.

"Ardashir did more than start a war. What is better than a war?" Octar said.

I shrugged.

"Two wars, Eochar. He started two wars. And he had planned it brilliantly. While Rome was fighting amongst themselves, he took their strongholds. But he is also learning from the best. He is doing what Rome has been doing for many years."

I had no idea what Octar was referring to and it must have been clear from my expression.

"His armies are encamped in the lands of the Alani", the Hun king explained. "He has not attacked them. He is negotiating with them. He desires for them to swear loyalty and fight alongside his own armies. In this way, he builds a mercenary army of his own which would assist him against any rebelling Parthian lords."

Octar might have been a barbarian of the worst kind, but he was politically savvy and far from stupid. I was deeply impressed.

He was not finished yet. "I need you for something. It will serve your purpose as well as mine. But enough talk for tonight. Now we eat and we drink! We will talk again tomorrow when we are sober."

Chapter 16 – Shahanshah

I sat with Cai, Hostilius and Vibius next to the hearth fire in the comfortable tent provided to us by the high king of the Huns. It was still morning, but a spring storm was raging outside and the sky was dark and ominous. I knew the weather well enough to realise that it would soon start to snow. We did not plan to venture outside until the storm had passed.

"There is trouble in the east", I said, and poured each of my friends a generous goblet of red wine and then filled mine to the brim.

While we savoured the wine, I took a moment to study them. Hostilius had grown a thick beard and Vibius even more so. The Primus Pilus had shaved his head. He reminded me of the guards the slave traders kept. Vibius's hair was longer, but not yet long enough to braid. They all wore the loose flowing robes of the steppe people. None would have thought them to be Roman legionaries.

I took another swallow of wine, savouring the rich fruity taste.

We were on our way to the lands of the Kangju, where we would join the Silk Road. But the tribes between us and our destination were warring.

Octar had earlier briefed me in detail on the happenings in the east and I needed advice in order to make a decision.

I drank and continued. "To the east of the Sasanian Empire exists the Empire of the Kushans. Long ago the Kushans were horse warriors, arch enemies of the Xiong-nu. They were defeated by the Xiong-nu and fled to the west. The remnants of the surviving tribes reunited, eventually founding the mighty Empire of the Kushans."

"But the Kushans have not forgiven the Xiong-nu, neither have they forgotten. They have allied with a wild people from the eastern steppes called the Xionites. The Xionities have been probing the borders of the Huns as well as those of the Persians. The lands between the eastern borders of the Huns and the Silk Road are crawling with them. They are a different people to the Huns – smaller, with darker features. They kill indiscriminately and they are as numerous as the stars in the sky. With that in mind, we have a slim chance of reaching our planned destination."

Cai nodded. "The Kangju are civilised people. Many years ago, they make war with Xionites. Maybe wild men failed to defeat Kangju? Maybe Xionites moved west? Who knows?"

Vibius looked increasingly worried while Hostilius sat with a smirk on his face. "I know you too well Domitius. Get on with it and tell us your plan, or should I say, Arash's plan."

He drank deeply and displayed the prominent smirk again.

I scowled. "As the Primus Pilus is suggesting, there is another way. It might not be less dangerous than risking the Xionites."

"Will there be an opportunity to wet our blades?" Hostilius asked.

"I believe that will be the case, Primus Pilus", I said.

"Then I need to hear no more. I say we do as Domitius suggests", Hostilius said.

Cai scowled and Hostilius grinned.

A servant entered, followed by a gush of icy cold air. He carried a small copper cauldron and placed it in a specially designed holder at the edge of the fire. We were handed bowls and spoons and soon we were laying into the thick mutton, herb and wild root broth which went well with the rich wine.

While we were feasting I shared my plan.

We spent the rest of the day inside the tent. Eating broth, drinking wine and telling stories.

Hostilius told them how I had saved his life during our scouting missions for the emperor Thrax. Vibius shared his experience of being a raw recruit in the legions, while Cai told us what it entailed to be a monk of the Dao during his years spent in the Hanzhong Valley.

We left the broth to simmer. Cai added water from time to time. Interestingly, the taste of the broth seemed to improve and develop with time. Maybe the wine also helped to that effect.

In any event, we went to bed content, and even better, we had agreed on a plan.

We woke up to clear skies. The whole tented village was covered by a thin layer of snow and it was bitterly cold.

Octar had gifted us each a long leather overcoat lined with sheepskin. We wore this over our armour.

Cai and I were preparing for the day's journey when Hostilius asked: "What in Hades are you doing, Domitius?"

I was rubbing mutton tail fat into the exposed skin of my face to prevent burns from the cold air.

"Your beard will protect most of your face, Primus Pilus." I handed him the fat and he rubbed it over his nose and lips.

"It works well, but is smells and tastes a bit rancid, eh?"

Cai made his own potion but Vibius also massaged the rancid mixture into his skin, wearing an expression of distaste.

Not long after, Gordas appeared and escorted us to where Octar was readying his army of five thousand Huns. Our horse caravan, laden with silk, had left the morning before, escorted by a hundred Huns.

We were on our way to the lands of the Alani.

We fell in behind Octar and his retinue, the place reserved for nobility. A mile out from camp the Huns increased the pace to a gallop. The strong, stocky horses could keep up the pace for hours, which they did. Fortunately we only travelled seventy miles that day, but even so, Hostilius and Vibius were dead on their feet by the time we stopped to camp.

Vibius dismounted and lay down on the grass. "Please tell me that it is out of the ordinary for these people to ride this far in a single day."

"You are correct, Vibius. To travel this distance is not normal for the Huns, my friend", I replied.

He looked relieved and I added: "They normally travel much farther."

Vibius did not reply, but just lay flat on his back in the grass. He groaned before getting up to take care of his horse.

Allthough I jested with Vibius, I was not all evil as earlier I had arranged with Gordas that two of his warriors take care of our horses and pitch the tents. "Vibius, we do not have to take care of the horses, the king has made arrangements for his guests", I explained.

As soon as the tents were pitched I asked my friends to light a fire. I left with Gordas and ten of his warriors to shoot game for the pot. I arrived back within the hour with six fat wild fowl. Cai had managed to get a dried dung fire going while I contributed a few pieces of wood, collected on the hunt. Soon the birds were spitted over the fire. I produced a round of hard cheese which I dissolved in water that I heated in a small pot. The nomad cheese is incredibly hard. When it is cold, you can easily break a tooth if you try to eat it without heating it first.

The cheese broth was bitter but very nutritious. I was used to it, but my friends struggled with the flavour.

"It tastes like vomit boiled with milk and butter", was the description Hostilius assigned to it.

"The body needs the fat, Primus Pilus. Drink it or you will fall from the saddle before the sun sets tomorrow", I said.

Hostilius did not desire to look the part of a weakling, especially when Gordas and his barbarians would be watching so he downed the cup of cheese broth. Vibius followed suit.

Exhausted, we retired early.

Before first light the following morning, I sneaked out of the tent and readied the horses for all of us.

Hostilius and Vibius could barely walk. They did not want to show weakness, forcing me to look the other way, mumbling some excuse as I wandered off to ask something of Gordas who was camped nearby.

It took us nearly a week to reach our destination. We forded the Volga River near the shores of the Hyrcanian Ocean and made camp. Messengers were sent to the king of the Alani to announce our arrival.

Early on the morrow the messengers returned, accompanied by an escort of warrior nobles of the Alani. I immediately realised why people thought that they were related to the Roxolani. The Alani were tall, jovial men with blue eyes and blonde hair. Even their horses resembled those of the Roxolani.

I was introduced to the leader of the Alani entourage and he clasped my arm. "I am Beorgor of the Alani."

"Well met, Beorgor of the Alani", I replied. "I am Eochar of the Roxolani."

"I have heard the name of Eochar the Merciless", he replied, "cousin of king Apsikal the Wise. The man who speaks to Arash. The slayer of giants."

I did not know whether to feel honoured or insulted. I had always thought of myself as merciful, but the name he afforded me could only assist me in my mission. I nodded.

As soon as the Hun king was ready, we rode for the nearby camp of the Alani.

Octar was accompanied by a select retinue of nobles. I was among that group, as was Gordas. I rode alongside Beorgor, who spoke much. Soon I learned that the king of kings of the Persians were camped a few miles to the far side of the Alanian tented village. Ardashir, the Persian high king, or shahanshah, was accompanied by his son, prince Shapur, and the Sasanian army, of course.

Octar would meet in private with Khuddan, the high king of the Alani.

The Hun king had shared his plans with me. Ardashir was demanding that the Alani provide him with a mercenary force of eight thousand heavy cavalry. In return he would depart from the Alani lands with his army, and the barbarian king would receive a handsome payment of eight hundred pounds of gold. This would be problematic for Khuddan, as it would weaken him and he would run the risk of being overrun by the Goths and their Western Alani allies.

Octar knew Ardashir held the balance of power and that the Alani king would have to agree to the Sasanian proposal. The Urugundi king had come with an alternative suggestion.

Octar would send Khuddan eight thousand Huns to assist him in his war against the Greuthungi Goths.

Khuddan in return would provide a force of two thousand heavy cavalry that would join the five thousand Huns that were camped close by. This Alani and Hun force would fight as mercenaries for Ardashir. They would negotiate that the payment be increased to a thousand pounds of gold. The Huns and the Alani would share this payment.

It was a masterstroke from Octar. He would gain leverage over the Alani, weaken the Goths, and earn a fortune in gold. He was facing one problem, though. To entrust command of the joint army to a Hun or an Alani would soon result in complications. He required a general of reputation who would be seen as impartial. He also needed someone who could stand up to the scheming Persians. I was the answer to his problems. I would lead the mercenary force with Gordas and Beorgor as my deputies.

Khuddan and his chief nobles rode out to meet Octar on the road. It was clear why the Alani was feared on the plains. They rode intimidatingly large horses. All the warriors wore conical bronze helmets with a neck guard of scales attached to the base. Horses and riders were covered with armour - scales of bronze and hardened leather. The thick leather was first soaked in hot water and then hammered while dried next to open flames. The end result was leather scales almost impervious to arrows.

Khuddan wore a magnificent suit of silver scale armour which matched that of his horse. Long blonde hair extended from underneath his helmet. The king's powerful features was framed by a neatly trimmed beard, specked with grey. His forearms were bare and even from a distance I saw the muscles rippling as he sat upright, expertly controlling his horse. The animal was without a doubt trained for war and the presence of strangers made it snort and shake its huge head, steam emanating from its flared nostrils.

As a sign of mutual respect both kings dismounted and clasped arms. Most probably it also prevented the stallions from having a go at each other.

In any event, the kings rode at the front, each followed by their guards, eyeing one another suspiciously. We entered the tented village, which was enormous, but so typical of the nomads. The kings dismounted at the tent of Khuddan and entered on their own. As a sign of trust, I noticed that Octar was not asked to surrender his weapons.

We waited outside and soon servants appeared carrying large bronze jugs of heavily salted hot milk, which was a favourite of the nomads. I had acquired the taste during my time with the Huns and I savoured every mouthful of the hot liquid.

I was enjoying my third cup of milk when the kings re-appeared.

All went silent.

"The Alani and the Huns are going to war", Khuddan said. "We will fight side by side against our enemies. We have renewed our bonds of friendship." The assembled nobles broke into loud cheers. The Huns among them howled like wolves.

The sun had just reached its zenith when we set off to meet with the Persians. Messengers had left much earlier to announce our imminent arrival. The shahanshah would be expecting us. The Persians had erected a tent a mile away from the main camp. As the Persians and the Alani were ancient enemies it would not be expected of us to enter their war camp. We waited near the tent and soon a Persian delegation of similar size detached from the army and moved towards us.

Octar and Khuddan were deep in muted conversation while the talkative Beorgor related some tale without end to a mute Gordas, who had a generally bored look about him.

I used the respite to study our delegation.

Octar was a true Hun with his elongated skull and scarred face. Swirling dark blue tattoos covered most of his exposed skin. Thick muscles bulged as he made animated gestures. His dark hair was plaited into a single braid and tied at the back with thin silver bindings. Khuddan was not much different, albeit without the deformed skull and the scarred cheeks. He was taller than the Hun, but more lithe and sinewy. It was clear that he was immensely powerful, the veins like thick cords on his tattooed forearms. Unlike Octar, he sported a thick beard which was plaited into many thin braids.

Each of the kings had three bodyguards in attendance, all champions of their tribes. They were not necessarily more muscular than the kings, but when they moved, it was with a predatory hint. Even a fool could see that these men were killers all.

And then there was Gordas, who, despite his barbarian facade and permanent scowl, radiated intelligence and cunning. Beorgor was a killer, that was clear, but he was a joker by nature and never stopped talking. A rare mix.

My attention was drawn to the approaching group which matched ours in number. The riders slowed down to a trot when they neared the tent. I could not keep my eyes off their horses. Horses of which I had never seen the like.

Beorgor noticed my amazed expression. "The horses are called Niseans", he explained. "They are the largest horses in the world. Even bigger than the ones our heavy cavalry use. Over the years we have taken a few in battle to improve our stock. They are bred near a town called Nissa at the foot of the Zagros Mountains in Persia."

The horses were truly magnificent. Two riders rode pure white specimens. "Only the members of the royal family are allowed to ride white Niseans", Beorgor said. "For any other it is seen as an affront to the gods, which carries the punishment of death."

I made a mental note to stay away from the white Niseans.

The party reined in and walked their horses towards us. The Nisean of the king was unencumbered by armour, but the rest, including the prince's horse, were clad in iron. The riders were similarly protected, and each carried a ten foot spear. They had no shields, but I noticed maces, bow cases and hand axes tied to their saddles.

Again, Beorgor enlightened me. "The shahansha commands ten thousand of these ironclad warriors who are called 'immortals'. The men of iron who guard the king are the veterans of countless battles. They are hand-picked from the ten thousand. They are the best of the best."

Ardashir wore a loose-fitting, long-sleeved tunic of finely woven wool, bleached to a brilliant white. All the edges were decorated with green and gold embroidery. The king's leggings matched his tunic. The soft leather boots were knee high and dyed green. Around his shoulders he wore a thick purple cloak, fastened at the front with a golden clasp. A leather belt trimmed with gold adorned his waist. The longsword at his side looked to be practical and well crafted, rather than the ornate kind preferred by royalty. It emphasized his warrior nature.

They came to a halt ten paces from us. Only then did I appreciate the size of the Niseans. Even Khuddan's huge horse appeared small. Octar's Hunnic horse was dwarfed. Yet, looks can be deceiving and all present knew that underestimating the Huns came at one's own peril.

The Persian king and his son both unbuckled their sword belts and passed it into the waiting hands of underlings. They dismounted. Octar and Khuddan followed suit and they all clasped arms and disappeared into the tent.

No words were spoken in front of the underlings.

The immortal guards stayed mounted and formed a line outside the tent, grounding the hafts of their spears while watching us in silence.

The Hun and Alani guards, on the other hand, looked like a disorganized mob in comparison.

Within a sixth of a watch Octar's face appeared in the door of the tent and a Hun bodyguard immediately attended, going down on one knee. The guard inclined his head to his king, and walked over to us. "Lord Eochar, your presence is required by the kings", he said.

I handed my sword to Gordas and entered the tent.

Inside the spacious tent the kings and Prince Shapur were reclined on separate couches, in the style of the Greeks. I went down on one knee and bowed my head. Octar gestured for me to take a seat on the sumptuous furs laid out on the ground. It would have been a sacrilege for me to be seated on the same level as the royals so I sat cross-legged on the furs.

Prince Shapur was the first to address me. He spoke in broken Scythian. "Lord Eochar, we have reached an agreement with your king. He has suggested that you lead the combined mercenary force. We will travel through the lands of the Persian Kingdom and we will not allow any violation of the locals."

"You may speak", he added.

Allow me to digress. Alexander of Macedon conquered Persia six hundred years earlier. Part of his legacy was that Greek became the second official language of the Sasanians, albeit mainly spoken by the nobility. Nik had tutored me in Greek from an early age, it being a requirement of any self-respecting Roman patrician.

"I will keep a tight rein on the warriors, my lord", I replied in perfect Greek.

I could see that even Octar was surprised as he was not aware of my hidden talent.

A hint of a smile appeared on Ardashir's lips. "I find it amusing. A man respected by the Huns and the Alani, who speaks like a Greek?"

This was clearly a question. "Lord, my tutor was a man by the name of Nikephoros", I replied.

Ardashir nodded. "Did you receive schooling in military tactics?"

"Yes, lord. Roman and Greek military tactics", I replied.

Ardashir raised his eyebrows. "The Parthian kings of Gorgan, Khorasan and Margiana are defying me. My son will lead the campaign against the rebels. I need you to obey him. What say you, Lord Eochar of the Roxolani?"

My eyes met Octar's and he gave me an imperceptible nod.

"Great king Ardashir", I replied, "I owe my allegiance to the high king of the Huns. I will obey, but I will not sacrifice my men."

Shapur nodded.

Ardashir dismissed me with a wave of his hand. "Leave us", he said.

Again, Octar nodded. I inclined my head while slowly walking backwards. Turning your back on a king is an insult of the worst kind and was punishable by death, at best.

Chapter 17 – Derbent

It goes without saying that the successful conclusion to the negotiations with the Persians had to be celebrated. Octar was pleased with me and I ended up seated next to him, although not in the seat of honour, which was occupied by Khuddan of course.

Octar slapped my back. "Well done, Eochar. You have gained the approval of the Persians. My proposal has been accepted. Ardashir conceded, we will be allowed to keep all plunder." He smiled slyly. "Knowing the Persians, this tells me that there will hardly be any fighting."

He leaned closer in a conspiratorial way. "Ardashir has also agreed to purchase your whole consignment of silk at the asking price. The merchandise is of a high quality and the price is reasonable. I will collect the funds and deliver it to Bradakos."

I smiled, as I had asked for four hundred pounds of gold. That translated to a hundred pounds of gold for each of us. Cai, Hostilius and Vibius would share in the bounty. I would not tell them until we were safely back within the Empire. If we did not return, well, then my widow would receive a windfall.

We retired to our tent as soon as the Huns and Alani were too drunk to notice our departure.

Hostilius and Vibius looked at me intently while Cai sat with his eyes closed, obviously deep in meditation.

"So, Domitius, what you are telling me is that I will be fighting on the side of the Persians", Hostilius said, frowning. "I know that we have a mission to complete, but it just feels wrong."

"It would be the ideal opportunity to study their tactics", Vibius said. "They would never suspect that people who look like this", he paused to point a finger at Hostilius, "are anything less than barbarians."

Hostilius turned red in the face. His anger always lay just beneath the surface. "What do you mean, duplicarius?" Hostilius growled. "You forget yourself."

Vibius realised that he might have overstepped the line. "No offence, Primus Pilus, I just meant to say that your disguise really works well."

"Next time try saying what you mean, eh", Hostilius growled, only partly placated.

I had trouble suppressing a grin. Vibius and Hostilius both looked as if they had crawled out of some barbarian backwater.

"And who are you laughing at Domitius?" Hostilius said, focusing his ire on me.

I extended both my open palms above my head. "Peace, Primus Pilus, it is just that all of us resemble the barbarians that we so love to fight. Only Cai still looks the same."

Cai descended from some distant abode. "I may look same on outside", he said, "but inside I am better man than day before. You all look different on outside, but inside, still same little boys as yesterday."

Hostilius and Vibius both dropped their jaws at the uncharacteristic insult from Cai. Even I, who knew Cai well, was shocked.

Cai grinned. "What wrong now?" he asked in surprise. "You not think it funny?"

Hostilius scowled. One could never be sure with Cai.

I changed the subject. "To answer your question Primus Pilus, we probably won't fight much. Our numbers will be used to cow some wayward Parthian king into swearing eternal fealty to Shapur. Once they have kissed and made up, we will move on to the next one."

Over time I have learned that predicting the future is best left to the gods. Even contemplating an outcome tends to anger them, as we were soon to find out.

* * *

A messenger from prince Shapur arrived three days later to announce that the Persian army was ready to leave.

The morning after, we struck camp early.

Beorgor and his heavy cavalry were waiting for us on the fringes of the Alani camp. Each Alani noble was accompanied by an entourage which included a young apprentice and three horses. Two horses were required for travelling - the warhorses were only mounted when battle was imminent. The Alani contingent thus consisted of six thousand horses and four thousand men. The five thousand Huns each had one spare horse. As we were travelling with the slow moving Alani and even slower Persians, there was no requirement for the traditional two spare horses.

I soon realised that Shapur did not trust his barbarian allies. We were instructed to travel behind the Persian cavalry and were followed by the Persian foot soldiers. Although the Huns and Alani knew no equal as scouts, we were requested to stay in formation. The real reason for this was to prevent groups of barbarians ravaging the countryside or deserting the army. Not unlike a man who keeps a vicious dog for protection, although he knows the dog might turn on him at any time.

To compensate for the palpable resentment in the air, we traversed an area endowed with unspeakable natural beauty.

We rode east, then turned south, travelling along the western bank of the vast Hyrcanian Ocean with the insurmountable mountains to our right. The local Scythians called it 'the mountains shining white with snow', which was a fitting description. Between the Caucasus Mountains and the water was a narrow gateway linking the Sea of Grass with the lands of the Persians. Some called it the Gates of Iskander, the Scythian name for the great Macedonian king Alexander.

We obediently travelled in formation for many days, feasting our eyes on the beauty surrounding us, hardly moving faster than a brisk walk.

On a pleasant afternoon, when we approached an imposing fortress looming in the distance, I was summoned by Prince Shapur. I gestured to Hostilius and Vibius to join me. All regarded my two companions as my bodyguards therefore their presence was expected.

Shapur rode with the vanguard, moving barely faster than normal marching pace. His immortal guards made way for us, allowing me to fall in alongside the prince. Vibius and Hostilius rode within earshot, but not close enough to threaten the person of the prince.

Shapur spoke to me without taking his eyes from the road ahead. "For an educated man, you keep a real rabble as bodyguards", he said in Greek. He swept his hand around to the fearsome-looking immortal guards. "It would stand you in good stead to have guards like the immortals. One of them would deal with those two without breaking a sweat."

I doubted it, but inclined my head. "I have known them for years and they are loyal, like faithful dogs. They are also handy in a fight."

Shapur snorted with contempt and changed the subject.

"We are now leaving the lands of the Alani", he said. "This land belongs to the Albanians and soon we will be marching through Armenia. The rulers of these lands will not dare to attack us."

He pointed to the walls of the imposing fortress towering above the flat landscape in the distance. "The area that we are traversing is called the Land of the Wolf, or the Gurgan, in the local language. This Armenian fortress guards the gateway. We call this 'the Fortress that guards against the wolves'. The wolves being the men under your command", he added. "There is a town adjacent to the fort. I do not wish your men to enter."

I nodded.

He waved me away and spoke to one of his guards in Persian.

Trotting back along the column, I asked Vibius: "Did you hear the words he spoke to the immortal as we left?"

145

Vibius nodded, and translated the words of Shapur. "If ever it is necessary, kill the ugly one first, he has the look of a killer about him."

Hostilius scowled. "The duplicarius doesn't really have a look of a killer, eh?"

There was treachery in the air so we had to be vigilant.

I informed Beorgor and Gordas who had a solution ready. "Let us infiltrate their camp tonight and kill them all", the Hun suggested.

I nearly choked on the piece of dried meat I was chewing on. "Peace, Gordas. It is only an off-hand remark. We will be ready, but we will not initiate violence against our allies."

Gordas nodded, having learned to trust me over the years. "I will heed your advice, Eochar, but know that I will unleash the Huns on these pompous bastards if they stab us in the back."

Before long we set up camp and I spent the evening with my friends as was the norm.

It was nearly mid-summer, with the weather being cold yet pleasant. Gordas and I had brought down seven wild ducks during the course of the morning. When he laid eyes on them, Cai claimed the bounty.

"Give to me. I prepare food tonight", he said.

He hung the ducks from his saddle and left them there for the remainder of the day. As soon as we made camp, he cleaned and seasoned the fowl.

Within a third of a watch they were spitted on stakes next to the open fire.

"Cai, you are going to burn the meat", Hostilius stated.

"You already look like barbarian. Best is not act like one", Cai replied.

Hostilius scowled, but he knew Cai by then and took the rebuke in his stride.

I still had red wine left, but used it sparingly. I did purchase an amphora of white wine from the Persian merchants trailing the army. Apparently this local wine was well-known and called Shirazi. The wine was a pleasant surprise. An excellent dry white with a distinct fruity nose.

I filled all of my friends' cups and Cai smacked his lips. "Will go well with crispy duck."

"Burnt duck", Hostilius interjected, but Cai ignored him.

Cai knew his business and we soon devoured the delicious roast duck accompanied by the Shirazi wine.

I slept like the dead and woke when Vibius shook my shoulder. "Best come with me, Lucius. There is trouble afoot."

I dressed and donned my armour, but left my sheepskin jacket as there was no chill in the air.

A brooding Gordas and scowling Beorgor were waiting for me outside my tent.

"Tell me", was all I said.

Gordas looked at Beorgor, who nodded.

Gordas slowly released his breath. "Five of my men and six of the Alani disobeyed orders and ventured into the town yesterday evening. To cut a long story short, three locals, two Alani and three of the Persians were killed in a brawl."

I sighed. "Bring the culprits to me."

Soon the five Huns and four remaining Alani were lined up in front of my tent. My hand rested on the hilt of my sword.

The leader of the group of Alani spat at my feet. "You are not one of us, we will not listen…" He never finished his sentence as my blade took his head and he collapsed in a pool of blood.

"Anyone else got something to say?" I asked. Predictably, no one did.

I turned to Beorgor and Gordas. "Cut off the little finger from each of their left hands and put them in a bag with the head. I am in a merciful mood today." They bowed their heads and the guilty ones were escorted away.

Hostilius looked at me as if he had seen me for the first time. "And I thought I was a bloody strict bastard. Remind me never to get on your wrong side."

"Discipline is a word that does not feature in the vocabulary of these warriors, Primus Pilus", I said, "but they understand fear, respect and reputation. Most of all reputation. I have to uphold my reputation as Eochar the Merciless. I would have preferred that the Alani returned to his comrades this evening. He unfortunately gave me no choice."

Hostilius had surely sent his share of legionaries to their death and his face turned sombre. "I know what you mean, Domitius." And in his eyes I could see that he did.

We were still talking when an immortal guard of Shapur's appeared to escort me to his presence. I turned to Hostilius. "Please tell Gordas I need the bag immediately", I said.

I mounted and followed the immortal with a bulging leather satchel tied to my saddle. Hostilius and Vibius rode at my side.

Shapur was still in his tent so I waited outside. My friends were forced to wait twenty paces away.

The Prince appeared with four bodyguards flanking him. "You have displeased me, Lord Eochar", he hissed. "My instructions were clear. Your warriors were not to enter the town."

I emptied the grizzly contents of the bag on the ground. "They have been punished, my lord."

Shapur grimaced. "I want eight more heads, general", he replied.

"Prince Shapur, I have done what I have done", I said, and turned around to leave.

I heard a sword being drawn from a scabbard. I drew my jian and deflected the killing blow from the immortal as I swung around. I allowed his sword to retain much of its momentum and as a result he overextended. I moved to the side and severed his head, my blade cleanly slicing through the chain mail links that protected his neck.

In a flash, Hostilius and Vibius were at my side. The remaining three immortals had drawn their swords.

"Hold!" Shapur yelled.

The immortals froze and I backed away two paces, followed by my friends.

150

Shapur knew that if this incident spiralled out of control, his campaign would be doomed. Consequently he would fall out of favour with the king. He was no fool.

"My sincere apologies, Lord Eochar. The guard acted without my approval", the prince said.

I nodded. "I accept, Prince Shapur. Forget that this unfortunate incident ever happened."

Then Arash spoke to me and I added: "I claim his armour and weapons, nonetheless. It is the law of the Sea of Grass."

In his eyes I could see his reluctance, but he nodded in an attempt to prevent the army from fighting among themselves.

Hostilius and Vibius were left with the grizzly job of removing the weapons and armour from the dead immortal.

We mounted and rode back to the camp. I have clearly underestimated the threat. We would need to be more careful.

Chapter 18 – Gate of the Giants

Cai, Gordas and Beorgor were waiting for us.

We dismounted and for a moment I was unsure of what to do. I feared that on hearing the tale, Gordas would string his bow, draw his sword and lead the Hun horde on a rampage through the Persian camp.

I gestured for them to join me on the old furs scattered around the cooking fire. I poured each one a cup of wine and drank deeply from mine.

Gordas looked at me and asked: "Is it that bad?"

Hostilius and Vibius could communicate in Scythian using three-word sentences by now, but I did not trust their language skills enough and relayed what had happened.

Gordas stood when I had finished. I was sure that my worst fears would materialise, but he said: "By all the gods, Eochar, why do I always miss the action!"

He wetted his throat and continued. "I studied the armour of the immortals. Their chain mail is thick and every link is separately riveted. Only a blade with strong magic can slice through chain like that."

Cai sighed. "Blade made many, many generation ago. In old days, in Hanzhong valley, when sky rain iron, people bring to monastery. Master forge swords using these pieces of metal. Some strong, some brittle, break soon. One day, piece brought to master, but he not able to melt it. For months monks labour, make bigger forge oven. They collect best quality charcoal. Eventually, master succeed and melt sky-iron, just enough for one blade. Master labour many month to forge metal into blade of magnificent sword."

Everyone present were warriors and they hung onto Cai's words.

"It only story. Not know if true", Cai concluded with a shrug.

"Either it's true or it is magic", Hostilius said. "No sword I know of is able to sever iron chain."

Beorgor held out his hand and I handed him the sword. He studied the blade reverently and handed it back to me. "I don't believe the tale about the iron from the sky. It is far-fetched and unlikely. I do believe that Arash has touched this blade. I can feel it."

Cai scowled.

In any event, I had to spend time to calm Gordas and Beorgor. The wine helped.

Over the following days, we rode south, keeping our formation. Vibius was fluent in the local language and he visited the traders most evenings.

"Lucius, I have heard interesting rumours while buying wine today", Vibius said. "The story doing the rounds among the Persian soldiers is that a barbarian general is the incarnation of Mithras, the god of light. Some swear that they have seen his sword glow with the power of Sol Invictus. They say that his sword had cut through the armour of an immortal as if it were not there."

I grinned, knowing that most soldiers are extremely superstitious. Exaggerated tales like Vibius had overheard would strike fear into the hearts of the Persians and make them less eager to cause mischief.

On the eighth day, the army changed direction from south to east.

Vibius pointed to the mountains on our right. "We are reaching the most southern extremes of the Hyrcanian Ocean. We will now travel southeast and then northeast. It may be that we have already crossed the border into Gorgan".

"I have heard a rumour that the Parthian lords of Gorgan, Khorasan and Margiana have united in revolt and a combined army is marching to meet us", he added.

The army continued its slow but consistent advance. We crossed what seemed like hundreds of small streams running down from the mountains into the sea. It must have slowed the Persian wagons, but we barely noticed. The days became increasingly pleasant traversing the countryside littered with fields and farms. The farmers and villagers were nowhere to be seen, as they had obviously fled into the hills, taking their livestock with. With great difficulty we restrained the Huns and the Alani from looting or killing the odd villager too slow to leave. Shapur was reclaiming the area for the Sasanians and only an idiot would stoop to raid his own people.

We passed many Parthian forts, but all were deserted.

Vibius returned one evening from his daily mission of procuring wine from the traders. We all waited in expectation. Not only for the amphora of wine, but also for the customary scraps of rumours and gossip that he would have overheard.

"We are travelling through an area called Mazandaran, the Gate of the Giants", Vibius said.

"It sounds pretty intimidating. Why is it called that?" Hostilius asked.

"They say that long ago gods and demons made their home along this coast", Vibius replied. "Let's just say that they were less than agreeable towards travellers."

"There is something else", he added. "This Gate of the Giants also refers to a narrow pass between the sea and the Alborz Mountains. There are rumours that the enemy is expected to meet us there."

The next morning we readied ourselves for the march, as usual, but we did not receive the order to advance. It was obvious that something was afoot. Less than a watch passed before I was summoned to attend the prince.

Shapur looked down his nose at Hostilius and Vibius. "Please don't bring the rabble closer, they smell. Come, join me, Lord Eochar."

We left my companions with the immortals and advanced to the summit of a low hill. From this vantage point we could see miles in every direction. To our right were the towering white peaks of the Alborz Mountains. To the left, the rocky shores of the Hyrcanian Ocean.

He pointed to the narrow passage between the Ocean and the Mountain, three miles distant. "Behold the Gate of the Giants, Lord Eochar."

In the distance I could see the multi-coloured formations of soldiers blocking the narrow passage. The opposing army was significant in number, giving credibility to the rumour that the three Parthian provinces had united in rebellion.

"My scouts tell me that the Parthian rebels have placed their heavy infantry at the front of their formation", Shapur said. "These men are called Dailamites. They are encased in scale, use oversized shields and carry heavy spears with tips designed for piercing armour. When they have expended their spears they take to wielding huge battle-axes with great skill. Four thousand block the pass. Behind them are at least another five thousand foot archers. The Parthian lords are holding their heavy cavalry in reserve, another three thousand."

I did not speak, as I was not asked to.

We studied the army in silence. After a hundred heartbeats the prince continued. "The immortals will not be able to break the line. Neither do I wish to waste my heavy infantry against even odds."

I nodded in agreement.

"I would hear your thoughts", he said.

"Prince Shapur, are you familiar with the arrow storm of the Urugundi Huns?"

He shook his head.

"Nothing in this world can stand against it. My Huns will break the line of the infantry to allow your immortals to crush them, but there is one problem. The foot archers are numerous

157

enough to break up the Huns. We need the immortals to dismount and use their bows to scatter the archers. Then the Huns will take over and break the infantry line."

Shapur stared into the distance. "My father would mock me for seeking the advice of a barbarian. I am no fool, Eochar. You are no more a barbarian than I am, although you seem to enjoy the company of the barbarian rabble." He spat in the dirt to emphasize his point.

"I trust your judgement because you know your men, but unlike most, you have been schooled in military strategy. I will deploy the five thousand immortals on foot to decimate the archers of the enemy. Their apprentices will stay behind with their warhorses. Once the enemy archers have been routed, we will see what your wild men are capable of. I still harbour doubts. I have never seen archers who are able to break the formation of the Dailamites."

It took the army of Shapur a full watch to assemble for battle. I sat in the saddle, staring out over the heads of the dismounted immortals. Shapur had been true to his word, my plan was unfolding.

Gordas turned to me. "My men are chomping at the bit, Eochar. I can hardly restrain them. You see an army. All my men see are scalps and loot, ready for the taking."

"Patience, Gordas. They will get their chance soon enough", I replied.

I had hardly finished uttering the words when I noticed a contingent of men moving through the Parthian line. They carried leafy green branches, the universal sign of parley.

"Allow me to take them out, Eochar. It may be a ruse by the enemy. Rather safe than sorry, eh", Gordas said, desperate for the fight to begin.

I scowled and held up my hand. "Stand down, Gordas."

The Parthian group stopped halfway between the two armies. A short while later they were joined by a delegation led by Shapur.

Soon the two groups separated. "No peace parley can be that quick. Your sword will still taste blood today", I said to a grinning Gordas.

I was proven wrong almost immediately as the Persian horn signalled for the immortals to stand down.

Gordas looked horrified. "How can this be?"

He turned his horse around and led the sulking Hun army back to camp.

I was as surprised as Gordas. Moments later I was summoned by Shapur.

"Lord Eochar, the Parthian lords have realised their mistake and have renewed their oaths of loyalty to my father", he explained.

"A wise decision, Prince", I said, and inclined my head.

He smirked. "The real reason for their sudden change of heart is that the northern border of Gorgan has been breached by the wild tribes of the steppes. We are to leave at first light. Ready your men."

"Prince Shapur", I replied, "the mercenary army under my command was hired to subdue the errant Parthian lords. It appears that the goal has been accomplished. We are no longer oathbound to continue and I will thus lead the men home."

Shapur was visibly unsettled. His olive complexion turned a reddish shade. He gestured for me to follow him. "Walk with me, Lord Eochar."

We walked and talked for a long time.

"You negotiate like a Persian, Lord Eochar", Shapur eventually conceded.

"I am sure that the rebellious lords will end up footing the bill", I replied.

Shapur smiled and clasped my arm.

Chapter 19 – Hammer and anvil

Hostilius looked inside the wagon that had earlier arrived from Shapur.

"By the gods, Eochar, how much gold is in here?" he asked.

"It is a thousand pounds", I replied.

Unlike Gordas and Hostilius, Beorgor was more interested in the twelve Nisean horses accompanying the wagon. "Nevermind the gold, the horses are magnificent. You truly negotiate like a god, Eochar."

"One Nisean will go to Khuddan, one to Bradakos and one to you, Beorgor. The Huns do not covet the large warhorses. The rest is mine." Beorgor gaped, then a smile formed on his lips which stayed there for weeks.

"We will send two hundred of the Alani heavy cavalry and their apprentices back with six hundred pounds of the gold. They will take the Niseans back as well. The gold is meant for Khuddan and Octar. Beorgor, can it be done?"

Beorgor nodded. "The lands we have passed through are filled with fear, and empty of men. No one will dare to attack four hundred men in iron."

"See to it", I said.

"And the other four hundred pounds?" Gordas asked.

"One hundred and forty pounds will go to the Alani and two hundred and forty pounds will go to the Huns", I said. "Distribute it amongst the warriors. Tell them that they have done well. Remind them to follow my orders and there will be even more loot."

I gestured for Beorgor and Gordas to walk with me. "Five pounds of gold I give to you, Beorgor. Gordas, you will have fifteen pounds, as you are not interested in the Niseans. You both have served me well. Just make sure that your warriors behave."

"I will rip the limbs from the warrior who disobeys your commands, Eochar", Gordas growled. "From the look in his eyes I could see that he did not mean it figuratively.

Beorgor departed in order to make the arrangements for the transportation of the gold and horses. I took the opportunity to speak with Gordas. "Are there any of your men who are, er…, good at stealing?"

Gordas raised his eyebrows, grinned and continued in a low whisper. "Just tell me what you need, Eochar. It will be arranged. Do you wish for the sword of Shapur? Or maybe his scalp?"

It was my turn to laugh. "No my friend, it is much less complicated, but I need you to send it away with the wagon at dawn tomorrow, to be delivered to Bradakos."

I explained to Gordas what I needed.

"I was hoping that it would be more challenging", he replied.

I slapped him on the back. "We ride at first light."

Later that same evening I sat with my companions around the cooking fire. Prime cuts of lamb were slowly roasting over the coals, compliments of the Parthian lords, of course. The evening was pleasant, so I wore no cloak over my armour.

Vibius drank deeply from his cup. "I have heard many rumours today", he said, "but I am sure that you know the truth of it, Lucius."

"The Parthian lords stripped their northern borders of soldiers to enable them to meet Shapur in the field. The army they have amassed is not insignificant, as you have seen earlier", I said.

Hostilius nodded. "The fight would have been bloody today."

"Octar had explained to me that to the east of the Sasanian lands lies the Empire of the Kushans. They are a powerful people and warlike by nature. They forever covet the eastern territories of Persia."

"You see, Lucius of the Da Qin, Rome not special", Cai added. "Many Empires same as Rome. All desire to steal neighbour's lands."

I ignored his wise words and continued. "The Kushans have been fighting with a people called Xionites for centuries, but recently they have subdued them and these steppe warriors have become their vassals."

I drank from my cup. "The weakening of the northern borders have not gone unnoticed by the spies of the Kushans. But they are crafty and did not attack the Sasanians directly, for fear of retribution. They have persuaded their allies, the barbarian Xionites, to invade."

"Where did they invade?" Hostilius asked.

"I remember you spoke about a wall built by the Parthians, Vibius", I replied. "It is built on the northern borders of the Gorgan Province to keep out the horse warriors of the steppes. It borders the shore of the Hyrcanian Ocean and extends for nearly one hundred and twenty Roman miles into the foothills of the eastern mountains. Many forts line the wall. But there had been peace for years and the Parthian lords have allowed the wall to fall into disrepair. Thousands of the barbarian Xionites have overrun the meagre garrison and they have breached the wall. They are swarming across the countryside. Burning, killing, looting and destroying prosperous farms.

The area is a major food producer, thus the Sasanian Empire cannot afford to have the land ravaged and farms destroyed."

"Will it not take time to make the journey?" Vibius asked.

"That is why we have been given a thousand pounds of gold, my friends", I said, and grinned. "The Huns will be the vanguard and ride to Gorgan with all haste. We will hem in the marauding barbarian war bands, but we will not engage the main force until the heavy horse of the Persians and the Alani arrive."

"I will ride with the Huns. Primus Pilus, you and Vibius will ride with Beorgor and the rest of the mounted Persians."

Hostilius started to protest, but I held up my hand. "The Huns will ride at speed, which means nearly a hundred miles a day. Every day. But do not be concerned, we will reach the ravaged lands within three or four days and you will only be a day or two behind."

Hostilius nodded. "You are not wrong, Domitius, but I don't like it."

"I go with you", Cai said flatly.

I have learned that when Cai had made up his mind, nothing in this world can persuade him otherwise. I nodded in acceptance.

"Huns talk less than Alani", Cai added. "Better for meditation."

We left earlier than usual the following morning.

Shapur had provided us with a couple of Parthian scouts who knew the area well. They appeared to be hardy men who knew the area like the back of their hands.

The scouts could speak a bit of Greek and I was able to communicate with them on a basic level.

"We no need ugly small horses. Sorry, no offence, great lord of steppes", one told me after I commanded them to exchange their horses for the Hun horses.

I scowled. "There is no choice. Your horses will die. Hun horses are the best in the world."

Again they held up their hands in protestation. "Small barbarian horse no. We take…" and so on and so forth.

In any event, it took Gordas to draw his sword. That did the trick.

Four hours later we were still riding at a good gallop. I was leading the army with Gordas and Cai, the three scouts riding alongside us.

"Lord", said one of the scouts in broken Greek. "Horses should be dead now. No understand. Is magic?"

"No magic. Best horses in the world. They never tire", I replied.

The scout just shook his head and carried on leading the way with a concerned expression on his weathered face.

We covered a great distance that day, yet still made camp early, adjacent to some unnamed stream. There was plenty of grazing for the horses. In addition, we had brought grain to help keep them in good condition for the forthcoming battle.

Three days passed without incident. We rode like only the Huns could. Even the Persian scouts seemed to struggle to maintain the relentless pace.

At noon on the fourth day we encountered the first signs of the wanton destruction brought about by the invaders.

We came upon a village where all the inhabitants had been slaughtered. The village square was home to a large tree in which some locals were strung up, their bodies riddled with arrows. It was obvious that they were used as entertainment by the barbarians.

We burned the bodies of the villagers and made camp although it was only just past noon. I sent out many scouts. In addition I set a line of double sentries to protect the camp. I even had Gordas and his commanders check on the sentries, which was highly unusual.

"Gordas", I said, "these people are like the Huns for all we know. They are hardy horse warriors of the Sea of Grass. It will not do to underestimate them."

He scowled, but nodded. "They may be what they like, but no one will prevail against the Urugundi Huns." He paused for a moment and added: "And they do not ride with the messenger of Arash."

What do you say in response to that level of confidence?

We did not have to wait long for the scouts to report back. They failed to locate the bulk of the Xionite army, but they did come across various small raiding parties enjoying the spoils of their raids.

I summoned the Persian scouts. The destruction of their homeland left them distraught. They listened in silence to my words, eager to play their part in driving out the invaders.

"Tomorrow we leave early", I said. "Gordas, you will remain here with two thousand men. The rest of the army will split into two groups. We will leave the spare horses and hunt down the raiders."

Gordas wanted to protest, but I silenced him by raising my hand. "Do not fear, Gordas, you have a role to play."

I drew a map of the area in the dirt and explained to all.

"We will circle around the raiders and drive them in the direction of Gordas's force. Gordas, we will be the hammer and you the anvil. We will smash these small raiding parties between us. None will live to tell the tale. You will be entitled to the loot that they carry." The opportunity to gain loot appealed to the barbarian within Gordas and he smiled and nodded, suddenly content with the plan.

We struck camp before first light the following morning.

With the guidance of the local Persian scouts we travelled at speed through the early morning gloom. We rode at a fast gallop for nearly a watch when the scout reined in. I signalled a halt.

The scout inclined his head: "This where you ask be, great steppe lord. River close. We ride south and west. Many raiding parties of barbarians ride here." He pointed in the direction where Gordas and the rest of the army would be waiting in ambush.

I signalled for my sub-commanders to approach. Our group divided into three groups of five hundred warriors each, which would scour the countryside. A Persian scout accompanied each group.

Many miles to the east, the same would be happening as the other Hun war band deployed in a similar fashion. Resultantly, six war bands would drive the enemy to the anvil.

I had given specific instructions to my men. They were allowed to loot, but only gold, jewellery, clothing and weapons. Small items that would not slow them down.

We encountered the first raiding party within five miles from the outset. We fell upon the sixty odd Xionites who had just woken up from their wine-induced slumber. It was not much of a fight. We outnumbered the enemy ten to one. The only injury on our side was when one Hun broke the nose of a comrade fighting over the loot in the aftermath of the clash.

While the Huns were looting and taking scalps, I inspected the bodies.

It was clear that these men were a mixture of diverse tribes, even cultures. The man I studied possessed strong eastern features - small slanted eyes and a flat nose. The body next to him belonged to a man of small stature with a long moustache and hawk-like nose.

Cai looked over my shoulder, not bothering to dismount. "They are of the Hu, as my people call them. Mixed bag of barbarians." He pointed to the corpse with the slanted eyes. "That one prettiest."

I scowled, mounted, and we rode off in search of more victims.

The next group we encountered consisted of at least three hundred warriors. After we exchanged volleys of arrows, their leader decided that discretion is the better part of valour and the war band raced off at speed.

We gave chase for a while, but not at full speed, just to make the ruse believable.

"No be concerned, great steppe lord, they go to where warriors wait", our Persian scout explained.

We came across more Xionite war bands. All were mounted, and fled before us. In a similar fashion my other commanders were also herding the barbarians in the direction of Gordas.

But things do not always play out the way we plan.

We were descending a low grassy hill when the other side of the shallow valley slowly filled with many hundreds of screaming Xionites, heading straight for us. Their number was difficult to estimate, but the Persian scout said: "One thousand and seven hundred, great steppe lord."

I eyed him with suspicion. "Father grow many sheep", he explained. "He farmer. I learn count sheep when boy."

In any event, I was in no mood for heroics and signalled the retreat. We raced away in the direction we came from.

Fortuna is one of the gods whose work is most often overlooked or ignored.

We were fleeing for our lives when our path crossed with the remainder of our war band. No skill or wisdom was involved. Only luck.

Our pursuers were on the other side of the crest of the hill and ignorant of our bolstered numbers. We were still outnumbered, but the odds were more even. I exchanged greetings and a few words with the commanders of the other group and again we changed direction, heading straight for the enemy.

Before we crested the hill we released three volleys of arrows into the unsuspecting enemy. I had trained with the Hun cavalry under Gordas and was familiar with their way. As we raced down the slope on the other side of the hill, my signifier gave the signal for the Hun warriors to form wedges. The Xionites were still reeling from the shock of the arrow storm when the Huns extended their line and hit them with a multitude of ten-men wedges, penetrating deep into their formation.

The Huns had stored their bows as close quarter work required hand axes, spears and lassos. Two things made the difference in the end. One being the natural ferocity of the Huns, and the second, their superior armour.

There was a third factor, also.

Halfway during the battle, Gordas arrived with his two thousand strong war band.

Chapter 20 – The Wall (June 240 AD)

It is difficult to estimate how many of the enemy escaped, but I believe that it could not have been more than two hundred. In fact, I had planned it that way.

When the commanders of the main Xionite army become aware of our presence, they would recall the small raiding parties. They would not desire a repeat of the happenings of the day. This time around, their forces would be united.

Normally steppe nomads would yield little plunder, but in this case they have been stuffing their purses with Persian gold for weeks.

Gordas had no qualms to participate in the looting. Later on, as evening descended, he came to seek me out.

"The warriors are content, Eochar. The dead yielded rich pickings. The enemy warriors carried much gold. In addition, we gained nearly eight hundred horses."

He thirstily drank from a looted skin that I was sure did not contain water. He offered it to me, but I declined.

"The men are cheering your name, my friend. They say that they have never seen the feigned retreat executed more convincingly. They are convinced that you are the messenger of Arash."

"Gordas, it wasn't a feigned retreat, we were running for our lives", I said.

He burst out laughing and slapped my back, the contents of the skin clearly having taken effect. "Your jests are even better than Cai's."

I tried a second time, but Gordas was not to be persuaded otherwise.

"Luck? You call it luck? There is no such thing, my friend", he said. "The gods decide the outcome of events. Arash intervened because you are his favourite."

Many horses were killed during the fight and it went without saying that we would eat well that evening. Gordas took it upon himself to organize an impromptu feast in my honour. The senior Hun commanders joined us around the fire where an unfortunate sheep was spitted along with choice cuts of horse meat. They had taken copious quantities of Persian wine from the raiders so there was more than enough to go around.

I drank sparingly. In contrast, the Huns celebrated their new-found riches with gusto.

Should we have been attacked that evening, it would not have gone well for us, but the gods were merciful.

The morning was pleasant and it was with no great difficulty that I rose before first light. I found Gordas already awake, lighting a fire. There was no sign of the drunken stupor he had succumbed to the evening before.

"How do you do this, Gordas?"

"Do what?" he replied.

"Drink that much without suffering from a hangover."

He produced a small clay flask. "Cai gave me this potion", he replied with a grin. "I can ask him to mix you some as well."

In any event, we were not going to war that day, but I did send a multitude of scouts in every conceivable direction. Some were to report back, while others would remain in the field and alert us should the enemy approach.

By early afternoon the first Persian scout reported back.

"Army approaching, great steppe lord." Obviously he had my immediate attention, but before I could pose a question he added: "Prince Shapur army."

Within less than a watch, Beorgor, Hostilius and Vibius joined us in camp.

Hostilius wore a generally dejected expression. "I knew I would miss all the fighting. I knew it."

"Don't be concerned, Primus Pilus, there is still a big fight coming. What you missed was little more than a skirmish", I said.

Vibius interrupted. "It's not exactly the story the Persian scouts are spreading in camp. They tell about a major victory won by the great lord of the steppes."

Before I could reply, one of the Hun scouting parties arrived back.

They reported to Gordas, but I was close enough to overhear. "General, we have found the camp of the enemy. Many thousands of warriors with much loot. All the time small groups of raiders are still arriving."

Gordas called me over. "Eochar, you would want to hear this", the Hun commander said.

The scout inclined his head and continued. "Half a day's ride that way." He pointed due north.

"How many?" I asked.

"Twenty thousand, lord."

I nodded. "Rest and be ready to ride in the morning."

I turned to face Hostilius and Vibius. "I need my bodyguards. We will go and speak with the prince."

When we arrived, servants had just finished pitching the not-so-insignificant tent of the prince. Shapur was standing close by, deep in conversation with his commanders. I was allowed to approach. He noticed my gaze linger on the tent.

"Lord Eochar", he said, "the tent can be transported in sections on packhorses, like we did during the last four days. Normally it would travel on a wagon."

"Prince Shapur, I need to share urgent information with you", I said.

He held up his hand to stop my response. "I have convened a meeting of my commanders. You will soon have the opportunity."

He walked towards the entrance of the large tent and gestured for the men to enter, which included myself.

He sat down on a low stool, while all the commanders sat on the thick woollen carpets or soft furs. Servants poured wine into silver goblets and distributed it with the help of silver trays. When all was done, the prince waved the servants from his presence. The immortal guards barred the entrance as well as the outside perimeter of the tent from unwanted ears.

Shapur nodded in my direction. "Lord Eochar. Please continue." He spoke in Greek and I was confident that his commanders possessed a good command of the language.

I continued in Greek. "My barbarian scouts have located the main camp of the enemy. They report numbers in excess of twenty thousand", I said. "Apparently the Xionites are preparing to return the way they came. They are encumbered by wagons heavy with Persian loot."

Shapur nodded his head in recognition of my report.

He stood, radiating confidence and superiority. I barely managed to restrain myself from smiling openly at the similarity between the Roman nobility and what I was experiencing with the Sasanians.

"I have devised a plan to crush the barbarian rabble", Shapur said.

He looked my way with half a smile. "No offence, Lord Eochar."

I spent nearly a full watch within the confines of the tent as Shapur explained his plan. He unfolded a velum map of the province of Gorgan and indicated all the troop movements. The plan was discussed in detail. Shapur asked probing questions to assure himself that all understood.

The sun had set by the time I joined my scowling bodyguards outside the tent.

"These immortal bastards didn't even share their wine with us", Hostilius said with a scowl. "If soldiers don't share their wine, it is a sign to watch your back, Domitius. Mark my words. I have been around the block a couple of times."

I took his words to heart. Hostilius was no fool.

"I have always believed that Shapur is a pompous bastard", I said. "But today I have changed my view. I now think he is a clever and extremely capable pompous bastard."

I explained the prince's plan to my companions, detailing the roles that they would play.

The next morning was overcast and gloomy.

"A storm is brewing in the east", Hostilius said.

"He means it literally, Cai", I interjected.

"Of course he does", was the only reply I received.

Gordas arrived while we were preparing for the journey. "We have the warhorses, Eochar", Gordas confirmed. "All ten thousand of them."

"Good", I replied. "I will join you as soon as the Persian scouts arrive."

Shapur did not only desire to chase the Xionites from Persia. He wished to destroy their army.

In order to crush them, they needed to be hemmed in. This was close to impossible on the open terrain on which they were camped. Should he offer battle near their camp, they would use their mobility to avoid the heavy cavalry and the vastly outnumbered Huns. They would scatter in all directions and happily raid their way across the countryside, eventually filtering across the border passes.

There was only one way to score a decisive blow. The heavy cavalry would strike when the enemy had their backs to the wall - the Gorgan Wall.

Shapur needed to create a ruse that his army was a lumbering giant of infantry and heavy cavalry marching inexorably towards the Xionite camp. That would ensure that the enemy would not flee in haste, but that they would slowly move north towards the breach in the wall. Thus they would retain their valuable loot. Their only concern would be to ensure that they were able to outrun the slow Persian army.

The nomads were acutely aware of the fact that the slower heavy cavalry of the Persians would be unable to give chase. As long as the Sasanian army remained at their rear, there was little risk to them.

The first phase of Shapur's plan was to send the warhorses of his heavy cavalry to the Gorgan Wall, close to where the ambush would take place, but not close enough to be discovered by the enemy scouts. The Persian horses would remain on the west side of the breach but the Parthian and Alani warhorses would be hidden on the east side of the breach. My Huns would give effect to this part of the plan.

When the Xionites neared the breach in the Gorgan wall, Shapur would send the riders of the warhorses and their apprentices with all haste via a back route, travelling through the night if necessary. They would meet with the Huns and their rested warhorses. They would be ready to strike at the enemy when they were about to cross the breach.

Shapur expected that the Xionites would become aware of the absence of part of the army, but with the heavy cavalry in place, it would be too late for them. The Dailamite infantry would advance on horseback to act as a stopper should the Xionites try to backtrack once they became aware of the ruse.

My Huns would wait in the hinterland north of the wall to delay their passage through the breach.

We rode the rest of the day, being led to the wall by way of a considerable detour to ensure that we were not detected by the enemy. We could not travel at speed due to the presence of the powerful warhorses who were prone to fatigue. The Huns knew horses well, therefore we stopped regularly to ensure that we did not overwork the huge beasts.

The farther north we rode from the snowy mountains, the drier the landscape became. Even the rain abated, leaving a heavily overcast sky. Soon we rode through what could only be described as semi-desert, the only vegetation being knee-high bushes that required little water to thrive. We did still encounter the occasional flock of short-haired sheep and goats, which seemed to be well adapted to the dry environment.

During the late afternoon of the second day, a Persian scout pulled his horse next to Simsek. I have come to know him. "Greetings Pezhman", I said.

"Greetings, great steppe lord", the scout replied.

He pointed into the distance. "Look, great steppe lord, red snake there."

Ten miles away, I noticed a winding, reddish structure.

"Where will we make camp?" I asked the scout.

"We camp next to Gorganrud River. Only place horses have water, great steppe lord."

An idea came to me. "Are you a Parthian?" I asked.

My probing question clearly made Pezhman nervous, but I pushed on. "How did you end up as a scout for the Parthian lord of Gorgan?"

"Great steppe lord, when me boy, Parthians war with Saka horse people. My family dead. They take me for work. Pezhman scout good. Pezhman good with horse. Work for high lord."

"Good", I said, dismissing the scout. Arash had given me a plan.

Pezhman led us to a ford soon after we reached the river. Even though the water was shallow at the crossing point, it took the rest of the day to cross the thousands of horses to the northern bank, which was less than a mile from the wall.

I left Gordas to supervise the crossing, and guided by the scout, my friends and I set off to inspect the wall.

The wall was built out of mud bricks. Pezhman enlightened us. "Soil and mud from river mixed with red sand and straw. Then bricks burn to make strong."

Vibius could speak Persian, but for my benefit he asked in broken Greek: "Who built?", and pointed to the wall.

"Parthians say it Parthians who built", Pezhman said with a smile. "Persians say it Persians of long years ago who built. Some say it great war god from Macedon, Iskander, who built."

He leaned in conspiratorially. "Great steppe lord, me think they all built piece. Some day will need new wall. Strong wall. Horse people always come. Wolves from Steppes grow stronger. Long-head warriors with scars in face that ride with you. Much dangerous men. One kill many Persians."

I was warming to Pezhman. He must have been a year or two younger than me, and although he was sinewy, he had a powerful look about him.

"My ancestors great Saka warriors", he added. "Even mighty Iskander not march onto Sea of Grass ruled by People of Wolf."

"Pezhman, if your father and mother were Saka, why do you speak Greek? Why do you not speak the language of the Sea of Grass?" I asked.

He looked at me in disbelief, as if the answer was obvious, continuing in perfect Scythian: "My Parthian lord does not wish for me to converse in the language of the Sea of Grass, lord."

Chapter 21 – Ambush

The plan of prince Shapur was to trap the Xionites between the river and the wall, then smash them from both flanks with the heavy cavalry.

We were camped fifteen miles west of the breach in the wall.

The five thousand warhorses of the immortals would remain at the camp, to be ready when their riders arrived. The warhorses of the Alani and the Parthian lords still had to be taken to the eastern side of the breach in the wall. We could not travel on the Gorgan side of the wall, as the passage of so many horses, and the inevitable tracks they create, would alert the enemy to our presence.

Forts dotted the wall at regular intervals. The strongholds were designed to accommodate up to five hundred warriors each, but the long years of peace has had its effect and less than fifty clearly terrified men garrisoned the fort that guarded the gate we would use as a passage through the wall.

It was with great difficulty that we persuaded the suspicious Parthians to open the gate, even though we were armed with the written orders of Shapur and the lord of Gorgan. Eventually it was the presence of Pezhman that did the trick, as he was recognised by one of the guard officers.

We passed the breach in the wall, and I briefly reined in to study it. The nomads had destroyed a fort and demolished a section of the wall, leaving a gap of at least forty paces across which was clear of debris.

Fifteen miles east of the breach we had to cross back into Gorgan, and surprisingly, we were welcomed. A messenger had arrived from the prince informing the guards of what was to transpire and the gates opened without a challenge, although we were eyed with suspicion.

I spent the night east of the breach and left early in the morning, accompanied by two hundred Huns, leaving eight hundred to guard the horses. By afternoon we were back in the main camp where a messenger awaited my arrival.

"Lord Eochar, prince Shapur says that Xionite army will arrive day after tomorrow. Tomorrow night, the immortals and the Alani will arrive and prepare." I nodded and sent him back to his master, confirming that all was in place.

I was confident that our part in Shapur's plan would be executed as planned. As soon as at least two thousand of the Xionites pass through the breach, the Huns would fall upon them. At the same time the heavy cavalry would strike the enemy in the flanks. The Dailamites would guard the southern bank of the river, ensuring that none crossed back into Gorgan.

But I had other concerns nagging at me so I called an impromptu meeting with my companions, as well as Gordas and Beorgor. I shared my thoughts with them.

"I do not trust Shapur to release us once we are back on the southern side of the wall", I said. "It is a feeling. Apart from the attack by one of his guards, it has been little things here and there. A look. A hushed conversation among his commanders. A sudden silence when I arrive. I would hear your thoughts."

Hostilius was the first to speak. "If they trap us on the inside of the wall, the heavy cavalry will slaughter us all. There are not enough of the Alani to stand against them. The Persians number in excess of twelve thousand. I have seen the way they look at us. They need us for the time being, but after the Xionites are vanquished we become just another band of barbarians that needs killing."

"Feels wrong to agree with Hostilius, but he speak wise words", Cai added. "Shapur using hand of enemy to catch snake. People praise him if we die. Stabbing barbarian allies in back, not seen as treachery."

"I agree", Vibius said. "I have heard whisperings around the camp, but nothing certain. We are at risk."

"We could kill all the Persians when they arrive and join the Xionites?" Gordas predictably suggested.

I shook my head. "We will stop the enemy in the breach as we promised to do, but we will not return to the south of the Gorgan Wall. We will travel back to the lands of the Huns along the east coast of the Hyrcanian Ocean."

I looked at Beorgor. "The challenge would be to extract the Alani after the battle. But do not be concerned Beorgor, we will not abandon our friends."

He nodded and drank from his cup.

I turned to Gordas. "Are the horses that you have taken in battle of quality?"

A hint of a frown appeared on Gordas's face, but he humoured me nonetheless. "They are not that different from Hun horses, maybe slightly taller and slimmer."

"Good", I replied. "I need two of the best geldings with saddles brought to me first thing tomorrow."

Gordas's frown turned into a sly smile and he inclined his head. "I will do as Arash commands you."

I nodded and continued. "Gordas, are you able to spare me two hundred of your warriors tomorrow? They will join the other eight hundred waiting with the Alani horses."

"Four thousand Huns will be more than enough to deal with the enemy who makes it through the breach", Gordas stated confidently. "I can spare two hundred of my men."

I retired early, but slept fitfully.

I woke up with a start when Hostilius kicked my leg. "It is the third watch of the night and the first of the Persians are arriving."

He helped me don my armour. "Domitius, I will join you on the southern side of the wall today", he said. "I need to witness the Persian heavy cavalry in action. I cannot sit idly on the other side of the wall."

I nodded. It would be our only opportunity to see the heavy cavalry in action.

Gordas was waiting outside the tent with two magnificent horses. I thanked him and took the reins.

Shapur would be with the immortals and I did not want to linger because I would be bending the orders of the Sasanian prince by taking the thousand Huns south of the wall and joining the Alani.

Cai had a bored look about him. "I go with Gordas. Someone with common sense need accompany Huns." With that he waved me away.

We had to repeat our route of the previous day, this time followed by thousands of Parthian and Alani cavalrymen and apprentices, all riding their spare horses.

As soon as we had crossed to the north of the wall, I summoned Pezhman. I passed him the reins of the two horses that Gordas had procured. He mounted, handing me the reins of his horse, inclined his head and rode off, smiling. Two hundred Huns peeled off from our group and followed him into the night.

"I don't even want to ask what all that was about", Hostilius said.

"Good", I replied.

We travelled slowly by the light of a partial moon. There was no need to hurry. The scouts had informed me that the Xionites were only expected to reach the wall by the second watch of the morning.

When the first light of dawn illuminated our way, we were still seven miles from our destination, therefore we increased our speed to a canter. Within a third of a watch we reached the gated fort in the wall on the east side of the breach and passed back into Gorgan territory without incident.

On the southern side of the wall the Alani and the Parthian heavy cavalry prepared for the ambush.

"Make sure you form up on the right flank, next to the wall", I told Beorgor. "The Parthian heavy horse can take the area bordering the river." He nodded and rode off.

I followed with the Huns in tow, keeping my distance. I could see Beorgor waving his arms, arguing with the commander of the Parthian cavalry, frequently pointing in my direction. The Parthian shook his head and walked away, clearly unhappy.

Beorgor walked his horse towards me. He was grinning.

"What was that all about?" I asked.

"The commander of the Gorgan heavy cavalry is Lord Yazdan. He told me that prince Shapur had instructed him to take the right flank, closest to the wall. I said to him that prince Eochar had told me the same. I advised him to come and discuss it with you, Lord Eochar the Merciless. I told him the last man who confronted you was the immortal, in the presence of the Prince. He heard that the immortal had lost his head and he decided that he was content to take the left flank."

Never underestimate the value of a reputation.

The scout jumped from his lathered horse. I held up my hand and offered him my wineskin. He took a long swallow. "Thank you, great steppe lord. Enemy crossing river. Vanguard crossing breach in wall."

We had begun our advance during the course of the morning but were still three miles away from the enemy. We walked the horses to minimise the dust cloud, but it was unavoidable that the enemy would soon become aware of our presence.

"It is time", I told Beorgor. "The heavy cavalry must immediately mount their warhorses. Is everything ready?"

"Yes, lord", he said, and inclined his head.

I looked over my shoulder at the deep ranks of Alani heavy cavalry. The horses were encased in scale, chain and boiled leather. The riders were all but impregnable. Thick iron helmets with chain protected their necks. Their bodies were covered with iron and bronze scale. Vambraces and greaves completed the picture.

"May Arash grant you victory", I said to Beorgor.

He nodded. "You should go to the back, lord", he said. "You are not dressed for the occasion."

I was not going to join the heavy cavalry. I was there only to observe.

Arash had other plans.

Chapter 22 – Wall of steel

Hostilius and I soon realised that we could see little more than the rear ends of the warhorses from our position. I waved one of the Hun warriors closer. "Follow us", I commanded.

"Yes, lord", he said.

"We need to get onto the wall", I said to Hostilius as I took my bow and two quivers from my saddle.

We rode up to the wall and when we drew alongside it, I crouched with my feet on the saddle and jumped to reach the battlements which were within my reach.

"I can't manage that, Domitius", Hostilius yelled. "I'm no horse barbarian."

I leaned over the battlements. "You don't have to jump, Primus Pilus, just give me your hand."

I grabbed his extended arm by the wrist and for a few moments he dangled with his feet in the air. The Hun warrior had the clarity of mind to push Hostilius up by his feet and soon he was standing next to me on the wall, albeit with injured pride.

"Now that was undignified", he muttered under his breath as he followed me in the direction of the breach.

I yelled to the Hun warrior who held our horses. "Wait here with the horses. Approach when I signal."

He nodded.

From the top of the wall we were afforded a hawk's eye view of the unfolding battle. The sky was overcast and I was sure that it was raining closer to the mountains.

On the northern side of the breach, outside of the wall, the Huns had engaged the Xionites. Rather than fighting at close quarters, the two forces were trading volley after volley of arrows. The Huns held not only the numerical advantage, but they were better armoured and their asymmetric bows were superior to those of the Xionites. Already the enemy was pouring back through the breach, trying to avoid the deadly Hun arrows with their superior range.

Inside the wall, thousands of barbarians were milling around, not sure of what was happening north of the wall. Warriors on the flanks had noticed the approaching heavy cavalry and were shouting warnings to their commanders. Within moments the Xionite commanders launched an attack on the approaching cavalry. The sky darkened as large groups of nomads galloped towards the heavy cavalry releasing thousands upon thousands of arrows, then turning back to regroup and launch another attack.

The sight of the approaching heavy cavalry knotted my stomach, even though I was merely an observer. They rode knee to knee, their line extending in excess of a mile, four ranks deep on both flanks.

The enemy arrow rain was relentless. From time to time I noticed an unfortunate rider clutching his head and falling from his mount to be trampled to death by his comrades. But the barbarian arrows were hunting arrows, not armour-piercing war arrows, therefore too few of the heavy riders fell to stop the flood of metal. When the men clad in iron were three hundred paces from the enemy they accelerated to a canter. All around the ground began to shake as forty thousand hooves pounded the dirt.

At eighty paces, the riders slowly lowered their heavy two-handed spears and spurred their horses to a gallop. Moments later they impacted the barbarian line with an audible clash. The spears sliced through mail and flesh, in some instances impaling two or even three of the enemy, the huge horses bowling over the smaller animals. The combined weight of the four ranks were almost unstoppable. The riders let go of the spears that were encumbered with bodies and drew either hand axes, maces or swords to finish what they had started.

It took many well-placed blows to take down even one of the metal-clad monsters and soon the battle turned into a one-sided slaughter. Hundreds of the raiders tried to flee back across the ford in the river, only to find their way barred by the heavily armoured, spear-carrying Dailamites. They presented their oversized shields, locked in a shield wall, to the nomads' arrows, and slaughtered them with their two-pronged spears and battle axes when they tried to force their way through to freedom.

Some of the enemy escaped down the flow of the river, miraculously weaving through the ranks of heavy cavalry, or by evading the Huns in the dust-filled confusion on the north side of the wall. Thousands upon thousands of dead men and horses filled the space between the two wings of the Persian army. The wounded yelled and moaned in pain and despair, knowing that no chance of salvation existed.

The hairs on the back of my neck raised when I realised what was happening. Or rather, what was not happening. There was no looting whatsoever.

At my side, Hostilius stood without speaking, affected by the horrific slaughter that he had witnessed.

My voice came out as a hoarse whisper. "The battle is only over when the looting starts, Primus Pilus. They are coming for us. That is why there is no looting."

I signalled to the Hun warrior, who trotted closer with our horses in tow. We lowered ourselves from the wall and mounted.

197

My mind was racing, trying to work out the best course of action. There was only one viable option. Shapur would certainly have strengthened the garrisons of the forts guarding the gates further along the wall. We had to pass through the breach in the wall.

I had issued my instructions to Beorgor earlier. There was to be no looting and he had to be ready to advance through the breach should things go wrong. I signalled for the commander of the Huns to join us and we rode towards Beorgor who trotted closer.

"We must ride through the breach now!" I said. As I pointed to the opening in the wall three hundred paces distant, I could see rank upon rank of heavily armoured Dailamites marching into position. Shapur was blocking our route of escape.

Two unexpected eventualities unfolded in our favour. Heaped corpses of men and horses blocked the advance of the five thousand immortals who had attacked the western flank of the Xionites. In contrast, few bodies obstructed the breach as most of the enemy in that area had fled north of the wall when the heavy cavalry attacked.

Most of the enemy warhorses were spent after the fight with the barbarians. Not being able to muster another charge from their tired mounts, the three thousand Parthians dressed their ranks and advanced towards us at a walk. We were trapped between them and the Dailamites. The Parthians were buying time for the immortals to pick their way through the field of dead, regroup, and hit us in the flank.

I was forced to use the Huns to keep the Parthian heavy cavalry's advance in check. They rode at the enemy and released arrows at short range along the line, all but halting the slow advance of the Parthians. Unlike the immortals, the Parthian heavy cavalry did not carry bows, leaving them unable to retaliate in kind.

"My men can do this", Beorgor growled. "They will crush the Parthian cavalry, but it will be to no avail. When the horses are spent, the immortals will kill us all."

"The best you can do, lord, is ask Arash to intervene", the Alani added.

He had barely finished uttering the words when two enormous clouds of dust appeared on the far side of the Gorgan Wall. It slowly rose, swirling to the heavens above the breach.

In the distance, above the sounds of the dead and dying, I could hear the howling of four thousand Huns. The whirlwind had arrived, and in its wake would come the storm.

Beorgor looked over his shoulder and pointed at the dust clouds. "What is that, lord? Has Arash sent us a storm?"

"Let your men mount their spare horses and be ready to ride", I replied. "There will be no more fighting on this side of the wall today. And yes, the storm of death is coming."

The Dailamite infantry blocking the breach stood ten ranks deep. Five facing either way. It was common knowledge that their huge shields and thick armour made them impervious to attack by arrows, which was the reason Shapur used them.

But they had never before faced the arrow storm of the Urugundi Huns. Thousands of Huns peeled off the counter-rotating circles, riding at an angle towards the breach. Every warrior releasing an arrow every three heartbeats, then re-joining the circle. This constant stream of arrows were concentrated along a twenty paces section in the centre of the Dailamite shield wall. Sixty arrows impacted each shield every heartbeat, causing them to waver. Arrows poured through the resulting gaps. Within less than a hundred heartbeats the Dailamite line broke. It was the moment the Huns were waiting for and rather than continue with the barrage of missiles, they engaged the heavy infantry. Plucking shields away with lassos, splitting skulls with hand axes. All done at break-neck speed from the backs of their horses.

The spearmen facing us turned around to support their floundering comrades. Beorgor seized the opportunity. The Alani heavy cavalry struck the Dailamites from behind like a giant fist of iron. The remaining spearmen fled, but most were slaughtered by a multitude of arrows.

The Alani went through first, with the Huns on our side of the wall covering their retreat.

As we rode away from the wall, I saw Shapur and his immortal entourage arriving at the breach. He stared at us intently, but did not try to pursue us. He knew that the open spaces of the plain were the forte of the nomads.

Under the leadership of Ardashir and Shapur I knew that the Sasanians would soon be a power to rival that of Rome.

Chapter 23 – The Black Sand

Soon we were north of the wall where a grinning Gordas waited for us.

"It is good to follow you, Eochar. Arash is never far from where you are", the Hun said.

Gordas pointed to a train of wagons in the distance. "The Xionites sent their wagons filled with loot through the breach ahead of the army. We waited patiently until they had presented us with this gift before we attacked."

"Huns so enamoured with loot, not even notice spearman blocking breach", Cai said. "Fortunate thing I follow way of Dao - place no value in shiny trinkets. Rather keep eyes on wall."

Gordas scowled. "I was making sure that Eochar's orders were followed", and he pointed to four carts heaped with empty looted waterskins.

Hostilius slapped my back. "We have done it, Domitius. We are safe."

From the east a dust cloud rose, warning us of the approach of horsemen. Gordas instinctively reached for his bow.

I held up my hand. "It is only Pezhman returning. I sent him away on a mission."

"Is he not the Persian scout?" Hostilius asked.

"Primus Pilus, Pezhman has wisely left the employ of Shapur. He now works for me", I replied.

Hostilius raised his eyebrows.

"The route home is not as easy as you might have thought", I said. "Between us and the Sea of Grass lie the great deserts of Kara Kum and Kyzyl Kum, the Black Sand and the Red Sand. Beyond the deserts are the fertile lands of Chorasmia. There is a road through the Kara Kum, used by merchants, which will lead us to the Valley of the Wolves in Chorasmia, the place the locals call Jurjan. I have heard that from Jurjan the road continues on towards the Sea of Grass, again crossing a vast arid plain."

By then, a smiling Pezhman reined in his horse next to us.

"I have located a man of my people who knows the road to Chorasmia. From here we will ride north to a ford in the Atrak River. We will cross the river, fill our waterskins and rest the horses. From there it will be three of four days' ride across the Black Sand."

He smiled broadly. "It will be easy, lord. We know the way."

The river was three days' ride behind us. Pezhman and the Saka scout led the way.

Hostilius and Vibius were riding at my side, both having the appearance of desert nomads, although Vibius's headdress resembled the real thing.

"The Persian girl who raised me had made me practise tying the 'shemagh' when I was a boy. It was probably just to keep me out of mischief", he explained, proudly pointing to the expertly tied cloth which covered his whole face, except his eyes.

We had cut up our spare tunics or looted clothing as we soon realised that the sun of Kara Kum was vastly different to the sun of the Sea of Grass. The nights and the mornings were cold, but we were all used to enduring low temperatures. Before the end of the first watch of the day, the temperature would rise to a level which I imagined could only be recreated in an oven. There was no wind, only a searing heat that drained the body of moisture and energy.

Our lips were chapped and our exposed arms, hands, and feet were blistery and red from sunburn.

The exception was Cai of course. His head was wrapped in a shiny white shemagh and his long white silk robe covered even his hands.

Hostilius looked at Cai with a sideways glance. "How come you look so cool and relaxed?"

"I not waste energy on idle chatter that drain body of moisture. Silence speak thousand words", Cai answered.

Hostilius rolled his eyes.

The Saka scout reined in his horse to draw parallel with mine.

"Lord, we will reach the Valley of the Wolf this afternoon", Pezhman said. "Chorasmia used to be ruled by kings with friendly relations to Parthia. When the Chorasmians were attacked by horse warriors, they hid behind thick walls until the allied Parthians came to relieve the siege. When high king Ardashir started fighting the Parthian lords, a new king took power. He is Afrig of Kath, a powerful warrior. I think it will be good if you speak with him before bringing the army close."

My Saka scout was correct of course.

Shortly after our discussion we stopped briefly to allow the horses to drink of the precious little water we had left.

I used the opportunity. "Vibius, come with me", I said.

As I turned my horse, I heard Cai say: "I go too."

I nodded.

We went in search of Gordas who was riding with the Huns about four hundred paces down the line.

I had earlier ordered Gordas to keep an emergency reserve of a hundred waterskins.

Gordas noticed our approach and reined in. "I had to issue sixty additional waterskins already", he said. "He smiled cruelly and continued. "It was only for horses that were close to collapse. The men have been rationing their water well. We are Huns. This heat is as nothing to us."

"Join me", I said, "and bring six skins of water for our horses. Five of us are going for a ride."

"Why six skins for five horses?" Gordas queried.

"It's for the sixth horse. Load it with a hundred pounds of the looted gold", I replied.

We rode for a full watch before we reached the fort at Jurjan. The gates were closed, with many soldiers manning the walls.

I was about to announce our presence when Cai nudged his horse forward. He addressed the captain of the sentries, using the language of the steppes. "Please inform honourable king that Lord Cai Lun of Empire of the East has arrived."

My friends gaped at me, as surprised as I.

The captain of the guard disappeared to consult with his superiors.

"Why didn't you tell us of your plan?" I asked Cai.

"No need waste breath. I heard of travellers on Road of Silk pass through Chorasmia. They say king of Chorasmia high regard for lords from Serica. Eastern lords come with silk caravans, spend much coin. No threat", Cai explained.

Soon the thick wood and iron-studded gates creaked open. To my surprise, a man similar in appearance to Cai shuffled through and started conversing with him in the eastern language of Serica.

He signalled for Gordas to bring the horse loaded with gold. I caught Gordas's eye and gave him an imperceptible nod.

Cai turned to me. "Secretary to king says must leave barbarian servants outside gate. Not welcome in city."

Again I nodded.

A third of a watch later the gates opened. Many wagons laden with water and provisions slowly exited, creaking under their heavy loads.

"Lord Cai Lun says not to bother him again today", the captain of the guard said. "The provisions and water is for his army.

They may camp three miles outside of the city. The wagon drivers will show you. Now begone from my sight, barbarians. Do as your lord Cai Lun commands."

Gordas and Vibius stared at me with blank expressions.

"What are you waiting for, barbarian rabble", I said and grinned. "Lord Cai Lun has spoken."

Chapter 24 – Return (September 240 AD)

I took a deep swallow of the purple-coloured red wine and placed the empty cup on the side table next to the couch.

Timesitheus said nothing, averting his gaze. I knew he wanted to believe. I could feel it.

Senator Crispinus was the first to speak.

He grinned, and slapped my back. "Remember, Timesitheus, Lucius is no deceiving Roman."

To my surprise, Cai took two scrolls from a leather bag and handed it to Timesitheus. "Wise man from Serica once said that to see is to believe."

He waited until Timesitheus had unrolled the scrolls. Both were written in Persian and Greek, the intricate seals glistening in the light of the oil lamps.

"I keep written orders from Prince Shapur and lord of Gorgan. Make nice souvenir", Cai said.

It was my turn to surprise. I walked to the pigeon holes above the desk and extracted two scrolls.

I handed a copy each to the governor and the procurator.

"We have compiled a detailed report on the army and the tactics of the Sasanians", I said. "You will find that it contains details regarding the reporting structure, composition and capabilities. I am sure that the emperor will find it useful in the near future."

"There is however one thing that I could not add to the report", I said, and sighed.

Crispinus raised his eyebrows. "How so? It looks as if this report deals even with the most minute of details."

"As I have mentioned in my report, Ardashir is called The Unifier. He makes the decisions - all of them. He does not suffer disobedience from the Parthian lords. When the Sasanian army takes the field, they now fight as one. But the most important factor I could not mention in writing is that everything about the army feels similar in professionalism to the Roman army. It is as if he has succeeded in creating a second Roman military in the east. The only difference being that Rome's army is built upon the might of the infantry, while the Sasanian army revolves around the heavy cavalry. If we do not change our tactics, we will not carry the day against them on the flat plains of Persia."

No one spoke.

I was sure that I had overstepped the line.

Timesitheus looked at Hostilius. "What do you think, Centurion?"

"I concur with everything the prefect has said", Hostilius answered. "These Persians are right hard bastards, sir. They have watched us and learned from us. We also need to change. We need to improve."

Timesitheus sighed. "It is hard to face the reality. I will discuss your advice with the emperor. We will not make the mistake of underestimating the enemy."

"The Empire owes you a great debt", Crispinus said. "All of you. You have accomplished something I would have thought impossible."

They stood to leave.

"If I may, I have prepared a demonstration for your benefit", I said.

Crispinus raised his eyebrows, but nodded his head.

"Please allow me time to prepare", I said, and added, "tell your guards to stay their hands." I left the entourage in the company of Cai and Hostilius, who escorted them out the gates.

Pezhman assisted me to don the armour of the immortal guard whom I had killed months earlier. First we fitted the heavy iron greaves and vambraces, then he helped me into the leather shirt with the thick iron scales. The scale shirt had slits on the sides to accommodate riding, and it extended to the knees. He strapped on the shoulder harness, to keep all tightly in place, and I fastened the weapons belt around my waist. The belt had space for a sword, a dagger and a mace. Leather straps extended from both sides of the belt, to which Pezhman tied my bow case and quiver. I fitted the reinforced plumed helmet decorated with silver and gold. The helmet sported an engraved brow guard and all along the rim, thick chain mail hung from the helmet, resting on the shoulders. The only exposed openings being the eyeholes.

Pezhman took a step backwards, grinned, and said in Greek: "Great steppe lord, you have become Persian immortal. I cannot help feel scared inside. I cannot even speak in language of Sea of Grass with immortal."

I slapped his shoulder and we exited the back way to where the monstrous Nisean was waiting. My Roxolani had fitted the armour that Gordas had 'procured' for me one night from the Persian camp. Its entire body was covered by an apron of leather, fitted with large iron scales. The head was encased in a bronze plate and the neck protected by scale and chain.

Pezhman assisted me into the horned saddle and handed me the thick wooden lance, eighteen feet long, and tipped with a wickedly sharp armour-piercing iron tip.

I walked the horse fifty paces in the opposite direction to where the imperial entourage was waiting out of sight, around the corner of the wooden walls.

The Nisean accelerated from standstill to a gallop in the blink of an eye. I rounded the corner at a blistering pace, thundering to where the spectators waited, now wide-eyed. The Germani guards' eyes moved from side to side, a tell-tale sign of men ready to turn tail and run.

I lowered the lance that I held in both hands, galloping at full speed, and reined in ten paces away from the group. The Nisean snorted, pawed the ground with its enormous front hoof and shook its head from side to side, clearly unhappy that I had aborted the charge.

I dismounted and removed my helmet, handing the reins to a wary Hostilius.

"I illustrated a charge by the heavy cavalry, which the Persians call the immortals", I explained. "As you will read in my report, Ardashir has a personal guard of ten thousand of them. I thought it better that you experience it, rather than just read about it. The horse, the armour, as well as the weapons are originals from Persia."

The whole group, apart from my friends, were visibly shaken by my demonstration. Timesitheus looked up at the horse.

"By all the gods, this monster will run right over a Roman horse. It gallops with armour as if unencumbered."

Crispinus asked, now clearly worried. "I knew it was you, yet I was still overcome with fear. Are there ways to defeat these monsters? Will the legions be able to stand against them?"

I spent a third of a watch answering questions about the heavy cavalry. In the end they were satisfied. I had succeeded in bringing the message home. The Sasanids were not to be underestimated.

Eventually I clasped arms with the governor and the procurator and they turned to leave.

Then a frown crossed Timesitheus's face. "It nearly slipped my mind, Prefect, but did you mention that Tullus Menophilus did not pay the Carpiani their, er... bribe, for lack of a better word?"

"That is what I was told by Thiaper of the Carpiani, Procurator", I answered.

"Hmm..., I will make a point of requesting the emperor to look into it", he said as if to himself. They walked away, followed by their burly Germani guards.

As soon as they were out of earshot, Hostilius turned to me and said in a low whisper: "Governor Tullus Menophilus is a dead man. If you steal from your comrades in the legions they find your bloated corpse one sunny morning floating facedown in the river. What do you think the emperor does when his comrades steal from him? Let me tell you. The same bloody thing."

"Don't be ridiculous, Primus Pilus, Tullus Menophilus is a well-respected governor", I replied.

"Well-respected my arse. In the end it's all about the gold. It always is, mark my words", Hostilius said.

Vibius was not privy to the meeting with the imperial delegation as his rank was not senior enough to allow his presence. We strolled over to where he was in discussion with one of our Roxolani guards.

I gestured for him to join us and my friends followed me into the main house. I walked down the stairs that led to the spacious wine cellar.

"I agree, Domitius", Hostilius said. "The completion of our mission calls for a celebration. It's never too early in the day to start drinking."

"And never too late in day to stop", Cai countered.

I walked to one of the shelves, grasped it tightly and opened it like a door.

Hostilius could not contain himself. "Good thinking, Domitius. Always stash the real good vintages where no one

215

else can lay their grubby hands on it. I do the same, you know."

To the disappointment of Hostilius, the small room did not contain a stash of the best vintages. It had the appearance of a store room. The back wall of the room was crude stone which had been chiselled to a near flat surface. I inserted a metal rod into a small hole and rolled the stone to the side, into a hidden groove, revealing a long, dark passage. Old wooden chests, some bound in copper and decorated with leather, were stacked against the sides of the passage.

Three similar chests stood awkwardly in the middle of the walkway.

The conversation died instantly.

"Open it", I said. "There is one chest for each of you."

Hostilius crouched down on his haunches and opened a chest.

"Each chest contains seven thousand eight hundred gold aurei", I said, "the equivalent of one hundred and twelve pounds of gold. It is a quarter share of our profits."

Allow me to digress. One gold aureus is equal to twenty-five silver denari or one hundred bronze sestercii. One hundred thousand sestercii is equal to the annual salary of a Primus Pilus, prior to deductions, of course. The same amount could buy one a small, yet profitable, farm in Italy. A net worth of four hundred thousand sestercii would ensure entry into the equestrian class, while three times that amount would make one a senator. Each chest contained the equivalent of eight hundred thousand sestertii.

"Never forget that gold is good servant, but cruel master", Cai said.

Hostilius, for once, had Cai's measure and replied in perfect Persian. *"Where may I find a tavern with decent women and cheap wine?"*

Everyone burst out laughing. Even Cai.

As Hostilius had predicted, we did start celebrating early. Segelinde, Nik and Felix soon joined us. With the reporting successfully completed, we could relax for the first time in weeks.

It was early autumn and already too cold to dine in the open. We feasted on fowl, wild boar and mutton. All prepared with the addition of the flavourful eastern spices that we had acquired during our adventure. We rounded off our meal with dates and cheese accompanied by a crisp white Shirazi from the personal cellar of Ardashir.

"When did you manage to get hold of this?" Vibius asked. "I doubt that it was a going away present from his highness the prince."

"I demanded four amphorae of Shirazi as part of the extension of our contract after the near battle at the Gates of the Giants", I said.

"So do each of us get a share of the wine as well?" Hostilius asked.

"I'd rather give you more gold", I replied.

He slapped me on the back and refilled his cup. "No need to. I already have more than I can ever use."

We had been given leave of our duties until the start of the month of October. The two weeks at home with Segelinde, Nik and my friends were godsent.

I went riding with Segelinde every day and even hunted a few times with Hostilius, who had blossomed into a keen hunter after his stint with Kniva.

An ecstatic Pezhman had joined the ranks of my Roxolani guards and was being trained as a warrior. My guards were equipped with the best of armour and weapons and Pezhman found it difficult to hide his joy about his spectacular reversal of fortunes.

We feasted every evening and the wine flowed freely.

But time passes like a raging river when you wish to slow it, and soon we found ourselves on the road back to the camp of the IV Italica.

As Marcus was the head tribune, we had the pleasure of reporting to him on our return.

"Gods, but I have missed you, Lucius", he said, embracing me like a brother.

Hostilius extended his hand to clasp Marcus's arm, but Marcus embraced him. "I even missed your scowl, Primus Pilus", he said, which obviously caused Hostilius to scowl.

Marcus invited me to dine with him in his quarters that evening, as he was keen to hear all about our adventures of the past months.

Marcus was the senior tribune of a legion, but before I divulged anything regarding the purpose of our journey, I swore him to secrecy. An unguarded tongue, when it came to the business of the emperor, could at best end in disaster.

Even while I was sharing the story with my friend, it had the ring of a tall tale.

Marcus just shook his head in disbelief. "On the one hand, it sounds unbelievable, Lucius. But on the other hand, it is exactly what I have come to expect of you. I, for one, believe every word."

He drank deeply from the cup with the crisp white Shirazi. "Where did you get this?"

"Would you believe me if I said that it is from the personal stash of shahanshah Ardashir?"

Marcus laughed and shook his head in amazement.

"Did you hear about the revolt that broke out in Africa?" Marcus asked.

I shook my head. "Nik usually keeps up to date with politics, but lately he tends to travel less and his news is not that fresh."

"The governor of Africa Proconsularis thought it wise to instigate a revolt against Gordian III. What was he thinking?" Marcus asked.

I have been away from Roman politics and the accompanying gossip for far too long, therefore I could offer no reply.

"Everyone loves the boy Gordian", Marcus explained. "The senate loves him. The soldiers love him. He is said to be respectful towards all. Why in Hades did Sabinianus wish to revolt? Idiot."

"What happened? Is the revolt still ongoing?" I asked, also saddened by the news.

"No, no. It was over nearly as quickly as it started. They made the mistake to assail the governor of Mauritania. They had obviously underestimated him, because he crushed the revolt severely, putting the fear of the gods into them. The conspirators became so scared that they delivered Sabinianus to Carthage and blamed him for everything. Last I heard, Gordian pardoned them after Sabinianus had lost his head."

He smiled at his own wit. "But there is more news. Your friend Timesitheus's daughter is marrying the emperor later in the year. I have heard a rumour that Gordian plans to appoint him as the prefect of the Praetorian Guard. What is your opinion of him?"

Normally I would not offer an answer to such a question, as judging the character of the rulers of the Empire was a dangerous game, but I trusted Marcus completely.

"Timesitheus is ambitious, but he has honour. He is intelligent and meticulous", I said.

I filled up both of our cups, swallowed, and continued.

"Let me tell you how it is", I said. "The Persians under Ardashir have all but dealt with their internal problems. They have also cowed the Kushan Empire to the east, mostly due to the defeat dealt to the Xionites. Word is that the Kushans will sue for peace soon. Then Ardashir will turn his attention on reclaiming their ancient lands to the west. Roman lands. Marcus, a war is coming between Persia and Rome. In my mind it is unavoidable."

"When it arrives, I can think of no one better to assist the young emperor. Timesitheus may desire power, but he would not have married his daughter off to Gordian if he wished to claim the purple for himself. With Timesitheus holding the reins, we have a chance. The Sasanians is a force to be reckoned with. Do not think them similar to the Parthians."

"I hear you, my friend", Marcus said. "We need to be ready. You will assist me to prepare the men as best we can for the coming threat. You know how the Persians fight and understand their shortcomings and weaknesses. The IV Italica will sell the lives of its men dearly."

Chapter 25 – Tribune (November 240 AD)

Marcus stared at Hostilius and me in turn.

"So how do we do this?" he asked.

Hostilius answered first. "We need to boost the discipline and toughen them up."

"I agree Primus Pilus, compared to the barbarians, these men live in luxury", I added.

"Leave it to me and the Primus Pilus", I said. "We will build a legion the equal of which you have never seen."

Hostilius grinned. "I like it. I can hear the rumours among the legions already. Stories of the IV Italica, the men made of iron."

Marcus grinned. "Good, I will leave it to you to get on with. I will inform the legate of our plans."

It was easy to train the men. I tried to mould them into Huns, following the ways of the barbarians.

I started slowly, one cohort at a time.

We marched with full travel kit, even though the snow lay thick on the ground. When evening came, followed by the bitter cold, we did not return to the warmth of the camp. We marched into the night and set up camp in the dark. We ate cold rations and made no fire. It rained, it snowed, but still we marched. Hostilius and I joined every march. We matched the legionaries step by step. We ate the same food and endured the same hardship. When men complained we punished them harshly, but fairly.

During one of these training marches we encountered a particularly bad snowstorm. The men were struggling with every step through the thick snow, but Hostilius and I were relentless - pushing on, no matter what. When it became too dark to continue, we made camp. I did allow the men to collect wood and light fires. Soon every contubernium sat around the cooking fire preparing the evening meal. Hostilius and I split up and walked among the men. We joined them around the fires, an act that greatly boosted morale.

As I struggled through the snow towards the next tent group, I heard a legionary say: "Prefect Domitius is a right bastard, he is. He grew up all rich and pampered, probably in one of them huge villas in Rome. Now he thinks he can teach us about hardship. I grew up in the Subura in Rome. That's hard."

They noticed my approach and all of them jumped up and came to attention.

"At ease", I said, and all of them sat down.

I needed to prove a point. I unbuckled my sword belt and removed the bear skin cloak draped over my shoulders. I unclasped my thick woollen cloak, folded it and placed it on top of the fur. I was left standing in only my tunic.

I pointed to the guilty legionary. "Do the same", I commanded.

They knew that I could have them crucified for their disrespect, therefore the legionary silently removed his layers of clothing until he was dressed as I was.

I moved two steps back from the fire and sat down on the frozen mud, gesturing for the legionary to join me.

"Legionary, state your name", I said.

"Titus Tullius, sir", he replied. "Second century, fourth cohort."

The rest of the contubernium looked decidedly uncomfortable, expecting some terrible punishment.

"Let me tell you about my childhood", I said. "It is a long story."

I told them how I grew up on the farm. Working like a slave from dawn to dusk.

I told them about my time with the barbarians. How the Huns endure the terrible cold and live for days with only the blood of their mounts as sustenance.

"These are the men that we will eventually have to fight", I said. "You are not tough enough to face them."

Before a third of a watch had passed, Titus Tullius collapsed facedown in the snow, blue from the cold.

We dragged him closer to the fire and I showed them how to rub his limbs with snow. I had them melt snow over the fire and placed his hands and feet in the lukewarm liquid to prevent frostbite. Only when Tullius was fully revived did I don my own cloak.

"Do not test my patience", I said as I turned to leave. "If I ever hear you speak like this again, my hand will go to my sword." I meant every word.

Less than a week had passed when Hostilius came to speak with me. "The news of your little stunt with Titus Tullius has spread like wildfire, Domitius. You have a brand new nickname."

"And what might that be, Primus Pilus?" I asked.

"They call you 'the man with his hand on his sword'."

Back in camp I made a point of visiting the contubernium of Tullius during the evening meal.

They were sitting around the fire and I walked into their midst, hand on my sword.

"Just making sure you have fully recovered, Tullius", I said.

He responded with an incoherent stutter. I slapped his shoulder. "Good, I am glad that you are well again, legionary Tullius. I will be keeping an eye on you."

Spring arrived earlier than usual. The men of the IV Italica were in better shape than ever. Hostilius and I had trained them harshly throughout the winter. To compensate for the severe training regime, Marcus, Hostilius and I funded the purchase of a herd of cattle to supplement the army food. It was unheard of, but the men ate well and trained hard. With the coming of spring and the increased fitness of the legionaries, the initial resentment caused by the hardship had turned into pride. Pride in their abilities and trust in their commanders.

The warmer weather came with better underfoot conditions and the cavalry joined the training exercises.

We practised the testudo formation for hours on end.

I had arrows made without tips. Using my old looted Scythian bow, I punished the odd legionary with well-aimed arrows that found the gaps between shields. Although the blunted arrows could not puncture mail, it still hit with incredible force, the culprits suffering mostly bruised ribs that hurt for days.

We trained to repel heavy cavalry and I showed them how to unhorse an armoured rider. They were shown the vulnerable parts of horse and rider and where to strike a debilitating blow.

Hostilius and I were watching another mock cavalry charge from a hillock close to the training field when he suddenly grinned. "I think they are ready to be tested", he said. "What do you think, Domitius?"

"I agree, Primus Pilus", I replied.

We noticed a horseman approaching from camp and soon Marcus was at our side.

As we were on our own, there was little need for formalities. "I needed to get out of the office. The administrative burden increased considerably during the last few months since Timesitheus had been appointed as prefect of the Praetorian Guard. He is a perfectionist, but I'm not complaining, because things have never run this smoothly."

He took a small scroll from his saddle bag. "But I have not joined you only to complain."

He clasped my arm and handed me the scroll. "Congratulations, Tribune Lucius Domitius Aurelianus."

Hostilius slapped me on the back. It was unexpected and I nearly fell from the horse.

"It seems like the powers that be are repaying you for services rendered", Marcus said, and grinned. "Vibius has been promoted to decurion, as we had discussed."

"What about the Primus Pilus?" I asked.

Hostilius answered the question. "When Senator Crispinus visited, he asked if I would ever be available for promotion. I told him that we can't all be pretty boys sitting on pampered horses."

"Well, Primus Pilus, he probably took offence, in which case you will never be promoted. Never ever", I said.

"Suits me just fine, it does", Hostilius replied with a twinkle in his eye.

Chapter 26 – Roxolani (April 241 AD)

Earlier, I had gifted the nine Niseans to the Roxolani who lived with Nik and Felix on my farm. They would look after the horses, but any offspring I would retain. It was a deal made in Elysium. The Roxolani almost worshipped the huge, powerful beasts and would ensure that they were cared for like royalty.

It was time for the next part of my plan. On a morning that was much too pleasant for early spring, Cai and I rode into Sirmium, steering a light legionary wagon.

The guards on sentry duty knew us well and saluted smartly as we rode through the gates into the town.

We headed straight for the area that housed the shops of the armourers and smiths. Months before, on my return from the east, I had requisitioned eight copies of the horse armour that Gordas had 'procured' from the immortals. In addition, I had eight copies made of the Sasanian horsemen's plumed conical helmets.

The armour was magnificent, and a close copy of the original.

We departed with a fully loaded wagon, leaving behind a smiling armourer whose purse bulged with gold.

"Only value of gold is buy useful item", Cai said. "Fool who keep chests of gold die with much gold. Wife's new husband spend quickly."

Once again he was right, which made me feel better about the purchase and at the same time guilty about having a hoard of gold stashed away.

With the necessary permissions, I summoned the Roxolani to the legionary camp. Marcus arranged for ten of the Roman cavalrymen to do duty on the farm during their absence.

"I will arrange the construction of a marching camp ten miles from our permanent quarters", Hostilius suggested. "The whole of the legion will march to this camp, one century at a time." He smiled cunningly. "We will ambush them on the march. I know of a good place."

* * *

I watched the century snake along the road from within the concealment provided by the trees. Behind me, the eight Roxolani were chomping at the bit. "This armour is of high quality, lord", one said. "It is all iron. It is a pity that this is only a mock charge."

"Play your part convincingly and I will allow you to take the armour home one day, should you so wish", I said.

"And the horses, lord? May we take the horses as well?"

I laughed. "I offer you my little finger and you wish to rip off my arm?"

The Roxolani warrior chuckled and I held up my hand for silence.

When exiting the trees at the bottom of the hillock, we would have fifty paces to accelerate. Then we would burst from the shrubs that offered concealment, eighty paces from where the legionaries were marching down the road.

I kicked my monstrous stallion in the flanks. The incredible acceleration of the Nisean breed never failed to amaze me, and when we burst from cover we were at full gallop. We rode boot to boot, a solid wall of iron, our long lances held in both hands.

Any fool could see that we were no Romans dressed as barbarians. We were the real thing. The heavy men in iron.

To their credit, the men of the legion did not turn and run. The centurion took charge, but the wall of shields was patchy. When we reined in at thirty paces, some of the legionaries in the front rank took a step to the back, cowed by the charge of the immortals.

I removed my helmet, which caused a collective sigh of relief from the bent column facing me.

Hostilius appeared from cover, after which we spent a third of a watch in discussion with the century. I ordered the legionaries to inspect the riders from close-up, and again highlighted their weaknesses. We reinforced the value of a solid wall of shields.

Over the course of the next few days, we repeated the ruse countless times, until the whole legion had been dealt with.

* * *

The legion did not abandon the marching camp to return home.

Hostilius was a fierce supporter of the ball game called 'harpastum'. "Domitius, it is your barbarian blood that keeps you from appreciating the game. It is without equal when it comes to conditioning the men for battle. Every century has to enter a team of twelve. Officers won't be allowed to play, else it gets ugly."

He was referring to an incident months ago when a centurion was tackled by a burly legionary. Afterwards the centurion

233

exacted revenge through use of the military system, which eventually resulted in the demotion of said individual.

"Exactly why I don't like it", I said. Hostilius ignored my jab.

"The men will enjoy it. They have worked hard. We will spend a couple of days by the river. During the day we will have the harpastum tournament and in the evenings we will feast." He held up a hand to stop any retort. "It has all been arranged. Just sit back. You don't have to like it to enjoy it, eh", and slapped my shoulder as he walked away.

It turned out that Hostilius was right. The soldiers immersed themselves in the tournament. The Primus Pilus had arranged prizes for the winning team, century and cohort.

Six evenings of leave for the winning team members. The winning century being issued with triple rations of decent wine for two days and the victorious cohort with double wine rations for two days.

Apart from the prizes, the bragging rights were substantial. Even though I viewed the whole tournament with suspicion, I ended up as a spectator most of the time, finding that contrary to my expectation, I also became absorbed.

I attended the final game accompanied by Hostilius and Marcus. Hostilius had cleverly located the field next to an area bordered by two sloping hills, which afforded the men a good vantage point from a seated position.

The winner was to be determined between the third century of the second cohort and the first of the fifth.

Although he denied it profusely, I was sure that Hostilius had bet a substantial sum on the outcome. "Don't be ridiculous, Domitius. I have a deep appreciation for the game. I don't expect you to understand it, but apart from the physical side, much strategy is involved." I narrowed my eyes but kept my counsel to myself.

I must admit that the legionaries involved displayed an inordinate amount of skill. A stocky soldier from the second cohort ran faster than any man I have ever witnessed before. Eventually the third of the second emerged victorious, resulting in Hostilius leaving the field with a broad smile. "I may not be allowed to play it, but I know the game. I told you the second would take it", he gloated.

In any event, the men were content and morale was at a high.

Slowly but surely we were building a legion capable of facing the might of the Sasanians.

Chapter 27 – Timesitheus's request

Back at the legionary camp in Sirmium I took the time to look up my old contubernium. It would have been problematic inviting them to join me in my quarters. A tribune was not expected to associate with legionaries on a social level, but to join them around their fires from time to time was viewed as good leadership.

Hostilius arranged duties for the new members of the tent group so that only my friends from way back remained.

After waving away the formalities, I produced an amphora of red. Ursa all but grabbed it from me and filled our cups to the brim.

"I nearly wet myself when them Parthians ambushed us, Umbra. It sure was a neat trick", Ursa said.

"We know you can't tell us, with you being a tribune and all, but word is out that you've been to the land of them barbarian Parthians", Pumilio said. "They tell us that no man can go there and come back alive. I told them that centurion, er… sorry, Tribune Umbra is no ordinary man, he is. We all believe that you've been there and spied out how to kill them good and proper."

"All I can say, Pumilio, is that in order to defeat the Sasanians we need to be as hard as iron. That's the reason why we have been training so hard", I replied.

"The new boys in the tent complained in the beginning", Pumilio added, "but we told 'em that it is the way of Umbra. We've trained with you before so for us it was no surprise. We told them not to mess with you and all, cause them barbarians call you 'the merciless one', don't they?"

I narrowed my eyes. "How do you know that?"

"The bookie came to pay Hostilius his winnings after the game and he overheard him speaking to his secretary. The bookie is a second cousin of Silentus's brother-in-law in the third of the second", Pumilio explained.

Silentus nodded in agreement.

I was enjoying my third cup when Cai arrived. "Head tribune Marcus ask you come now. He say it urgent."

I had heard most of the gossip and bade my friends farewell, Cai probably having saved me from consuming too much wine.

Marcus was standing behind his desk when his clerk showed me in. He motioned for me to take a seat, but he remained standing, pacing up and down with his hands held behind his back.

237

From an ornate silver amphora he poured two large cups of wine and handed me one.

"I have just returned from the office of the legate", he said with a sigh.

He drank deeply from his cup and continued. "A missive arrived from Rome earlier today. It was written by Gaius Timesitheus, the praetorian prefect, and carries the seal of the emperor. With it arrived a wagon accompanied by two hundred mounted praetorians."

I raised my eyebrows. "The wagon must have a precious cargo to warrant a retinue of two hundred praetorians."

He nodded. "Both our names were mentioned in the missive. The wish of the emperor is that we recruit a force of three thousand infantry and three thousand mounted archers from the tribes north of the Danube. I have been tasked with it and you are obliged to assist me. We have been entrusted with one thousand five hundred pounds of gold to achieve this."

He sat down heavily, resting his elbows on the desk, with his face in his hands. He rubbed his eyes and continued. "I do not even know where to start, Lucius, but I know that arranging this will be as nothing to you."

Marcus was right, I did not believe that it would be overly difficult to come to an arrangement with the Roxolani and the

Goths. I always enjoyed my time on the Sea of Grass and I knew that Segelinde would be ecstatic at the opportunity to visit her family yet again. I was in for a surprise.

As I mentioned before, I had purchased a house in Sirmium to enable my wife to live close by. Because of my rank, I was allowed to spend most evenings at home.

We employed two cooks, a cleaner and a body slave for Segelinde. The body slave was a young Goth girl I had purchased at the slave auction at the insistence of my wife. I had paid far in excess of the amount I believed she was worth, but when one's wife's happiness is at stake, no price is too high.

She hadn't been with us a week when Segelinde insisted that she be manumitted.

"She is a sweet, innocent Thervingi girl, Eochar. A girl taken from her parents who were killed by Romans. I will not stand for it that she remains a slave. She will stay here out of free will, or leave."

That was that and we ended up with Adelgunde staying on as a paid servant.

Apart from the servants, I had also arranged for a bodyguard to reside on the premises. Egnatius retired from the legions the year before and, like Felix, he had nowhere to go. I investigated him thoroughly before offering him the job. He was an excellent swordsman, rarely drank too much and was decent and dependable. He never rose through the ranks as he had assaulted an optio years earlier. The officer was about to violate a young Marcomanni girl after a battle when Egnatius intervened by kicking him in the head. Egnatius was lucky to escape execution, but was doomed to stay a ranker for the remainder of his service.

In any event, I walked up to the door and used the brass knocker. Shortly afterwards a peephole slid open. Egnatius opened the door, came to attention and saluted.

"Good evenin', Tribune."

I had given up weeks before on my efforts to de-militarise Egnatius. I have come to accept it and played along.

"At ease legionary", I said.

"All is well, sir", Egnatius replied. "Nothing out of the ordinary to report."

I nodded, entered the house and left him to go about his business.

Segelinde was in the kitchen with Adelgunde and the cooks. My wife was showing them how to make traditional Gothic honey and wheat cakes. We had brought back vast quantities of spices. As an experiment, Segelinde had added ground ginger to the biscuits.

Even now, years later, I have to confess, ginger and honey wheat cakes are still my favourite sweetmeat.

Adelgunde had prepared a bath so I could rid myself of the dust and sweat.

I emerged refreshed, excited to share the good news with my wife.

I poured us each a small goblet of crisp white and broke the news, smiling, while seated next to her on the couch in the dining room.

Segelinde buried her face in her hands, bent over and started to weep, shaking with grief-filled sobs.

I was flabbergasted. I sat watching her like an idiot, the glass hovering close to my mouth. As soon as I had recovered a modicum of wit, I shuffled closer and put my arm around her. Eventually the sobbing subsided. It did not go unnoticed, though, because I caught a glimpse of Adelgunde as she lurked near the doorway with an accusatory look in her eyes.

"I am so sorry, Eochar", Segelinde said and sat upright, reaching for her untouched wine.

I nodded, waiting for her to enlighten me.

241

"You are going to be a father, Eochar", she said.

I stared back at her, now utterly confused. "Then why are you crying? It sounds like joyful news to me?" I said.

She hit me on the arm. I remember thinking that, had she been a man, she would have been a formidable warrior because it hurt more than a little.

"I am pregnant and you are leaving to visit my family. I will be all alone when the child is born, while you are hunting with Kniva." She started to sob again.

A watch passed before we reached an agreement. I summoned Egnatius and he rounded up all the servants in the dining room for an impromptu meeting.

They all stood there, wide-eyed, not sure what to expect.

"I am going away for a short while." No one moved or showed emotion.

I continued. "We are relocating the household to the farm in the meantime. Make your arrangements, you will be leaving the day after tomorrow." They were still staring at me.

"Lady Segelinde is with child", I said.

Adelgunde and the two cooks started to cry. Moments later Segelinde joined them. Women.

Chapter 28 – Foederati (May 241 AD)

It is an understatement to say that the news of Segelinde's pregnancy was well received by Nik, Cai and Felix.

Cai's face contorted in horror as I explained that Segelinde would ride with us to the farm. "You have taken leave of senses, Lucius of the Da Qin. I will go now and arrange for litter in Sirmium."

As he left the office he was still shaking his head and muttering incoherently in the language of the east.

Nik and Felix crooned over Segelinde, hence I was ignored for the most part. Even the Roxolani seemed more protective towards her. One of them enlightened me. "Princess Segelinde's child could be the future king or queen of the Roxolani. Remember, she is the daughter of king Bradakos."

Eventually, following a tearful goodbye, I rode off alone, with five Hunnic horses in tow.

Cai had made it clear. "I watch over wife. No time babysit you. You big enough look after yourself. Just not be stupid."

I left, harbouring feelings of abandonment, which were soon forgotten as I entered the legionary camp at Sirmium.

Marcus slapped me on the back on hearing the news, and we celebrated with an excellent red. "I am sorry about the timing of the mission, Lucius, but the legate is becoming anxious", he explained.

"We will leave the day after tomorrow", I replied. "I need to make some arrangements with the Primus Pilus."

Hostilius was unconcerned about my upcoming mission, but overjoyed at the news of me becoming a father.

"It is as it should be, Domitius. A man is supposed to have a wife and father children. One day I would want to do the same."

"When will you be venturing down that road, Primus Pilus?" I asked.

I never realised that Hostilius was the family type. He fell silent and turned his face from me. "The legions have always been my life, Domitius", he said, "but two years from now I can choose to go my own way if I desire it. I am tempted to leave and start a family of my own."

We talked and drank wine for a long time and I think I learned more about the man that evening than I had in all the years before. I eventually arrived at the real reason for my visit and even though we were both slightly inebriated, he approved my request.

"Domitius, I know you now outrank me and could just tell me what you want", he said. "I appreciate that you have discussed it with me first. Leave it to me, I will personally make sure that the arrangements are in place."

I spent the next day catching up on my administrative duties. In the absence of Cai, I had to pack for the journey. We would wear barbarian clothing, as I had personal experience of the dangers associated with parading on the Sea of Grass dressed as a Roman.

At my request, Hostilius had arranged for the gold to be taken from the chests and packed into amphorae used for oil and wine. To further the deception, they poured oil, flour and legionary issue wine into the containers filled with coin.

On the day of our departure, Marcus and I were waiting at the gate with two wagons filled with what passed for provisions. The gate was closed as it was still half a watch until first light. We heard the sound of approaching footsteps. Ursa, Pumilio and Silentus appeared from the gloom. Within heartbeats, Vibius rode into view on his Hunnic horse, also leading a spare.

The threesome saluted.

"Tribune Domitius tells me that you are the men who assisted us when the Thracian wished to kill us", he said.

"Yes, Tribune", Pumilio replied, "that will be us, won't it?"

"I thank you for what you have done. During this mission, there will be no use of rank. You will address me as Marcus and Tribune Domitius will go by the name of Eochar. The familiarity will stop once we are back across the Danube."

All of them nodded and we were let out the gate with a wave of Marcus's hand. Two of my Roxolani guards were waiting for us on the road to Onagrinum, a crossing point on the Danube. Marcus had made the arrangements. A ship of the imperial fleet was anchored close to the auxiliary fort. The fast vessel, called a navis actuaria, was seventy feet long and designed for transporting troops and horses. The flat hull grounded on the banks so we had no trouble loading the horses and amphorae.

It took six days to reach the port of Novae where two sturdy horse-drawn wagons were waiting for us on the northern bank of the Danube.

The three legionaries were in charge of driving the wagons while the rest of us rode next to them, the spare horses tethered to the trailing wagon. The Roxolani guards ranged far and wide to warn us of approaching danger.

My bows were strung and stored in the holders on each side of the saddle. In addition I carried two quivers containing thirty arrows each.

During the day I took the opportunity to hunt, as did the barbarian guards. When evening came, we made camp and cooked the kills of the day over the fire.

"So tell me, Umbra, are we taking a gift of oil and flour to your friends?" Pumilio asked. "When we get there, will we bake them some proper bread as well?"

I chuckled. "Pumilio, I am sure you already know what's in the amphorae?"

"My second cousin's brother-in-law was one of the men who put the gold in them amphorae", he said, confirming my suspicions.

I nodded. "We are recruiting mounted archers in the event of a war with the Sasanians. We will negotiate a treaty, a 'foedus'. Rome will pay them gold and in return they will supply us with warriors when we are in need of them."

The wagons kept us from travelling at speed on our way to the home of my people, the Roxolani. I knew that I would be able to come to an agreement with Bradakos. The same applied to Kniva, iudex of the Thervingi Goths, my brother-in-law. I looked forward to spending time with the people of the Sea of Grass. The mission was a welcome break from the monotony of everyday life in the legions.

Vibius had been promoted to decurion subsequent to our mission in the east. We enjoyed one another's company and shared stories with Marcus about our recent mission to Persia.

Although I did not expect any hostilities, I habitually wore my full armour as well as the yellow silk undergarment gifted to me years before. We were in the tribal lands of my people and I did not fear an attack. At our back was the Empire and no threat would emerge from that direction. Or so I thought at the time.

We were jesting and laughing when Simsek's ears pricked up. Having learned the hard way not to ignore such signs, I immediately held up my hand and strapped on my helmet.

"Prepare yourselves", I yelled. I spurred my horse towards the wagons, my strung Hunnic bow already in my left hand and five arrows in my draw hand.

The wagons had come to a halt. Ursa, Silentus and Pumilio were no fools and they had the horses secured and the rim brakes in place before I pulled up alongside them. Their legionary shields were held at the ready with their backs to the wagons.

On the far side, eighty paces from the track we were on, a group of men on horseback burst from the shrubs at full gallop. They wore chain with good helmets, their whetted spear blades gleaming in the sun. I breathed deeply, exhaled to give me stability, and then they died. Simsek again showed his worth, remaining motionless like a rock as arrow after arrow left the terrible Hunnic bow. But there were too many.

The riders, at least twelve, streamed around the wagons. I let go of the calm and embraced the fury of the god of war and fire. And I became a Hun, a demon. I gripped a wickedly sharp battle axe in each hand. The first of them came at me with his spear arm pulled back, ready to strike. The blade of my axe embedded itself in his face and he toppled from his horse, crashing against the side of the wagon. I drew my jian and deflected a spear thrust aimed at my throat while the axe in my left hand all but severed the arm at the elbow. A third slashed at me with a sword I was sure was of Roman cavalry issue. The edge struck my shoulder, but the hoof scales held and I opened his throat with the tip of my blade as I spun around. Enemies were all around me. Ursa roared like a beast and I heard a horse scream and fall. From the periphery of my vision, I saw Marcus fighting for his life, assailed by two attackers. A sword blade came at my face and I turned my head, taking the impact on my helmet. My jian entered the exposed armpit and another body fell from a horse. Something struck me on the back of my shoulder, spinning me around. The attacker pulled back the spear to strike again. I had no way to parry.

I heard the howls of my Roxolani guards and as my adversary's eyes darted away, a bloody arrowhead appeared from his neck, showering my face with gore. Two still faced me, one with sword and one with spear. I dispatched the sword bearer, then the other swung his horse around and fled. I spurred Simsek after the faster horse, which outpaced him with ease. But Simsek did not tire easily, and soon I returned to the wagons, dragging the unconscious man behind my horse, his body snared in my lasso.

Marcus nursed a wound to his thigh where a spear point had scored a deep cut in the muscle. Ursa had taken a terrible hit from behind which dented his helmet. He was still delirious. Silentus and Pumilio escaped with flesh wounds only. Vibius was uninjured.

The Roxolani was already looting the corpses, clearly pleased with the unexpected windfall.

I had a closer look at the dead men, who were Roman for sure. The man I had snared with my lasso moaned softly. I cut a purse from his belt, heavy with coin. Freshly minted coins from Rome.

I was in no mood for mercy so I signalled for the Roxolani to join me.

I spoke to my friends. "I will return shortly, after we have taken care of this man."

Torture was a necessity I never relished, yet I handed the man to my barbarian guards as he regained his senses.

"I will tell you nothing", I remember him shouting. The Roxolani was watching. Silent amusement visible on their faces.

"It will be easy, lord", one said, grinning. "May I borrow your axe? I will clean it afterwards."

Less than a third of a watch had passed when we trotted back to my friends, the Roxolani still wiping gore from the axe.

Silentus was cradling Ursa's head on his lap.

"We heard the bastard scream for mercy", Pumilio said, and spat in the dirt. "They were praetorians", he said, and kicked a corpse in the head. "I recognise this one. He was with the wagon when they brought the gold."

"They are Romans, trying to kill their own", Pumilio added. "They don't deserve mercy."

"Then you will be pleased, Pumilio, as my Roxolani's understanding of Latin is even less than their grasp of the concept of mercy."

Chapter 29 – Agreement

We slowly made our way to the home of the Roxolani, nursing our wounds.

Ursa had recovered well. Marcus's leg was still heavily bandaged, but healing.

"Lucius, when are you going to tell us?" he asked, not taking his eyes off the road.

"The poor sod we interrogated uttered one name. Gaius Julius Priscus", I said.

Marcus stared at me blankly, but Vibius recalled. "Is he not the haughty praetorian tribune who you er… incapacitated when the Carpiani attacked us all those months ago?"

I nodded.

We shared the story with Marcus. "If I had not hit him, we would all have been killed", I explained. "I humiliated him in front of his men and he is hungry for payback. I can hardly believe the lengths some men will go to, to exact revenge." Unsurprisingly, my conclusion as to his motives could not have been further from the truth.

In any event, we reached the Roxolani camp safely, where we were treated like royalty. Marcus, Vibius and I shared a tent close to that of the king.

At my request, Ursa, Pumilio and Silentus were accommodated in a separate tent of generous proportions. They were provided with food and drink. I visited them on the second evening.

Ursa had torn a joint of mutton from the carcass roasting over the fire. In his other hand he held a cup filled with mead. The juices were dripping down his chin. "These people sure know how to live the high life. By all the gods, Umbra, why did you ever decide to come to Roman lands? I'm sure you could have been the king's champion or somethin' like that. They would have taken care of you all good and proper."

"It's a long story, Ursa, but I agree with you", I replied. "These people live well."

"And the women are real pretty, with the golden hair and all", Pumilio added.

"Just a word of advice. The women around here are warriors, like the men", I cautioned. "Keep your hands to yourself or you might find a blade in your gut with a pretty blonde holding the hilt."

Silentus nodded and stared longingly after a female warrior strolling past.

The arrangement I proposed to Bradakos turned out to be a gift sent to him by the gods. "We are at peace with our neighbours and the young warriors are restless. When there is no war, they fight amongst themselves. Idle hands work for the evil one, is it not? Less than a moon ago I had to order the execution of such a warrior, following a most unfortunate incident. All brought on by deeds of idleness, I tell you. You are paying me fifty thousand gold coins and solving the problem for me." He slapped me on the back. "Eochar, you truly are the messenger of Arash."

We were feasted and entertained. I told my mentor that his adopted daughter, Segelinde, was with child.

Predictably, this joyous news ushered in a brand new round of feasting. Days passed before we were escorted to the lands of the Goths, worn out and tired.

To ford the river bordering the lands of the Goths proved to be a challenge, but with the assistance of the Roxolani, we eventually reached the eastern bank with the heavy wagon.

On the first day we were intercepted by a patrol of Gothic cavalry. Due to the persistence of Segelinde, I was fluent in the language. Their leader, an oathsworn warrior of Kniva, recognized me. "Lord, you saved us when you defeated the men of Werinbert the usurper. The warriors speak of it still. We will escort you to the hall of the iudex."

Pumilio looked at me suspiciously. "Umbra, how come all them barbarians seem to know you? You even know how to grunt in what goes for a language around these parts."

"I am married to the sister of the king", I replied truthfully.

They looked at me with wide eyes and Ursa burst out laughing. "Sure thing, Umbra. And my father is the emperor, isn't he?"

Kniva, now married to a beautiful Greuthungi girl, spent most of his time since I had last seen him to cement his kingship. He was the great lord of the Goths, binding all the minor lords to him through oaths and favours.

My brother-in-law was presiding over the Althing of the Thervingi. This was the forum where disputes were settled and laws were made. As no foreigners were allowed to participate, we had to wait four days for the proceedings to end and for his lords to return home. My friends and I enjoyed the hospitality of my parents-in-law who were over the moon upon hearing the good news about their daughter. I swore them to secrecy, as I wanted to be the one who broke the news to Kniva.

Eventually, when all the lords had departed, I met with Kniva.

Initially he seemed reluctant to commit his men. "Eochar, I need the men to guard my borders against the Roxolani and the Huns. If they sense my weakness, they will spill over the borders, killing and burning at will."

I had already discussed this with Bradakos and I smiled. "I am buying peace with the Huns at a cost of three hundred pounds of gold. Bradakos of the Roxolani is arranging it."

In the end he agreed, subject to one condition. "I will personally lead my men and not throw away their lives."

We reached agreement and he made his mark on the scroll. Only then did I tell him about Segelinde. We feasted for days. We left, worn out and tired.

Kniva arranged for a contingent of Thervingi to escort us to the edge of their tribal lands where the Roxolani warriors were waiting for us.

We had left the wagon with Kniva, who gave us six horses in return. My legionary friends could ride, but Ursa looked especially awkward on horseback as his feet kept hitting stones in the roadway, to the endless amusement of his friends.

We had earlier arranged not to stop over at the Roxolani summer camp, but headed straight for Novae where an imperial ship would be waiting for us. The ride to Novae passed uneventfully. Elmanos, the Roxolani noble, and sixty of his best warriors escorted us, which meant that there was no threat of attack.

We hunted, enjoyed evenings around the fire and consumed copious quantities of red wine.

I grew closer to Marcus and Vibius. All of us felt positive about the future of the Empire under the young Gordian and his guardians.

"He is already liked by the senate as well as the legions", Marcus said. "He could be the one who brings stability to the Empire once again. Thirty years from now he could still be emperor. He is young enough."

"The coming war in the east will determine our destiny", Vibius said. "Should the emperor emerge victorious, he will gain much needed reputation. The Scythians and the Goths are waiting, watching and biding their time. They will be reluctant to anger the man who subdues the Persians, but they will swarm over the border and raid deep into Roman lands should the legions be crushed."

"Then we had better make sure that Rome wins", I said, and drank deeply from my cup.

Chapter 30 – Wisdom of age (July 241 AD)

It was with mixed feelings that we were greeted by the sight of the mighty Danube. I was sad to leave the jovial Scythians behind, but excited at the prospect of being re-united with my family and friends.

A navis actuaria from the imperial fleet was waiting for us just off the bank. We boarded the ship and in the absence of wind, the rowers propelled us upriver. The sleek little ship was built for speed, with fifteen oars on a side. Towards the afternoon, an easterly breeze picked up, and soon we were racing up the river with the wind at our backs.

The gods were with us, the wind remained for the duration of the six day journey.

Our first priority upon reaching Sirmium was to report to the legate. He was pleased with the outcome and speed at which we had completed the mission. Our success would stand him in good stead with the emperor, as well as with Timesitheus.

Back in his office, Marcus promptly signed the orders that provided me with five days of leave, allowing me enough time to visit the farm.

The Roxolani had ridden straight home with the spare horses after disembarking, hence I knew the news of my safe arrival would have reached my family.

I left the fort during the second watch of the afternoon and allowed Simsek to open his legs. We rode at a gallop all the way to the farm, a feat that could not be accomplished by any other breed of horse.

Nik and Segelinde stood on the rampart, waiting anxiously for my return. I immediately felt a stab of guilt. Although I missed them terribly during the last two months, my thoughts had many times been preoccupied by the mission.

The watchers disappeared from the ramparts. As I approached the gate and reined in, I heard the thundering of hooves approaching from behind.

It was my Saka scout, Pezhman, who yelled to Nik in broken Latin. "Apologies, great Roman lord Nik. I not catch Lord Eochar. Ugly horse too fast."

He turned to me, suddenly realising that he might have used the wrong words. He continued in Latin. "No offence meant, great steppe lord."

They had sent Pezhman to escort me, but somehow I took a shortcut and missed him, with the result that he desperately chased after me for the last few miles.

I was soon immersed in a hot bath, washing away the sweat, dirt and grime of the last couple of days. Nik knocked twice and walked in. The old man slowly lowered himself onto the bed at the other end of my room.

He held up his hand and said: "Don't get up, son. We can talk while you bath."

Although I had pushed it to the back of my mind, the attack by the praetorians weighed heavily upon me. I told Nik. He sat quietly, absorbing all, only nodding now and again or interrupting to clarify.

"I believe that Priscus wanted revenge for my actions", I said.

Nik nodded, but said nothing, milling over the problem in his mind.

I left him to ponder and closed my eyes, allowing the tension to slowly drain away, relishing the feeling of safety, surrounded by my friends and family.

Nik may have been old, but his mind was as sharp as ever.

"Son, you are not wrong in your deduction that the most likely cause for the attack is the tribune's need for revenge. But it is dangerous to discard other possibilities. It is possible that you were attacked for other reasons. Maybe they wanted to stop your mission from succeeding, or it could have simply been an attempt to steal the gold. Who knows?"

He sighed. "There is a risk that the legate is involved. If he discovers that you are aware that the men who attacked you were praetorians, or even worse, that you have been given a name, you are as good as dead. I will immediately send Cai and four Roxolani to bring Marcus to us. We need to talk before he makes his report."

A watch later, a tired Marcus and I sat with Nik and Cai in the study. Nik poured a delicate, nearly transparent red for each of us. "It is a new cultivar. Try it", he said.

The old man sat down on the couch and savoured the wine. "We live in dangerous times. Just three years ago Rome had six emperors in one year. Six!"

He drank again, clearly enjoying the wine.

"At the time of the death of Marcus Aurelius, Rome has had only four emperors over the preceding eighty years, each one ruling twenty. It brought stability and strength to the Empire."

Marcus had the utmost respect for Nik and trusted him implicitly. "Sir, I know that you have an extraordinary insight into affairs such as these. I will heed your advice."

He looked at Marcus and nodded. "Tribune, you have to be extremely careful. I suggest this not only for the good of my son, but also for your benefit. To me, you are the brother Marcus never had. Two reports need to be submitted. One to the legate, stating that you were attacked, and another to Timesitheus and the emperor, which provides more detail."

Nik assisted Marcus with the drafting and soon he rode off into the night with the report meant for the legate. Four Roxolani guards escorted him.

Nik held the missive for Timesitheus in his hand. "Leave this with me. I have ways to ensure that this is delivered directly into the hands of the praetorian prefect. It will take a bit longer, but it will be secure."

Segelinde was now more than halfway through her pregnancy. In light of the attack, she decided that it would be wiser to remain on the farm for the time being.

I returned to the legion four days later, with Cai in tow.

We reached the camp by the second watch of the day and I immediately reported to Marcus, my senior officer. His clerk recorded the date and time of my return to duty.

A substantial amount of administration awaited me on my arrival back at my quarters. Cai waved me away. "Go train with men. I take care of writing."

Grateful, I went to seek out the Primus Pilus.

Hostilius had not let up with the training of the legion and I was forced to wait for him to return from the forced march he was leading.

I was sitting in his office when he walked in, still sweating profusely.

He clasped my arm. "Welcome back, Domitius. I heard that you had returned a few days ago, but before I could get hold of you, you left for the farm. Coincidentally, when I went to speak to Tribune Marcus, he had also mysteriously disappeared for the evening. What are you up to?"

Hostilius had always been good at sensing when something was out of place. "Allow me to enlighten you, Primus Pilus", I said.

I trusted Hostilius with my life and therefore I told him about the attack, as well as my suspicions regarding Tribune Gaius Priscus.

"I had a good look at him the day you put that haughty bastard in his place", Hostilius growled. "He has shifty eyes, Domitius, a real nasty piece of work."

Hostilius filled two oversized beakers half with white wine, topped it up with water and handed one to me. He drank thirstily. "Do you remember Tullus Menophilus?"

Without waiting for the obvious answer he continued. "Heard he is going to be dealt with back home in Rome." He noticed my confused frown and drew his finger across his throat menacingly.

263

"I hate to say it, but I told you so, didn't I. He took the one thing that is dearest to the emperor. Gold, that is. And he is going to have his head removed as a reward."

He drank again. "Must have stolen a lot, because the rumour is that his name will be removed from all official records as well."

I must have looked surprised, but Hostilius put me in my place. "Don't look so shocked, Domitius. Not long ago you were the favourite of the Thracian, then suddenly he turned on you."

"Truth be told, I like the young emperor Gordian" I said. "I even find Timesitheus agreeable, yet I do not fully trust them."

He stood, and drank the last swallow. "Enough talk. The men are progressing well. They are combat ready, and tough. Come, join me, the second cohort is training at the posts."

Much later, tired from the weapons training, I lay on my bed. I rarely had trouble sleeping, but that evening I lay awake, thinking on Hostilius's words. Priscus had made an attempt on my life. Could the reasons behind the attack still be alive and well? Will he try again?

I was pulled from my fretting by a slight creaking sound to my left. Someone had opened the door to my quarters. I went from half asleep to wide awake in less than a heartbeat.

Nik taught me to sleep with a dagger at hand. I have never had to use it, but it had become a habit. My left hand tightened around the hilt of the wicked Hunnic blade, a present from Gordas. It came with a tight-fitting, felt-lined leather scabbard. I could draw it without fear of alerting the intruder, who was advancing in my direction, keeping to the shadows on the opposite side of the room.

I did not move, but watched him through the slits of my eyelids, remembering the words of my Hun friend. "It might appear more like a spike Eochar, but it is practical, not fancy. It will pierce armour as easily as it will pierce a skull. Believe me, I have tried it more than once."

The dark assailant stopped beside my bed and I saw the blueish glint of a slightly curved, footlong blade. He slowly lifted the weapon with both hands clenched tightly around the hilt, thumbs pointing skyward, ready to plunge it down into my neck.

Cai had taught me that before a man exerts himself, he gathers energy by inhaling deeply. It is something fighting men have in common and I gambled that it would be no different that day.

I heard the slow, calm intake of breath as the deadly blade rose even higher. It was the moment I was waiting for. Halfway through his drawn breath, with the blade still rising, I struck with the speed of a viper. The point of my dagger entered his head at the base of his skull. My right hand swung around, grabbing an elbow to stop the killing stroke, but it was unnecessary. The assassin went limp and crumpled to the floor, the tip of my dagger protruding from the top of his skull.

The dim light of Mani entered my room as clouds shifted high above. From the corner of my eye, again, I sensed movement. I had been so focused on the immediate threat, I missed the presence of a second assailant. As the killer lunged, I stepped aside, blocking the blade with my open left hand. I stepped in and struck him full in the face with my right elbow, the cartilage fracturing with an audible crunch. He fell backwards, allowing me enough time to grab the blade of the dead attacker.

He moved the tip of his blade in a circle to distract me, then struck like lightning, slashing the blade horizontally from left to right, in an attempt to open my throat. I knew the move well. I moved into his swing, blocked with my right hand, and head-butted him in the face. I was in no mood for mercy, and as he stumbled backwards, I took another step forward and skewered his neck with his accomplice's weapon.

I felt the rage leave me and I sat down to steady myself.

"Cai!" I called.

No answer.

I was filled with a sudden fear that my friend had been killed in the adjacent room and I called out louder, with even more urgency. "Cai!"

"Why you bother me in middle of night? You have bad dream?" came the reply from the room next door.

Cai walked in with an oil lamp and looked around my room. "I get Hostilius", he said, "you bring Marcus."

A legionary camp was never fully asleep. Guards patrolled the ramparts and between the barracks. Nobody would deem it suspicious should I be seen outside.

Hostilius and Marcus soon joined us in my room.

Marcus leaned over one of the corpses with an oil lamp in his hand. "These men are surely from the Province of Arabia."

Hostilius leaned in, drew his dagger and cut a purse. He emptied the contents in his hand and raised his eyebrows. "Gold. Looks to be minted in Arabia." He fingered a coin. "This one is Persian." He cut the other purse as well and pocketed the gold.

"They have no use for it anymore!" Hostilius said, and shrugged.

"Do we inform the legate?" Marcus asked.

"Marcus, I believe the fewer people know about this, the better. I suggest we get rid of the bodies and keep this between us", I replied.

"What about the blood stains on the wood?" Marcus said, pointing to the huge pool of blood next to the second assailant.

"No need be concerned, Tribune. I know of mixture for cleaning blood off wood. Works well. Nobody notice", Cai said.

We all stared at Cai in wonder.

"How in Hades do you know a recipe that cleans blood off wood?" Hostilius asked.

Predictably he did not receive an answer.

Chapter 31 – The twin gates of Janus

The days grew shorter, and before long we were in the grips of a harsh winter. The passes across the Alps were snowed shut and ships remained in the harbours with little news reaching us from the capital.

I visited the farm twice a week and had secured the services of a midwife, whom I paid to stay on the farm until Segelinde's time arrived.

Since the night attack, I had not let down my guard, yet all remained peaceful.

On a freezing, clear morning at the end of December, I was training at the posts when the watch officer arrived, trailed by a Roxolani guard on a lathered horse.

He appeared genuinely distraught, and spoke in the language of the steppes. "Lord Nik says you must come", he said.

That was all he needed to say. I had made arrangements in case of emergency and jumped on Simsek to collect Cai from the camp.

Less than half a watch later Cai and I stood next to Nik and Felix. Inside the bedroom, Adelgunde and the midwife were taking care of Segelinde. Time seemed to stand still and after what seemed like a watch, the distraught midwife appeared, closing the door behind her.

"It is not going well. It is a difficult birth", she said, and wiped the sweat from her brow.

She turned to go back, but Cai placed his hand on her arm, holding out a small cup filled with a vile-looking liquid. "Give to drink. Will help make easy."

The midwife frowned and I could see that she was about to spurn the offer. Fortunately I had commanded men for years. I stepped up to her, towering over the woman. My hand went to the hilt of my sword and I growled: "Do as the man from the east commands."

Within a sixth of a watch, I was holding my daughter in my arms, staring at her in wonder. I sat next to Segelinde, who was exhausted, but well.

The midwife still hovered around us, cleaning up and collecting her tools. "Lord, it is most concerning. The lady mumbled strange words when the baby was coming", she said.

Evidently, Segelinde reverted to Goth during the pain of the delivery, but it would not do to have rumours of her barbarian heritage spread around Sirmium.

"Do not concern yourself. Sometimes the gods speak through lady Ulpia. She has the sight, you know. I am sure that you noticed?"

"O yes, lord. I sure noticed, I did", she said, nodded, and went about her business.

My guards appeared to escort the wide-eyed woman home. She was clutching a fat purse in one hand and an amulet in the other. "Anytime, lord. I will help out anytime. Just send for me, lord. Thank you, lord."

Childbirth is fraught with risk so I was relieved that both mother and baby had emerged healthy from the ordeal. I spent three days at home, feeling clumsy, like a fifth wheel on a wagon.

A cavalry officer arrived on the fourth day with a missive from Marcus, summoning me back to camp.

Reluctantly, I left a tearful Segelinde behind.

I was adjusting the tack of my horse when Nik walked into the stable.

He placed his veined hand on my arm and I turned to face him. I could see that he had something to say, but had trouble getting the words out. "Lucius, it feels like the gods are giving me a second chance. Aritê, your mother, was so much like

271

Segelinde." His eyes became moist and he wiped away the tears with his sleeve.

I pulled him close in an embrace. "Go enjoy your granddaughter, father", I said. "You truly deserve it."

I mounted and trotted out of the gate, tears rolling freely down my cheeks.

Cai wisely followed a hundred paces behind.

Five miles from the farm, he pulled his horse next to Simsek. "Can we talk now?" he asked. "You done crying?"

I nodded.

"Great war is upon us, Lucius of the Da Qin. Enemies in front of us and enemies at back. We will need more than skill with blade to survive."

He tapped his right index finger against his temple. "Use this like use sword. You have mind sharp as sword."

I went to see Marcus immediately upon my arrival.

I walked into his office, unopposed by his secretary who knew me well. To my surprise a cloaked and hooded figure was seated opposite Marcus, with his back to the door.

"My apologies, Tribune", I said, and turned around to walk out again. Marcus held up his hand. "Join us, Lucius, we have been waiting for you."

I closed the door behind me. Marcus gestured towards the only open chair next to the mystery guest. "Good day, Tribune Domitius", Gaius Timesitheus said, turned towards me, and clasped my arm.

Timesitheus was not a man for small talk. "I have received the missive regarding the er... brigands who attacked you north of the River. Tribune Marcus has also told me of the visitors you had during the night. My people have been watching Tribune Priscus closely ever since. He has not put a foot wrong."

The prefect of the praetorians stared at the floor for a while, gathering his thoughts. "It might even be that someone is trying to blacken the name of Priscus. Apart from the incident, he has an exemplary record, military and otherwise."

"The easiest thing in the world would be to have Priscus executed. But is gets complicated. Priscus's brother is married to the daughter of Governor Octacilius Severianus. He looks after Moesia and Macedonia and he does it well. So do we grab them as well?"

"Soon the whole bloody East and the senate will be revolting and baying for my blood!" Timesitheus sighed.

"Be careful, Domitius. We will as well." He waved his hand, dismissing the incident.

"But do not think that I have come all the way from Rome only to tell you this", Timesitheus said. "I am making one final trip to ensure that the legions are ready. A few weeks ago, the young emperor opened the twin gates of the temple of Janus, the two-faced god of boundaries. Thereby he unleashed war upon the enemy who threatens our borders in the east."

I raised my eyebrows, being familiar with the gates of Janus. "Was Vespasian not the last emperor to open and shut the gates? That must have been nearly two hundred years ago?"

Timesitheus nodded. "One hundred and seventy to be precise. The people of Rome are solid in their support of their emperor. The stores and armouries are filled. The legions are ready. Even the omens are good."

Knowing how fickle the gods can be, I flinched on the inside at his last remark.

Unsurprisingly, while we were dining with Timesitheus that evening, we received a missive from a dust-covered, sweat-drenched messenger.

The Carpiani horde had breached the limes and invaded Moesia.

Chapter 32 – Carpiani

Timesitheus held out his goblet for more. "Domitius, I don't understand how it is possible for you to lay your hands on better wine than the imperial cellars are able to procure?"

I shrugged. "My father is a man of many talents, Prefect."

"We need to deal with the Carpi incursion swiftly and decisively", Timesitheus said. "This cannot be the cause of the Sasanian campaign faltering."

"Prefect, I have an idea", I said. "Will you allow me the opportunity to elaborate?"

He nodded and I shared Arash's idea with the prefect of the praetorians.

Initially he kept shaking his head. "It cannot be done." In the end he sighed heavily, closed his eyes and said: "I will arrange it, for the good of Rome."

Five days later the whole of the Fourth Italica, save for one cohort, boarded the ships, urgently commandeered from the imperial fleet. We headed for Durostorum on the lower Danube, close to where the Carpiani had breached the defences.

It took nine days to reach our destination. In fact, the river ice forced us to disembark as the ships were unable to pass, which left us fifteen miles short.

It took the best part of a day to unload and construct a marching camp, which was necessary as the Carpiani had free reign of the countryside. Six cohorts of the XI Claudia, based at Durostorum, tried to hunt down the Scythians, but due to the wild horsemen's mobility it was a near impossible task.

Morning came, bringing clear skies accompanied by an icy wind howling in from the northeast.

I found Hostilius on the ramparts, staring far into the distance.

He acknowledged me with a nod. "They are watching us, Domitius. I spied two of the bastards on horseback over on that rise", his eyes scouring a low hill three miles away, "and just now I saw the sun glint off metal over yonder." This time he motioned with his head, not wanting to let the enemy know that they had been spotted.

"Excellent, Primus Pilus", I replied.

Hostilius scowled. He motioned for me to follow him and we descended the rampart, stopping out of earshot of the legionaries standing guard.

He eyed me with suspicion. "You bloody well better tell me your plan, Domitius. I know you well enough by now to know you have one. When you brood and keep to yourself, that dark god of yours is whispering into your ear. And you haven't spoken to me in days. Now you seem all chirpy and happy while the weather is going to shit and the barbarians are eyeballing us."

He stared at me menacingly, tapping the tip of his vine cane on his left palm.

I smiled disarmingly. "Peace, Primus Pilus. I will tell you all today. What I need you to do is bring me three legionaries who grew up on farms in this area, close to Durostorum. I will be waiting in my tent."

He did not like my reply, and turned formal. Hostilius saluted, scowling: "Thank you Tribune, will that be all."

I nodded and Hostilius stormed off, legionaries scrambling to avoid the brooding Primus Pilus.

Less than a third of a watch later, three worried legionaries sat outside my spacious tent, with Hostilus watching their every move.

"Primus Pilus, please join me inside", I said, and motioned for one of the legionaries to join us.

The man was clearly terrified, probably expecting that some or other hidden infringement had come to light. "At ease legionary", I said, and handed him a cup of heated wine. He nodded and half-smiled gratefully.

"Tell me what you think the weather is going to do the next two days", I continued, the legionary nearly choking on his wine.

"It's going to be real cold, Tribune", he said.

"Tell me more", I said.

He started to frown, but thought better of it. It must have dawned on him that I was genuinely interested in the weather and he visibly relaxed. "It won't snow today, Tribune, not with the northeasterly blowing like it is. Tomorrow, if the wind runs from the north and west in the morning and picks up during the day, turning north, we will see the crop-killing kind of snow during the night. The morning after tomorrow will be bitterly cold and the snow will come halfway to the knees."

He took another swallow of the wine from my personal stash. "My father used to say that…", but he didn't get to finish his story because Hostilius interrupted. "The tribune is not interested in what your father had to say soldier. Dismissed. If I hear that you didn't keep your mouth shut about this meeting, you will be on latrine duty for the rest of your life." I could see that Hostilius meant it. The legionary swallowed nervously, saluted and left the tent, still clutching the cup of wine.

The other two legionaries corroborated his forecast.

When only Hostilius, Cai and I were left in the tent, I shared my plan.

"It is bloody dangerous, Domitius", he said while plunging his hissing, red-hot dagger in the wine to heat it. "Bloody dangerous and I like it."

Cai sat sipping on some potion that he referred to as tea. "Wise general from land of Serica said war based on fooling enemy. Enemy see what they expect to see. Then surprise and strike like viper."

I woke early the next morning. Although reluctant to leave the warmth of my furs, I was eager to see what the weather had in store.

While I was gathering the courage to get out of bed, Cai walked in from outside, warmly dressed in a sheepskin jacket and cap, compliments of the Huns.

"Wind strong from north and west." He held up his hand to stop me from getting up. "I prepare food. Get up when I finish."

The smell of fried smoked pork and eggs soon persuaded me to leave the comfort of my furs. I stacked the meat and eggs on a flatbread and drizzled honey on top. I swallowed down the food with heated milk sweetened with honey. Cai mixed in an eastern spice made from the ground bark of a tree. He poured me a second cup for good measure.

"I wait in camp", he said. "No need for man my age to run around in snow like rabbit."

Cai looked no more than ten years my senior, but I was no expert at gauging the age of easterners.

In any event, at that moment Hostilius's face appeared in the tent opening. "We had better get going Domitius, we still have a lot of ground to cover."

Within less than a third of a watch, the sixth, seventh, eighth and ninth cohorts were lined up in marching order outside the main gate. Hostilius and I led the two thousand soldiers from horseback. It was not our way, but we had to preserve our bodies for the coming days. Marching in strength was the only possible way for us to reconnoitre the lay of the land, as lone scouts would soon fall prey to the Scythians who were swarming all over the countryside. Six miles from camp I found what I was looking for.

We called a halt next to a densely wooded copse. While the men were resting, Hostilius and I took the time to scout the treed area.

"It is perfect Domitius, is it not?" Hostilius asked.

I nodded. "Make sure you know exactly how to get here. Remember, you will have to find it in the dark."

On the return trip to the marching camp, we remained acutely aware of the groups of horsemen watching us from the hills.

The rest of the day we continued with our preparations for what was to come. Late afternoon the wind strengthened and gushed from the north, true to the legionaries' prediction.

The temperature dropped significantly after sunset, and the first snow fell. The time had come for Hostilius to lead the first five cohorts on their covert mission.

All the men were dressed in the clothing adopted by the legions stationed on the Danubian frontier. Underneath all, a long-sleeved cotton tunic, covered by a padded felt undergarment over which chain mail was worn, accompanied by the normal belt and harness. Depending on the temperature, a woollen cloak or an additional sheepskin overcoat kept out the cold. Fur braccae were not worn by legionaries based in warmer climes, but in this part of the world it had become standard throughout the winter. The men protected their feet from frostbite with fur-lined socks they wore underneath legionary boots. I had made it compulsory to carry two spare sets of socks. One pair to warm the hands and a spare in case the original pair managed to get soaked by the snow.

Through the eyes of a Roman soldier from the time of Julius Caesar we would have appeared to be a barbarian rabble, but our clothes were comfortable and functional. Just another weapon to provide an edge to the legions.

Roman legionaries never campaigned during winter, so the last thing the Carpiani scouts would expect is Romans leaving the camp at night during a snowstorm. But the men of the IV Italica were used to these conditions. They were trained to march all night through thick snow and sleep in the open under fur blankets.

I spent the night in my tent under warm furs, feeling guilty about Hostilius and the nearly three and a half thousand men sleeping in the open.

Sleep did not come quickly as I mulled over my plan, weighing all the scenarios in my mind.

Cai woke me early the following morning. He was preparing a hearty breakfast of cooked oats, honey and fresh mare's milk.

When I had eaten my fill, I sat down on the bed, tucked the fur braccae into my knee-length sheepskin boots, and draped my bear cloak over my shoulders for extra warmth.

I went outside and immediately noticed that the ground was covered by a layer of snow half a foot thick. My prayers had been answered. Smiling, I marched off to the horse corral.

Timesitheus had to dig deep in his pockets to pay for the ten white horses. They were irreplaceable, so I kept them separated from the rest of the herd. The horses were magnificent with long, broad necks and massive chests. Their strong, muscular hindquarters emphasized their power. They moved gracefully, manes and tails swirling in the breeze. I had assigned a cavalryman to each horse to constantly groom, feed and look after them on the trip and it had paid off. They were in prime condition.

White horses are treasured by the steppe nomads. Rarely ever do you come across specimens. Any self-respecting barbarian noble would, at the least, strongly consider selling his children into slavery for the opportunity to acquire a white horse. Owning such a creature would not only boost his social status, but it could also be sold or traded for a large amount of silver or gold. These horses were originally bred for war, but one of the wealthiest merchants in Sirmium had imported them from Hispania Baetica to use in the chariot races. Fortunately for me, the prefect of the praetorians is hard to refuse. The barbarians would drool at the sight of these horses. They would endeavour to acquire them by any means. I would use this greed to our advantage.

I gave the order for the groomsmen to ready the horses. Every white horse was equipped with a horned saddle made from the best leather, dyed red and stitched with silver wire. The saddles were truly works of art. I had to suppress an urge to claim the horses for myself. To the Carpiani, these specimens would be irresistible.

I decided on the size of our force after careful consideration. It had to be large enough to deter a small band from engaging with us, but small enough to pose no threat to the horde. A third of a watch later, eight turmae trotted through the main gate, escorting a passenger wagon that would normally be used to transport dignitaries. I chose a massive white stallion as my mount. Every now and again I would ride ahead and make it rear up on its hind legs to demonstrate its spirit. I could imagine the talk of the Carpiani scouts at the sight of these horses.

Before long I noticed riders appear in greater numbers, now openly watching from the ridges. Scouts would be riding to their commanders to gather the horde. The king of the Carpiani would gladly forego all the loot in Moesia to acquire a breeding herd of these Hispanic steeds.

Meanwhile back at the camp, Marcus was furthering the ruse. All the orderlies and functionaries were dressed up as soldiers, lining the ramparts.

The sixth, seventh, eighth and ninth cohorts were deployed in front of the main gate in battle formation. The front ranks closely packed, but the rear ranks loosely, to create the impression that the whole of the legion was either in front of the gate or watching from the ramparts.

We rode, seemingly unaware of our precarious situation, until the planned disaster struck. Close to the wooded area, the rear wheel of the wagon came off, causing it to lurch and come to a grinding halt. I estimated that the invading barbarians numbered around ten thousand, but they would be spread out over an extended area, unable to muster their full force to engage us.

We made a show of attempting to fix the wheel. Two thirds of a watch later, when the job was nearly done, I saw hundreds of riders silhouetted on the low open ridge between us and the camp. In mock panic, I dispatched three riders to the camp, but they were cut off and chased back to us. Shouting orders, we abandoned the wagon and formed a half-circle with our backs to the dense wooded area.

The Carpiani streamed over the ridges and surrounded our position. I knew for a fact that they would not attack outright. The white horses were valuable without measure hence they would not risk injuring them. The nomads outnumbered the Romans eight to one.

The horde came to a halt a hundred paces from us, their ranks bristling with lances. A lone rider walked his horse towards us. I followed suit.

To ensure that I was not recognised, I wore a full face plumed helmet of polished bronze with an integrated mask. There were holes for the eyes and nostrils, with a slit for the mouth. These masks were mainly used in the arena to entertain the crowds, but it would be useful as a disguise.

The Carpiani commander was a grizzled warrior who I guessed had seen forty summers. He wore iron scale armour extending to his knees, with a matching open face iron helmet. Scales attached to the helmet protected his neck. His face and bare forearms were crisscrossed with a variety of white and red scars. His hard eyes of greenish-blue stared at me in open amusement.

He spoke in broken Latin. "Give white horses. We kill you quick then. No suffer."

He grinned and continued. "Carpiani keep man alive for five days without eyes, tongue and arms. Think good before decide."

I knew exactly what to do and how to. I dropped my reins and pointed my index finger straight at him, a huge insult in the culture of the nomads. I spoke in the language of the steppes. "Get out of my sight, coward. You ask for peace because you are scared. Run back to your mother or fight me like a man." I reared up the stallion for added effect.

The Carpiani was so infuriated that his surprise at my use of the language did not even show. He backed his horse five paces and yelled to his men. "We will fight."

The ranks of two thousand barbarians erupted into cheering, yelling and howling. They banged their lance shafts on their small shields. I could not even hear myself think, which was exactly what I wanted.

An underling approached and the Scythian dismounted, drawing his sword in the same motion. I signalled for Vibius to approach and he led my horse away. I slowly drew my blade. The face mask limited my vision, but there was no other way.

The sword of the Carpiani struck out for my right lower leg. I wore my iron greaves underneath my braccae and allowed his sword to strike a glancing blow. An almighty cheer erupted from the horde whose attention was focused on the duel.

I feigned injury and hobbled back a step or two. My adversary circled around me, stepped forward with his left foot and cut horizontally from low to high, a difficult strike to parry. I skipped back another two paces, avoiding the cut when cheers of "coward Roman" and "kill him like a dog" emerged from the enthralled horde.

Again the Scythian cut horizontally, aiming for my throat. I managed a weak parry before once again stumbling backwards.

Over his shoulder I managed to catch a glimpse of the last of Hostilius's men moving into battle formation as they emerged from the mogshade of the copse to surround the barbarians who were still oblivious to the danger.

The commander was obviously annoyed by the cat-and-mouse game and moved in for the kill. He lunged at me with a well-executed thrust, stepping in with the blow. I moved to the side, allowing him to continue his motion and head-butted him with my helmet. As he staggered backwards, I hit his hand with the flat of my sword, causing him to drop his blade. In desperation, he drew his dagger and came at me again. I blocked the blow, spun him around using his own momentum and gripped his head in a death lock - his own dagger at his throat. My forearm pressed against his windpipe, rendering him unable to speak.

I let him struggle for air and he collapsed at my feet, unconscious. I only had a few precious moments to act before the nomads would realise the danger.

I unstrapped my helmet and yelled in my best centurion's voice: "Who commands?"

Then Fortuna smiled down on me when a hulking bull of a man in full armour rode forward.

Thiaper of the Carpiani removed his helmet, smiled and said: "I do, Lord Eochar."

Chapter 33 – Nomad king (January 242 AD)

The steppe warriors surrendered their weapons. I gave them an oath that they would not be harmed and that their weapons would be returned, hence their honour would remain intact. In return they swore not to try to escape. I left them under guard of Hostilius and his cohort.

Thiaper and I rode to meet the king of the Carpiani. I had taken all the white Hispanic horses as a present for the king, save for two mares. One magnificent mare I gave to a brooding Rhemaxos, the warrior whom I had defeated in combat. The other mare I gave to an ecstatic Thiaper.

Within less than half a watch we located the entourage of the king. Thiaper and Rhemaxos first had to explain the absence of their men to Tarbus, who was a powerful and wily warrior. They had yet to camp for the night. After leaving my weapons and horses in the care of Thiaper, I was allowed to approach.

I inclined my head in respect and drew my horse level with the king's.

He indicated for his guards to afford us room for privacy and they fell back at least twenty paces.

"I am pleased to meet you, Prince Eochar of the Roxolani", King Tarbus said. "It is a pity you follow the blood of your father rather than that of your mother."

"It is the will of Arash", I said.

"Still is a pity", he replied.

I gestured towards the horses. "It is a gift for the king from the emperor of Rome."

He inclined his head in acceptance. I could see that he tried not to stare at the horses, but his gaze remained on them for some time. "Thank you, they truly are splendid and no doubt worth a fortune in gold."

He took a swig from a skin on his belt which probably did not contain water. "Do you know the history of Rome and my people?"

"The Carpiani had been allies of Rome for many generations. Then, a few years ago, governor Tullus Menophilus insulted their honour. Since then, things have gone downhill."

He laughed out loud. "It is a very accurate summary. Are you aware of the fact that I was part of the delegation who was insulted by your esteemed governor?"

I shook my head and could see the visible signs of anger rising within him as he recalled the memories.

"Do you believe that eight horses will be enough to restore my honour?" he hissed. "If you do, you are gravely mistaken."

I felt certain that the horses were enough, but I still had another arrow to my bow and I remained quiet.

"It will take much more than that to persuade me to travel back to my lands", he added. "I am even willing to sacrifice the men you hold if it comes down to it."

I knew that Tarbus was aware of my relationship with Bradakos, the king of the Roxolani. He would not dare to harm me as he could not afford to be at war with the Roxolani as well as with Rome.

I decided to take the bull by the horns. "King Tarbus, in the lands of Rome I am known by the name of Lucius Domitius. Since we are in the lands of Rome, I will speak to you as Lucius Domitius, the Roman Tribune."

He nodded.

"During the past year, Rome has assembled a mighty army. Ten legions at least, and an equal number of Germani, Gothic and steppe warriors. This army will be passing by here soon enough. They would prefer to deal with the Persian threat in the east, but will not hesitate to turn their wrath on the Carpiani. It will mean the end of your people."

I could see that I had angered him, but I pushed on.

"Now let me speak to you from my heart, as a prince of the Royal Scythians", I said. "I do not wish harm to come to the Carpiani. I wish for the restoration of your honour which had been tainted by the actions of Menophilus."

"And yet you would try and give me eight horses as payment for my honour?" Tarbus sneered.

"Hear me out, Tarbus of the Carpiani", I replied.

He realised that he was dangerously close to insulting me, which came with its own set of problems, so he sighed deeply. "It is Rome and the memory of Menophilus that angers me. Please forgive me and carry on, Prince Eochar."

"To regain your honour, the Roman Emperor is willing to deliver Tullus Menophilus into your care, since he had acted against you of his own accord. Yet, he is not to be harmed, but be allowed to live out the remainder of his life amongst the people he so despises."

Tarbus did not expect that. He was at a loss for words and I continued. "Your two thousand warriors will return unharmed, with their weapons and horses. In recognition of the restoration of your honour and the release of your warriors, you will agree to supply two thousand horse archers for the campaign against the Sasanians. And you will return to your lands immediately with your loot. Rome will not oppose you."

A watch later I was joined by Thiaper and we rode back to our men. The foedus agreement had been agreed on and Tarbus made his mark. Best of all, we had taken the blood oath and I knew he would honour it.

In Rome, the scribes would hail Timesitheus as the victor of a bloody campaign against the Scythian Carpiani. He would be honoured for securing their services against the Persians. My name would not be mentioned. It did not matter, I was content.

Chapter 34 – Prefect of the Guard

The victorius Timesitheus left the following morning to ensure all was in place for the upcoming campaign.

The Fourth Italica was to return to Sirmium. Timesitheus required the fleet for his own arrangements and subsequently the legion marched back to Pannonia by way of the Roman road.

I drew Simsek level with Hostilius, who insisted on marching with his men rather than riding. I rode, as was expected of a tribune on campaign.

"Is it a ruse, or are they really going to deliver Menophilus to the Carpiani?" Hostilius asked with a frown.

"As far as Rome is concerned, it will be recorded that Menophilus was executed for his crimes, but yes, he will be delivered to the Carpiani", I replied. "Gaius Timesitheus is a man of his word."

Hostilius shook his head in amazement. "The men's morale is high. They know that you persuaded the Carpiani to fight with us in the coming Persian campaign. Better still, they know that you did not pay the nomads anything. They hate it when the barbarians are paid for peace once they breach the borders.

It smells of cowardice, but more importantly, they prefer to feel the coin in their own purses."

I nodded and changed the subject.

"The snow concealed the tracks of the cohort exactly as we had anticipated. While I was fighting their commander you surrounded them. You did well, Primus Pilus."

He nodded ever so slightly in recognition of the compliment.

"When do we march for the east? Did Timesitheus brief you?" he asked.

"The second Parthica is ready and waiting for Timesitheus to return to Rome. When he arrives back in early spring, they will march immediately and the emperor will join them", I replied.

"It is four hundred and fifty miles to Sirmium, Domitius", Hostilius said. "This march will toughen the boys up. We will rest for a day or two at the major towns or forts on the way home to resupply."

The journey home turned out to be uneventful. As Hostilius had said, it was a test for the legionaries as they travelled with their full kit every day. We traversed friendly territory and no fortified camp needed to be constructed, thus we could travel farther.

The gods favoured us with agreeable weather, never did we need to march in snow more than two inches thick.

On the thirty-second day after leaving Durostorum, the IV Italica marched through the gates of their home camp in Sirmium.

The news of our victories outpaced the legion, and we were welcomed as conquering heroes. Their families as well as the townspeople had heard stories of the IV Italica defeating the vicious barbarian Carpiani in a bloody battle. The legionaries basked in the glory. No doubt existed in my mind that rather than talking down the rumours, they would inflate it.

As soon as I had seen to my duties, Cai and I set off to the farm. As ever, I felt apprehensive. Cai knew me well enough to notice. "No need fret, Lucius of Da Qin. All will be well", he said.

I harboured a suspicion that, due to his closeness to the Dao, Cai was afforded glimpses of the future. He always denied it, but his words did set me at ease.

Unsurprisingly, Cai was right. We were met at the gate by a beaming Segelinde cradling a babe in her arms. She was accompanied by an equally beaming grandfather. Cai gave me a sideways glance. "You worry about them? They play with baby, not worry about you."

297

I scowled and jumped off my horse to embrace my wife.

Following the initial greetings, Segelinde said: "Did you ride while Hostilius marched with his men?"

I smiled, impressed with my wife's insight. "Yes, it is expected of me. You seem to know how it all works. Did Nik explain the workings of the legions to you?"

"No, husband, you smell like a horse", she answered.

Needless to say, I found myself immersed in a hot bath within less than a third of a watch.

As was his custom, Nik came to my room with a pitcher of wine.

He looked ten years younger and had a spring in his step. Even the slight limp was less noticeable.

"Try this, it is a new consignment from Aquileia", he said.

The wine was a dark purple, appearing almost black in colour. I swirled it around in my cup and inhaled the fruity aroma.

"The winemaker has outdone himself", Nik said. "It is a new cultivar developed somewhere in Gaul. Apparently it grows well at a high altitude."

We both drank slowly, appreciating the flavours.

I shared the details of the campaign against the Carpiani with Nik.

"You have done well, son. But there is one piece of bad news that I need to share with you. A message from Senator Crispinus was delivered to me a few days ago. It took some time to reach us as he used, er… more confidential channels than the imperial courier."

Nik had my full attention. He drank deeply and smacked his lips in appreciation before he continued. "The tribune who tried to have you killed, Gaius Priscus, has been appointed as the second prefect of the Praetorian Guard, answerable only to Timesitheus and the emperor. It seems that Priscus's brother pulled some strings. This brother of his is prefect of Mesopotamia and is nicknamed 'the Arab'. Philip the Arab married into a very powerful and ancient family, the Octacilia. The Arab's father-in-law, old senator Octacilius Severianus, governs Moesia and Macedonia."

"Could the emperor not do anything?" I asked, which probably highlighted my ignorance when it came to politics.

"They planned it well, Lucius", Nik explained. "Old Governor Severianus must have been lobbying for months, if not years, to garner enough support within the senate. They waited patiently until Timesitheus went away on campaign.

Remember, the old families rule on behalf of the boy Gordian until he is deemed old enough."

I heard my daughter cry in the background.

Nik smiled, narrowing his eyes. "But the good news is that your enemies have revealed their intentions."

I looked at Nik with a blank expression.

He stood to leave. "And are you going to leave me in suspense?" I asked.

"I have to attend to my granddaughter, but we will continue our conversation over dinner. Think on it", he said, and winked as he left the room with a speed belying his age.

I donned a clean tunic and wrapped myself in a brand new fur overcoat that Segelinde had bought at the market in Sirmium.

Segelinde was unsuccessfully trying to hush my daughter so I went to find my friend from Serica.

I related to Cai that which Nik had told me. He handed me a cup of some evil brew and poured one for himself as well. "Huns drink this powdered root to better endurance. We try."

"How you know when barbarians invade?" he asked. "How you know who barbarians?"

"They cross the river and breach the defences", I answered. "They look different and wear different clothes."

300

He nodded and continued. "What barbarians want most when they cross River?"

That I knew the answer to. "They covet what is important in their cultures. Horses, livestock and silver. They want to fight us to blood their young warriors."

Cai sipped his tea. "Good, Lucius of the Da Qin. You know barbarians good."

"No River for Roman enemies to cross. You know they attack when try to kill you. They attack when they get elders to appoint tribune as prefect. Men of Rome wish for power. Power with no end."

It dawned on me. Gaius Priscus and his brother Philip the Arab wished to rule the Empire.

"They have support of elders in Rome and many legions in provinces", Cai said. "Patient enemy very dangerous enemy. They wait like hungry wolf, but dress like sheep."

I tried to push these dark thoughts from my mind and spent the rest of the afternoon in the company of Segelinde and my daughter.

When evening came, we all congregated in the dining room. A servant took care of my daughter and Segelinde joined us, sitting at my side. Cai and Nik shared a couch and while Felix sat on his own.

Servants brought platters of roast boar, mutton and wild fowl cooked with exotic spices and laid them out on a central table. On a smaller table they placed cheese, dates, olives and a variety of diced fruit. I even spied a plate of the sweetmeats made with honey which I loved so much.

Nik whispered some instructions and moments later a servant appeared with three amphorae of wine, which was placed next to the food.

Nik stood and poured wine into silver goblets. "We may speak freely", he said. "I have placed a Roxolani guard at the door."

We spoke in detail about the happenings of the last months and the possibility that a group of powerful men were conspiring against the emperor. All had their own opinions and views.

I had been on campaign for months and found it difficult to control myself when it came to the delicious fare, mostly listening to the comments of the others while stuffing food into my mouth.

Eventually it was Segelinde who wisely said: "It is not for us to decide on the destiny of the Empire. Emperors come and go. Were the boy Gordian's father and grandfather not also usurpers?"

All present went quiet, listening to the wisdom of a woman.

Nik nodded. "You are correct, daughter."

Segelinde smiled. "Most worrying is that Priscus seems to desire the campaign against the Sasanids to fail. He knows that only Eochar commands the loyalty of the nomads and the Goths. I think that is the reason why he wishes you dead. Mayhap he believes that, should the Persian campaign fail, the boy and Timesitheus would be discredited."

We all stared at Segelinde, knowing that her perspective was the most likely.

"But", she continued, "we do not know that for certain. Lucius, if you act against Priscus in any way without proof, you will be the one who will be branded a traitor. No, all you can do is warn Timesitheus and be a good soldier."

She drank from her cup and added: "And make sure you stay alive."

Chapter 35 – Month of the war god (March 242 AD)

There is a reason that the first month of spring is named after Mars, the Roman god of war. Spring also happens to be the start of the campaigning season when the legions set off to war.

We received word that Caesar Gordian and his entourage had already left Rome with the II Parthica and were crossing the Mare Adriaticum headed for Salona, the capital of Dalmatia. It would take them the best part of a moon to cross Italy and arrive at the port of Salona, given fair weather. Another moon of hard marching would see them arrive at Sirmium.

Vexillations from the Rhine legions, based at Mogontiacum and the like, would need two moons to reach Sirmium, with the army of Pannonia arriving at the gates in less than five weeks.

It would be one of the largest armies ever to assemble within the Empire.

There was a knock on the door and moments later Cai appeared, ushering in Marcus's secretary.

He bowed respectfully. "The tribune laticlavius requests your presence in his quarters, Tribune." I nodded and dismissed the haughty clerk with a wave of my hand.

I took time to select a small amphora from my collection and strolled over to Marcus's office.

Marcus stood up from behind his desk when I was announced, walked over to me and clasped my arm. He closed the door behind him and sighed.

He pointed to the heaps of scrolls and writing tablets stacked neatly on his desk. "My secretary takes care of most of it, but I still need to read through everything and follow up to ensure that it is done. I have developed a habit of falling asleep behind my desk most evenings. I have come to the realisation that war is mostly paperwork."

He grinned. "I do the paperwork so killers like you can be clothed, armed and fed."

I answered by pouring two cups of wine and handing him one. "At least you don't have to be fully sober to do paperwork", I said.

He gestured towards a chair and I took a seat. Marcus sat down behind his desk and rummaged through the scrolls until he found what he was looking for.

"This arrived earlier today. It carries the seal of the emperor, but is signed by Timesitheus. Lucius, I have been given command of the foederati you enlisted into the army. Three thousand Roxolani, three thousand Goths and two thousand

Carpiani. Once the whole of the army is assembled, these eight thousand men will constitute nearly a tenth of the force."

He sighed. "You know as well as I do that I am able to command cavalry, but I am no fool, Lucius. I know that these men will follow my orders, but for you they would be willing to die. They would ride through Hades to please Eochar, the favourite of the god of war and fire."

"Will you assist me in this?" he asked.

"I have been waiting for you to ask", I said. "I will have it no other way."

"Earlier today, a messenger passed through here", Marcus added. "He was on his way to rendezvous with the emperor. Apparently, shahanshah Ardashir has died. Maybe it will weaken the resolve of the Sasanians?"

I shook my head. "Marcus, from what I have seen, Shapur, his son, is an even more formidable enemy than Ardashir. Any victory will require effort and time."

That same afternoon I rode to the farm with a heavy heart. I knew that the campaign could last years.

Will my father still be alive when or if I returned? What would happen to Segelinde and my daughter during my absence?

Cai interrupted my thoughts. "Enough bad things in life. Waste of time to imagine bad things that never happen."

My father had arranged for a private family dinner, but I also requested Felix's presence.

Normally female babes are named eight days after birth, but due to my commitments with the legions, it was delayed.

I sat with Segelinde in the courtyard. The sun was shining, but it was still necessary to have a cloak draped around the shoulders.

"Segelinde, I would like to name our daughter Aritê, in honour of my mother, whom I never met", I blurted out.

She put her hand on my arm. "It would be an honour, Eochar. Your father, for one, would appreciate the gesture. He is such a dear old man. He spends time with her at every opportunity he finds."

I nodded. "I fear for your safety during the time that I will be away. The attempts on my life might just be the start of something much worse."

She frowned and I knew what was coming. "Eochar, you confuse me with a Roman woman. I am a Gothic princess. I have trained with Kniva for years and I can handle myself as well as any man."

Then her blue eyes softened. "I know that you are concerned. It is good. But focus on staying alive and do not worry about us. Nik is as wily as ten men and Felix is an experienced legionary. We will be vigilant."

That evening I slaughtered a sheep as a sacrifice to the gods and we named our daughter Aritê. Nik had tears in his eyes. He had to leave us for a while to gather himself.

"It is done then", I said, and handed an amulet in the shape of a crescent moon to Segelinde. It was a tradition for Roman girls to wear such an amulet until the day of their marriage. Aritê would do so as well.

A short while later Nik appeared with red eyes and embraced Segelinde and me in turn.

He said nothing, only nodded. Words were unnecessary.

We feasted that evening and I drank in every moment, treasuring my time with Nik and Segelinde.

Cai and I set off early the following morning. I dreaded the goodbyes and therefore did not wish to delay it.

On the road back to Sirmium, little was spoken. When we approached the gates of the camp, Cai said: "Lucius of Da Qin, you did well with name of daughter. Make heart of father content. Sometimes small thing worth more than many chests of gold."

As the Fourth Italica was not based at a border fort, we soon received word that all but one cohort would be marching east with the emperor. The men of the legion were eagerly awaiting the arrival of the emperor and the legions from all over the Empire.

Marcus and I sat with Hostilius in his office. "Word is that in less than a moon fifty thousand warriors will be encamped around Sirmium. There will be as many auxiliaries and foederati as legionaries. It will be a sight to behold. Pity you two won't get to see any of it."

I scowled and Marcus grinned. "Remember, Primus Pilus, with Lucius and me gone, you will have to take care of the additional paperwork."

It was Hostilius's turn to scowl.

He changed the subject. "The legate has informed me of the route that we will be taking."

He unrolled a map scroll and flattened it with lead weights designed for the purpose. We all bent over the map of the eastern provinces of the Empire.

The Primus Pilus traced his finger along the route.

"From Sirmium, we will march east through Singidunum to Viminacium. We will then turn south and east, following the broad Via Militaris through Naissus and Serdica to

Trimontium in Thrace. I've marched with an army of this size before. It's nearly four hundred miles to get to Trimontium. If we make good time, we will be there in two moons. Fifty thousand warriors with their equipment, carts, siege engines and hangers-on move at the speed of an ox-cart."

"We are meeting the barbarian foederati at a ford in the Danube, ninety miles north and east of Durostorum", Marcus said. "The shallow river-crossing is guarded by a Roman fort called Carsium."

"Marcus, our Hunnic horses could get us to Carsium in seven days, but for the sake of the Roman horses, we will travel at a leisurely pace. We should be in Carsium in half a moon. We will spend a couple of days in Carsium and then ride for Trimontium once we have gathered the horde."

I traced my finger from Carsium, west along the Danube. "We backtrack west until we reach Novae and then turn due south to Trimontium. It's only three hundred miles, so it will take ten days at most."

I frowned. "Timesitheus instructed us to follow this schedule, so we have no choice but to spend a month in Trimontium, until the emperor arrives. Barbarian warriors sitting around with nothing to do is a recipe for disaster. We will have to train hard in order to keep them busy."

On the eve before we departed, I visited Hostilius to attend to one last issue. "Primus Pilus, I have had word from the smiths in Sirmium that my… er, the legion's order will be completed within the week."

He held up his hand to stop me from elaborating. "I know Domitius, I know. It is the third time you have asked me this. I will make sure that the wagons join the baggage train." He slapped me on the shoulder. "I will see you in Trimontium. By the gods, man, at least look excited, we are going to war!"

Marcus, Cai and I left the following day with a turma of hand-picked cavalrymen. Our friend Vibius was appointed as the decurion to lead them. I rode Simsek, my favourite horse. Pezhman, my Saka scout who would travel with us, had arrived at camp the evening before with Hunnic mounts for Marcus and Vibius.

The road east was crowded with people travelling in the opposite direction. Mostly merchants travelling with their goods, who wanted to exploit the huge market created by a travelling army. We stayed over in military forts every evening. Since Marcus and I were tribunes, we were afforded good accommodation and fare. It turned out to be a blessing that we travelled on the same route we would return by. We could warn the officers of the legions not to be alarmed should they wake up to the presence of eight thousand barbarian warriors outside their fort.

311

Fifteen days after departing from Sirmium, we arrived at Carsium, the Roman fort guarding a fording point in the Danube. Marcus announced us at the gate and handed our written orders to the watch officer. A century of the Legio V Macedonica garrisoned the fort, supported by a turma of Thracian auxiliary cavalry. We were escorted to the senior officer commanding the fort, who turned out to be none other than Centurion Flaminius, whom we had saved from the Heruli four years earlier.

He came to attention and saluted smartly.

"At ease centurion", I said, clasping his arm.

I turned to Marcus. "Tribune, meet Centurion Flaminius, the hero who saved his century and many civilians during the sack of Histria."

Flaminius beamed at the praise and clasped arms with Marcus.

"I am pleased to see you again, sir", he said. "I have received a missive that the foederati will be gathering across the Danube. We have certainly seen an increase in barbarian activity over the last couple of days, sir, but there is no way to know whether they are there to help us or to kill us. Only a fool would venture across the river to find out."

An hour later, Pezhman and I led our horses to the Danube's edge. A mounted Flaminius joined us as he knew the river well and had to guide us through the shallows.

"I meant no disrespect, sir. Are you sure this is safe, sir?" a clearly nervous Flaminius kept jabbering.

We crossed without incident and ascended onto the tree-lined northern bank of the Danube. We kept going and soon emerged from the trees into a shrubby clearing. I knew the barbarians were watching, as the usual sounds of nature were absent. I held up my hand, halted, and unstrapped my helmet.

Moments later Elmanos appeared, flanked by four of his warriors.

They dismounted as a sign of respect. Pezhman and I followed suit.

"Now would be a good time to get off your horse, centurion", I said, nearly causing Flaminius to fall in his haste to comply.

Elmanos inclined his head and spoke in Scythian. "Welcome back to the lands of the Roxolani, Prince Eochar. The king sends his best wishes."

I clasped his arm. "I can see that the king places great trust in you, Elmanos, son of Masas. Do you command the warriors?"

"I command only in your absence, lord, but I will assist you where I can."

We all mounted. "Take me to the camp", I said.

Elmanos nodded. "I would like to apologize in advance, lord", he said. "I do not wish to anger you, or Arash, for that matter."

"The King did not wish it so, lord, but he relented in the end", Elmanos stammered on.

"Elmanos, I have no idea what you are talking about, but if you are trying to worry me, you are succeeding", I replied.

Just then, Gordas and ten of his Huns appeared from the trees, howling like wolves, racing in our direction.

I scowled at Elmanos. "Now I know what you are referring to."

"He insisted, lord", Elmanos said. "The king forbade him initially and he sulked for weeks. Eventually, the king capitulated. Gordas and his men swore an oath to be your bodyguards throughout the campaign."

I sighed inwardly and jumped off my horse to embrace the wild commander of the Huns.

At the time of my previous visit to Bradakos, I had asked him to keep Gordas and his men home for the duration of the campaign. I harboured concerns about allowing the Huns to travel through Roman lands. I knew how their minds worked and that eventually they would covet the wealth and prosperity

314

of Rome. Yet, Gordas was a friend and I could not send him home. At least, with the Huns lurking about my person, no one would be foolish enough to try and do me harm.

Elmanos informed us that Thiaper commanded the Carpiani foederati and was camped three miles to the north. Kniva and his Goths were expected to arrive within three days.

I left a visibly nervous Flaminius in the care of Elmanos and rode to greet Thiaper, escorted by Gordas and his Huns, who were now oathbound to protect me.

"Thiaper, how come Rhemaxos is not in charge? Is he not your senior officer?" I queried.

Thiaper smiled broadly. "I gifted my white mare to the king on the same day that you left us, lord, which made me his favourite. Rhemaxos wished to keep his horse, which was bad for his health in the long run. The king took his horse after his demise."

I smiled at the savvy of my friend and clasped his arm. "Send a messenger to the Roman fort when your allies arrive."

"Allies?" he asked. "I do not understand."

"You know what I mean, Thiaper", I replied.

He smiled slyly. "I will let you know when the iudex arrives, lord."

It was nearly dark when I passed by the Roxolani camp to escort Flaminius back to the fort.

He was clearly relieved. "Thank all the gods that you have returned, tribune. I was worried that them barbarians had slit your throat."

Chapter 36 – Trimontium

A messenger from Thiaper arrived late the following morning.

Pezhman came to summon me soon after. "Better come to the rampart lord, before a Thracian puts an arrow in the yelling Carpiani", he said.

I could hear a messenger hailing the fort in unintelligible Latin from outside the walls. I commanded the duty officer to open a sally gate and walked out to the messenger who was sitting on his horse two hundred paces from the wall.

"Thank you, lord", the messenger said.

I nodded in acknowledgement of his gratitude and he continued. "Commander Thiaper says to tell you that the king of the Goths will arrive this afternoon. That is all, lord."

I waved him away. "Go with Arash and thank your commander for the message."

I flicked him a gold coin and he rode off, smiling broadly.

I went to fetch Marcus. The two of us rode across the river with a very relieved Centurion Flaminius waving us off from the safety of the walls.

We were joined by Elmanos and Thiaper on the northern bank of the Danube. Soon the four of us were on our way to meet

317

with my brother-in-law, the iudex of the Thervingi Goths. An advance scout spied us as we neared the Goth camp. He turned his horse and rode back in the direction whence he came. I called a halt and we dismounted in the shade of an ancient oak.

Less than a third of a watch had passed when we noticed the approach of a small group of horsemen. As they came closer, I recognized Kniva leading the group. Next to him rode a hulking warrior with blonde braids extending from underneath his helmet. His scarred and muscled arms were decorated with a multitude of gold and silver bands, all inscribed with the magic markings of the Heruli.

The riders dismounted and removed their helmets.

All of us inclined our heads as a sign of respect towards the iudex. Kniva embraced me as he would a brother and clasped Marcus's arm, whom he knew well from our previous visit.

"It is good to see you, brother, and you too, Tribune Marcus." All of it was spoken in Gothic, a language I had a good command over on account of being married to a Goth.

I translated for Marcus and clasped the muscled arm of Rodoulphos, the Erilar of the Heruli. "Well met, Red Wolf", I said.

"Well met, Prince Eochar, favourite of Teiwaz", the Heruli replied.

I grinned, and introduced all.

Kniva turned to Rodoulphos and after a short, muted conversation, the Heruli excused himself and rode off at speed, followed by Kniva's oathsworn.

"I suggest that we talk over a cup of wine at the camp of the Carpiani", I said.

All agreed.

Thiaper led the way with Elmanos riding alongside. Marcus and I flanked Kniva.

True to his nature, Kniva's first concern was for the welfare of his sister.

"How is my sister?" the king asked.

"Your sister cannot be better, uncle Kniva", I said, and grinned.

He slapped me on the back. "Congratulations, Eochar. Is it a boy or a girl?"

"A beautiful little girl", I replied.

"It is good that she looks like her mother", he said, chuckling at his own jest. "We will have to celebrate the addition to our family soon, brother."

Marcus could not understand any of my conversation with Kniva, but I had prepared him for it and continued. "Kniva, brother, I need to clear the air before we talk with the Roxolani and Carpiani commanders." He nodded, probably expecting something of the like.

"You are the great king, the iudex of a mighty nation, a powerful man. I am but a commander in the Roman army. We will be fighting a dangerous enemy. For us to succeed, you will have to submit to my command, otherwise we will be a divided force. I will not put you in a position I do not wish upon myself, that I promise."

"Are you willing to submit to my command while we are on this campaign? Will you be able to do it?" I asked.

Kniva remained quiet for a while. "Brother", he said, "I owe you my life twice over and I have sworn an oath to you." He breathed deeply. "It will not be easy for me, but I do know that you are a favourite of the god of war. So yes, I will submit to your command without hesitation during this campaign."

Then he added with a smile. "Just like you are subject to the command of my sister when you are at home."

We both grinned at the truth of his words as we entered the camp of the Carpiani. A great weight has been lifted from my shoulders.

Kniva returned to business. "I have hired Rodoulphos and his thousand Heruli to bolster my army. I know that we will have to cross the channel of the Dark Sea to reach the eastern provinces. We will not be left at the mercy of the Roman navy. Rodoulphos will take us across, and his longboats will wait for our return."

"I understand your thinking brother, but there is no reason to be concerned. The guardian of the emperor, Timesitheus, is an honourable man. Nothing will go wrong", I said with confidence.

Although we were supposed to be a single foederati unit, we would travel as three different groups. The Goths and Roxolani still harboured ill feelings towards each other. Seeing their iudex and their prince working together would go a long way to assist in quelling these emotions, but only a fool would ignore animosities of old and intermix the tribes.

Marcus and I allowed the army two days of rest, specifically for the Gothic horses to recover after their arduous trip. Although the Goths fought mainly on foot, the whole of Kniva'a army travelled on horseback.

On the morning of the third day, the barbarian foederati crossed the shallow ford at Carsium and entered Roman territory.

The warriors were threatened with harsh punishment should they in any way harm the local folk. I, for one, would not hesitate to act upon such a threat as I was well aware of the tenuous hold barbarian commanders have over their subordinates.

The route to Trimontium had been well supplied by Timesitheus. Ample stockpiles of provisions ensured that my men were well-fed along the way. Wine rations were provided to keep the warriors content, but not enough to place them in a constant state of inebriation.

The locals were well-informed about the fact that a friendly barbarian army would pass close by their hovels and farms. They were told they had nothing to fear. The predictable result was that all of the local folk, without exception, gathered their coin and livestock and fled to the hills, trembling with fear. From experience, they preferred to rather be safe than sorry.

The turma of Roman cavalry led by Vibius ranged far ahead to ensure that we did not by chance encounter a Roman force unaware of our intention. Once we approached Roman forts, the cavalry gave notice to the garrison commanders to enable them to prepare for our arrival. Oxen and sheep were slaughtered and the meat, together with grain and wine rations loaded on carts, ready for delivery to our hungry army.

Gordas and his Huns rarely left my side once we had crossed the river as he had given an oath to Bradakos that he would protect me from harm.

Gordas's gaze drifted over the countryside and the large villas that studded the slopes of the hills. "This looks to be a rich land, Eochar."

"Don't get ideas, Gordas", I said. "The Romans bought this land with blood and they are willing to spill much more to hold on to it."

He pointed at the huge stones embedded in the Roman road. "People who are able to build a road in stone must be a formidable enemy."

I nodded. "A Roman legion is a fearsome predator of iron, muscle and discipline. Above all discipline. In its own way, it is as deadly as the storm of arrows."

He looked at me sideways. "I do not fear the legions, but I will never attack the Empire."

"Why is that?" I asked.

"Because, Eochar", he explained, "the Romans will send the legions and they will send you, with Arash riding at your back. What man will dare attack the favourite of Arash?"

He steered his horse closer to mine and leaned in conspiratorially. "We all know what you did with the Carpiani. They are only alive because you desire that they fight by your side."

In less than half a moon, we arrived at the fortified town of Trimontium. For obvious reasons, we skirted the town and made camp on a flat plain, close to the massive stone and brick pillars of the aqueduct. It had been built during the time of Marcus Aurelius and channeled fresh water from springs in the forested Rhodope hills, twenty miles to the southwest of the town.

"Did the gods build this?" Gordas asked reverently.

"The legions did. In times of peace, they build, rather than destroy", I answered.

"Bloody waste of time", he scoffed. "It is much easier to camp next to the river than bring the river to the camp."

Contrary to popular belief, barbarians are not averse to training. They train at their craft, be it with the spear, sword or bow. The challenge was to get the three groups to work together. Romans had overcome their tribal heritage generations before, but these warriors were still divided along those lines.

Fortunately for me, their respect for, and fear of their leaders outweighed their petty differences.

Our role, as light missile cavalry, would be to attack the enemy infantry or heavy cavalry while staying out of their grasp. In addition, we would keep the Sasanian horse archers away from the flanks of the legion. The Goth and Heruli infantry were extremely mobile and would function well as a surprise attack force, or as a reserve that could be rapidly deployed.

We practised various manoeuvres during the day and feasted in the evening. No warrior was allowed to venture into town. Before long the merchants and traders had set up their mobile stalls close to our camp to relieve the warriors of their gold and silver.

One evening I sat with Marcus, Cai and Vibius, discussing the happenings of the day. Later Kniva, Elmanos and Thiaper joined us to share the sizeable sheep that was slowly roasting over the raging fire. As ever, Gordas was also present. The aroma of the meat combined with the hissing and crackling of the fat and juices in the fire, made the wait almost unbearable. I swallowed down another generous gulp of red, then filled up my friends' cups from the large amphora. Over the years

Marcus had acquired a basic understanding of the language of the steppes, hence he was able to follow the conversation.

On more than one occasion, we discussed the fighting style of the Sasanians, especially the emphasis that they place on the heavily armoured cavalry.

"We have a major weakness. Vulnerability to the attack of heavy cavalry. I have a solution, but it will require practise, if it can be done at all", I said. I spent the rest of the evening sharing my plans and discussing the campaign with my friends.

"Lord, we do get to keep the loot that we take?" Thiaper asked.

"Yes. That is the agreement", I replied.

"If your plan works", he said, "I would like to lay my hands on the armour of the immortals. My men would too."

I held up an open palm. "Let us first practise, but yes, it would be good. The more we sweat, the less we will bleed, eh?"

The next day on the training ground, Thiaper and Elmanos instructed every warrior to gather five large pebbles from the nearby stream. For hours we tried to execute what I had planned, without success.

Come evening, I was close to despair. I sat with Cai when Gordas entered. "Tomorrow I will show you how Huns would do it. It will work with your plan."

Gordas turned out to be right. Yet, it took the best part of two weeks to perfect the manoeuvre I had in mind. In the end, the horsemen could do it with their eyes closed.

Gordas looked on proudly. "Not bad, not bad. But they will never ride like Huns."

Chapter 37 – Hellespont (June 242 AD)

The army of Gordian arrived later the same week.

My friends and I ascended one of the rocky hills which afforded us a panoramic view of the approach to Trimontium. The Roman road bordered the hill and was less than four hundred paces distant.

We made ourselves comfortable on a ridge while Gordas took two bulging wineskins from his saddle. "It is not good to watch a show with a parched throat", he said as he filled the cups. A cloud of dust was already visible on the northern horizon, heralding the imminent arrival of the legions.

In the distance, the approach to the city was lined with civilians. Thousands throwing flowers and leaves on the road as a sign of reverence and respect.

The emperor, mounted on a pure white Hispanic stallion, led the procession. It was too far away to distinguish his features, but I noticed the sun reflecting off his silver cuirass and his purple cloak fluttered in the breeze. Caesar Gordian was flanked by two richly dressed officers and I was sure I recognized the idiosyncratic movements of Timesitheus as he fiddled with his silver helmet. I assumed that the second officer would be my nemesis, Gaius Priscus.

Thirty muscled Germanic guards with wolfskin cloaks rode behind the trio, one carrying the standard of the emperor. The golden disks on the shaft, detailing his victories, reflected the sun like a mirror. The elite mounted praetorians followed, their black shields decorated with the silver emblem of the guard. Some mocked these mounted men for their immaculate grooming, but I knew only the best veterans of the legions were selected to the ranks of the speculatores. These men were experts with a blade and rode almost as well as barbarians, but what distinguished them was the fact that they were ruthless killers. Often they would be sent to do the dirty work of the emperor. Making a problem go away by wielding a blade in the night.

Then came the legions. The Praetorian Guard with their distinctive blue cloaks. The II Parthica, the legion of the emperor, stationed on the Alban hill close to Rome.

Then followed the Pannonians, or rather the vexillations from those legions. For reasons of practicality, the vexillations from legions, normally stationed close together, had combined for the duration of the campaign to march under a single standard and be commanded by one legate. Among them, I recognised the IV Italica with Primus Pilus Hostilius marching at the head, just behind the mounted officers. The sight of the golden Aquila, carried by the standard bearer, caused me to almost burst with pride.

The auxiliaries and foederati trailed in the dust of the legions. Thousands upon thousands of horsemen and infantry. Never had I laid eyes on such a host. I felt small and insignificant, inwardly laughing at our efforts over the past weeks. I felt a fool to have thought that we could make a difference to the outcome of a battle.

Cai read my mind. "One man turn around and run. Soon whole army running. One man break line of enemy, soon all enemy running."

He was right of course, and it helped me to understand. One small action in a battle, even by a few warriors, could change the outcome.

The emperor and his guards entered the town of Trimontium with the rest of the army camped on the flat plain surrounding the city. No marching camps would be built, but as a precaution, the barbarian auxiliaries camped on the outskirts.

We returned to camp. A messenger arrived late afternoon, summoning Marcus and me to the Praetorium of the emperor. On his insistence, Gordas accompanied us. I also allowed Pezhman to come along. He would hold our horses, the actual reason being to satisfy his curiosities regarding the Roman legions.

We were challenged by guards and sentries along the way, but rank and written orders gave us access to the Praetorium. The tent was surrounded by a ring of shield-bearing guards. Timesitheus was not taking any chances.

We left our weapons with Gordas and entered the command tent.

Timesitheus stood with his back to us, stooped over an enormous map. Marcus coughed in his hand and the prefect spun around with a frown, but smiled disarmingly when he recognised us.

"Peace, tribunes", he said. "It is just that I am constantly harassed by pampered politicians who play at being soldiers. Men who should be able to think for themselves. I could have conquered the world if Mars had given me more warriors like the two of you."

The man who governed the Empire in all but name walked to a low table and filled three silver goblets from a golden jug. We each took one and he led us to couches arranged in one corner of the spacious tent.

"Forgive me, I complain too much", Timesitheus continued. "The campaign is progressing well. All the hard work done over the past years is finally bearing fruit."

He emptied the goblet with one swallow. "I wake up every day with the intention to arrange for larger goblets, but I never get around to it", he said. "In any event, the reason why I

331

summoned you is to find out whether all is proceeding according to plan?"

Marcus was in charge and he answered. "The three foederati tribes provided the number of warriors as had been stipulated. We have had no problematic contact with the local populace on the way, mostly because they all fled to the hills."

Timesitheus smiled. "As I expected."

Marcus continued: "We have been practising manoeuvres for the last three weeks and the groups are working together as well as can be."

He emptied his goblet. "Prefect, there is one change of plan that I have to highlight."

He explained the fact that the Heruli would transport the foederati under his command, across the Hellespont. At first Timesitheus frowned. He was a man who planned everything in detail and saw those plans through to fruition. Any change in plan came with its own set of potential problems.

Timesitheus appeared to be deep in thought for several moments, but then he visibly relaxed. "Of all the unexpected things that could happen, this is but a minor item. In the end, it might even be beneficial to us. I will immediately dispatch a messenger to the imperial navy to ensure that they do not engage with Heruli longboats active in the area."

"I am pleased with your performance, tribunes. Now you have to excuse me, I have much to arrange."

We left the Praetorium to retrieve our horses and weapons. As we mounted to leave, Prefect Gaius Priscus, followed by a few of his speculatores, rode past us and entered the Praetorium. I could see Pezhman curiously studying the group, but made nothing of it at the time.

Before we returned to our camp, I sought out Hostilius. I found him overseeing the digging of the latrine trenches. "The soil is very rocky in this part of the world, Domitius. If someone doesn't make sure its deep enough, the camp will be swimming in shit within two days." I tried to interrupt, but he held up his hand. "I know what you are going to ask, Domitius." He pointed to two medium-sized wagons, parked separately from the rest of the baggage train. "That's the merchandise that you are worried about. I will have it delivered to your camp at first light. We will probably rest here for a week."

We left Hostilius to attend to his tasks.

For the first time in my life, I travelled as part of such an enormous host. Seeing that we commanded barbarian foederati, we were relegated to travel at the rear of the army. It does sound inconsequential, but there is a practical implication. Thousands of feet and hooves grind the dust on the side of the road into a fine powder that finds its way into any conceivable orifice in the body. In addition to that, thousands of horses, oxen and mules cover the road with manure. As a result we rode through a layer of shit for most of the way.

On the second day after our departure from Trimontium, Pezhman fell out of the column, spurred his horse and reined in alongside me. "Lord, there is something that bothers me."

I did not answer, but allowed him time to continue.

"You and Lord Marcus were visiting with the great Roman lord in the large tent two days ago", he said.

I nodded, confirming my recollection.

"I saw a man that I had seen before. Seen in Persia, lord."

He now had my full attention. "Where in Persia, Pezhman?"

"When I was a scout for the Gorgan lord, I rode with him to visit king Ardashir, to scout the way. That man also visited at the same time. He wore a shemagh around his head like the desert nomads, but I saw his face when he greeted Prince Shapur. He must be their friend. I do not understand lord? Why is he a Roman now?"

I did not ask Pezhman if he was sure of his facts. He obviously milled this around in his mind for two days and would not tell me something he was not sure of.

"You have done well, Pezhman of the Saka. You do your ancestors proud", I said.

I could see that referring to his Sarmatian heritage pleased him. "Keep this to yourself", I said. "I will think on it and try to understand." He nodded and fell back to join the Roxolani.

Cai was talking to Marcus when I fell in beside them and shared the information.

"It could have been a diplomatic mission to the Sasanians", Marcus said, "or Pezhman could be mistaken, but something tells me that whenever Prefect Priscus is involved, some kind of evil is afoot. But what it may be, we will never know."

Cai nodded in agreement. "He is planning, keeping true intention hidden."

The advance to Hadrianopolis took fifteen days. Half a moon of eating dust and being spattered with horse shit. Gordian entered the city, but the army did not linger and we continued our march to Perinthus, a town bordering the Propontis. The Propontis being the inland sea connecting the Mare Aegaeum to the south with the Dark Sea in the north.

From Perinthus the army marched south and west to reach the Hellespont, the narrow channel separating Thrace from the eastern provinces. Our destination was a small settlement known only by its Greek name, Sestos. I could hardly hide my excitement to reach the town.

"Why are you so chirpy?" Marcus queried on the morning of the day we would reach Sestos.

Gordas, true to his oath, was riding just within earshot, next to Cai.

I pointed to the narrow channel, a mile wide at this point. The eastern shore could be seen clearly.

"Seven hundred years ago, Xerxes, son of Darius, high king of the Persians, built a pontoon bridge at Sestos by lashing together three hundred and sixty triremes", I said. "He built a walkway across the decks with wooden planks and covered it with soil. Brushwood was stacked on the sides to calm the animals. The army was so large that it took seven days and seven nights to march them across." I spoke in Scythian so Gordas could understand.

"Did the great king cross to fight the Roman emperor?" he asked.

"No, he went to fight the Greeks", I answered.

"Where is the Empire of the Greeks, Eochar?" Gordas asked.

"They were defeated by Rome many generations ago. It is now part of the Roman Empire", I explained.

Gordas raised his eyebrows. "So did the great king with many warriors win a great victory?"

"No, they lost against the Greeks", I said.

"Sounds like a weak king with pathetic warriors", the Hun sneered. "His time would have been better spent staying at home, warm under the furs with his wife and a mug of hot salted milk."

I nodded, suddenly robbed of my enthusiasm. "Gordas, you really have a talent for making a huge feat like Xerxes's pontoon bridge feel like a waste of time."

Gordas grinned. "A king may build a bridge around the world, but if he loses the battle, it is a waste of time."

"Gordas not that far away from enlightenment", Cai added.

Needless to say, I did not continue to elaborate on Alexander of Macedon's crossing one and a half centuries later. But Gordas wasn't done yet. "Did you know the great Iskander crossed here by ship?" he asked.

I looked at him in wonder, which he took as a lack of knowledge from my side.

"He crossed here then defeated the Persian king of kings, Artashata, in a legendary battle", Gordas said. "Now that's a story worth telling."

337

Chapter 38 – The East

More than a hundred Roman ships were anchored just off the beach at Sestos.

Timesitheus, as was to be expected, had upgraded the capacity of the harbour to allow five ships to be loaded simultaneously.

Worryingly, the Heruli longboats were nowhere to be seen.

We were assigned an area for our camp. Once I had taken care of duties, I went in search of Kniva.

The iudex of the Goths was sitting on furs outside his tent, enjoying a horn of ale with Rodoulphos.

I started speaking, but Kniva held up his hand. "You may be the war leader, Eochar, but you still have to follow the rules of hospitality."

He motioned to a servant, who poured a horn of ale and held it out to me.

"Come join us brother, you are welcome at my hearth", Kniva said. "I have seen far too little of you during the journey."

I decided that the best course of action was to surrender. I took the horn from a relieved servant and sat down opposite Kniva and the Heruli.

I drank deeply, appreciating the quality brew. "I have missed your hospitality, brother. When I see and hear you, it reminds me of your sister."

"I miss her", he said. "Maybe I should visit her in the lands of Rome when we return." At the time, he did not realise that his words were prophetic.

I nodded and turned to Rodoulphos. "I notice that there are no Heruli longboats in the harbour."

"I can understand your concern, Lord Eochar, but I will explain", Rodoulphos said.

He drank from his horn and wiped the ale from his beard with the back of his hand. "My people have been building longboats for generations. Many years past we raided the Thracian coast and up the Danube, or so the stories go. Rome became strong and they built more and more boats which patrolled these areas. The most terrible of weapons were mounted on the decks of the Roman ships and they destroyed our craft whenever they encountered them."

He smiled evilly. "But it is not so easy to defeat the Heruli. The longboats are able to sail in shallower waters than the Romans' and they can outrun a trireme any day. The Heruli adapted. We started to operate at night and hide during the day when we rowed in waters protected by Rome. My captains are cautious. They will arrive during the night. Be

339

patient, it will take the Romans at least a moon to ferry their army across the channel."

Five days later, I woke up and rode to the seashore, as had become my habit. Fifty longboats were drawn up on the sandy beach. Rodoulphos and Kniva were engaged in a discussion with the captains.

It took the Heruli four days to ferry the warriors, horses and baggage across the mile wide channel. I was impressed by the longboats. They were well built, sturdy yet sleek, and incredibly fast. Rodoulphos arranged for Kniva, Marcus, Cai and me to travel in luxury. He proudly led us onto a boat with twenty oars a side, rowed by brutish Heruli. As we were the lords and nobles, we travelled without the encumbrance of horses and baggage. The Erilar stood at the stern with his hand held against the mythical creature carved from the wooden prow.

He shouted commands and the ship accelerated. I nearly fell backwards, were it not for Cai's hand that steadied me.

"How do you like the ship?" he shouted above the noise. "She is one of mine. Twenty rowers a side and can outrun anything with oars", he exclaimed proudly. "She is called 'Blood Serpent' and her magic is strong."

Well, needless to say, 'Blood Serpent' delivered us safely on the opposite bank and she returned to ferry the last of our baggage across.

The only memorable thing about the three-month-long trek to Antioch was the brutal monotony of the affair. To be fair, the landscape was breathtaking, as was the wealth and beauty of the towns and villages, but it was overshadowed by the boredom and constant petty infighting amongst my foederati warriors.

We travelled along the coastal road, skirting Pergamum, Ephesus and Seleucia. The road was longer than the inland road, but during the height of summer, the temperature along the coastal road was bearable. Another advantage was that the army could be supplied by the imperial fleet, rather than by costly and slow overland transportation.

I sighed with relief when we eventually reached Tarsus, the capital of Cilicia, the last major supply point prior to entering Syria. By that time I was weary from the travelling so Marcus and I decided to venture into the city.

It was a grand place filled with palaces, temples and monuments. We trained in the gymnasium on the banks of the Cydnus River and spent at least a watch in the baths. I felt refreshed and relaxed for the first time in weeks. On our way back to camp we paused at an upmarket inn to enjoy a cup of wine. Marcus and I had become close friends, and discussed a variety of issues. During the course of the afternoon, Marcus said something that I believe planted a seed in our minds. Something that would later change our lives.

"Lucius, the Empire has brought much wealth and prosperity to the whole of the known world", he said. "In many instances, it has brought peace for generations. Yet we allow the greed of a few, who covet power, to destroy it all by weakening the borders. Maybe one day the gods will give us an opportunity to set it right."

I still remember his words as if he had spoken it yesterday. Even today after all these years have passed.

Chapter 39 – Winter camp (October 242 AD)

Late one afternoon, Timesitheus came to visit Marcus and me in camp after we had completed our march for the day. He was accompanied by four Germanic guards, all built like oxen.

It was a pleasant afternoon. We walked and talked as the tents had not been set up yet.

His guards trailed twenty paces behind. Gordas and three of his Huns followed us at a distance, as they did not trust the 'scheming two-faced Romans', to use his own words.

"I am very aware of the challenges that exist when travelling with barbarian foederati, yet you have done remarkably well, my young friends", Timesitheus said. "We are two days away from Antioch and then the first stage of the campaign will be successfully completed. We have built the army, gathered reinforcements and the provinces to the west are secure and at peace. The imperial navy is already unloading supplies at the Antioch harbour. The city has in the past served as the base to eastern campaigns and it will suit us well. The Orontes River borders Antioch, so there is ample water and more than enough space for the army on the surrounding plains."

He sighed then. "I must share this with you. I am increasingly worried about the motives of Prefect Gaius Priscus. Priscus's brother Philip, the former prefect of Mesopotamia, has joined his entourage. While I spend my days working on the campaign, Priscus and Philip court the emperor. They have not set a foot wrong, but in light of what you have told me earlier, I am concerned."

I told him then about the revelation of Pezhman who saw Priscus with Shapur.

"You did well not to spread this information", he replied. "It cannot be proven, but I will stay vigilant."

He half turned around, stared at Gordas and added: "At least with those men guarding you, no living soul would even try to lay a hand on you two. By the gods, they even scare my Germani guards."

The army arrived at Antioch two days later.

Although we were in Roman Syria, we were effectively within enemy territory - Shapur had taken the whole of the Roman province of Mesopotamia and raided deep into Syria. I volunteered to camp upstream of Antioch, on the eastern bank of the Orontes River. It seemed to be a vulnerable position, but for the Scythians it was perfect. We had access to clean water, grazing and open spaces. Our scouts ranged far and wide. No enemy would be able to approach undetected.

We practised manoeuvres daily, rain or shine. Timesitheus kept us supplied with grain and wine and the warriors hunted game in the foothills of the mountains to supplement their diet.

I spent most evenings around the cooking fire with Marcus, Vibius and Gordas. On occasion we were joined by Kniva and Elmanos.

I made a habit of visiting Hostilius once a week and I even spent an evening or two visiting with my old contubernium.

"It is good to see you Umbra, we heard that you have gathered a horde of them barbarians to fight at our side", Ursa said as he refilled his cup from the amphora I had brought along.

"For once all of us feel the same about the emperor", Pumilio added. "He's got respect, even for us common soldiers. My cousin in the fourth said the emperor clasped his arm the other day when he went walking among them. He didn't even try to wipe his hand straight after!"

Silentus nodded and Pumilio said: "See, even Silentus likes him, doesn't he? He never liked the others. Even Prefect Timesitheus is a good soldier. We always see him walking on the ramparts, eyeballing the men to see whether they are doing their duty good and proper."

Ursa leaned in conspiratorially. "Timesitheus doesn't take shit", he whispered. "I heard him talking to a tribune the other day. The tribune ordered the gate to be left open, against the prefect's wishes. Let me tell you, the tribune will do his job proper from now on, won't he?"

Chapter 40 – Road to Edessa (February 243 AD)

The arrival of the vexillations from the eastern legions heralded the start of the campaigning season.

Each of the five legions that were based in Cappadocia, Cilicia and Judea sent two cohorts, bolstering the army with six thousand men.

Two days before we marched to Zuegma, the VI Ferrata joined the army, leaving the III Cerenaica to man the fort at Raphana, two hundred miles south of Antioch. This strategic fort guarded the approach from Parthia to Judea and could not be left undefended.

On the morning of our planned departure, Marcus and I waited patiently for the vanguard of the army to arrive. As was the norm, our contingent would act as the rearguard.

A rider delivered an unexpected message from Timesitheus.

Marcus unrolled the small scroll. "The prefect wants us to ride to Zeugma", Marcus said. "He wishes for us to scout the way. We are only to report to him if we find any sign of the enemy. His orders are not to cross the Euphrates at Zeugma until the arrival of the rest of the army."

We were much relieved, as none of us looked forward to a three week march trailing through the dust and manure of the army.

The road from Antioch to Zeugma was a major trade route, so we encountered trade caravans on the way. Neither the Sasanids nor the Romans would dare attack a merchant caravan from the east. War was one thing, but to kill the lifeblood of trade, which provided coin to both empires, would have been outright foolish.

Pezhman reported to me after using his initiative to question some of the camel drivers of the first caravan he came across. "Lord, the bridge at Zeugma is still intact. The traders used it to cross the Euphrates only a week ago."

Three cohorts of the IV Scythica garrisoned the Roman fort at Zeugma, but they had been ordered to abandon their position months ago and had subsequently retreated to Antioch to bolster its defences.

We completed the one hundred and thirty mile ride to Zeugma within three days, riding at a leisurely pace. The nomads ranged far and wide but failed to find any sign of the Sasanians.

Arriving at Zeugma, we found the small town functioning normally and the Roman fort deserted.

The elders of the town initially thought that we were a band of steppe nomads come to attack them, but Marcus and Vibius eventually managed to set them at ease. By the look in Gordas's eyes, it would not have bade well for the townsfolk if my barbarians had been unsupervised.

We set up camp next to the Euphrates and before long Timesitheus joined us with the main army. I had been keen to cross the river and scout the eastern bank, but we did not wish to anger the prefect by ignoring his orders.

Ten turmae of Numidian cavalry were sent across the river to scout the lay of the land.

I visited with Hostilius, not having seen him for weeks. Come late afternoon, we walked to inspect the famous pontoon bridge. Our rank allowed us access. While walking the bridge, the Numidian scouts returned. I noticed a familiar face and tribune Adherbal reined in next to me. He was riding a fine Hunnic horse, an offspring of Simsek's, which I had gifted him nearly five years before.

Adherbal smiled broadly and clasped my arm. "Every Numidian is envious of me. No other horse can keep up with him." He stroked the neck of the stallion lovingly, the horse whinnying in response.

He leaned down and whispered: "We found the enemy. Twelve thousand horse archers and five thousand cataphracts are encamped at Edessa. I am on my way to report to Prefect Timesitheus."

I nodded and he spurred his horse.

"It seems like the fun and games are about to start, Domitius", Hostilius said. "Mark my words, you will be in the Praetorium before the sun sets."

When I arrived back at my tent, Marcus was waiting for me in the company of a messenger who appeared to be close to a state of panic.

"Prefect Timesitheus requires your presence in the Praetorium immediately, Tribune", he said, and handed me my orders. Marcus held a similar scroll.

We arrived at the Praetorium where a scowling Hostilius was waiting outside the tent. "I told you, didn't I?" he said as a guard gestured for us to enter.

Timesitheus was alone.

On the table stood three large goblets filled with a fruity dry white. He was already savouring the wine and motioned for us to help ourselves.

"As you might have heard, a Sasanian force awaits us on the road to Edessa", Timesitheus said.

We nodded, confirming his suspicion.

"This opposing army is problematic in many ways", he said. "As you know, it is typical of the Sasanians. All the warriors are mounted."

"If I deploy the full might of my army, they will simply ride away. Should we give chase with, say the Numidians or your horse archers, the heavy Sasanian cavalry will certainly slaughter them. I require the Sasanian army to give battle and be defeated. It will boost the Roman morale, especially if we are able to defeat them with a force similar in size to theirs. In addition, it will stop them from joining with their main army, which is apparently still on the way."

I played with my goblet, a plan slowly taking shape in my mind.

"Is the wine not to your liking, Tribune?" Timesitheus asked, and I realised he was speaking to me.

I spilt some of it in shock, but when I looked up, I saw that he was smiling.

He held up his hand to stop me from offering an excuse.

"Senator Crispinus told me that you and Tribune Marcus Claudius are crafty when it comes to hatching plans. You have already proven your ability many times. Besides, the three of you know the Sasanians better than any other Roman alive."

351

"I need you to come up with a plan", Timesitheus concluded. "Report to me at first light. Dismissed."

We walked out, Marcus wearing a flabbergasted expression. Hostilius, in contrast, was smiling and appeared nonplussed.

"Do you appreciate the difficulty of the position he has just placed us in?" Marcus said. "It is nothing to smile about, Centurion. If we do not come up with the goods, he will lose faith in us."

"Do not be concerned, Tribune", Hostilius replied. "I have known Domitius for many years. He already has a plan." He slapped me on the shoulder. "Tell us your plan, Domitius."

So… I told them.

A third of a watch later, Hostilius was grinning from ear to ear and Marcus was frowning.

"Domitius, let me get the lads ready", Hostilius said. "The sooner we get it over with, the sooner we can pocket the loot."

"Hold your horses, Primus Pilus", Marcus replied. "We first need to get Timesitheus's approval."

"He won't have a better plan than the one Domitius's god whispered into his ear", Hostilius said. "Isn't that right, Domitius?"

We eventually succeeded in calming Hostilius and shared a meal complemented by fine wine. We went to bed early and I woke up relaxed.

Timesitheus, to the contrary, had the look of someone who had slept little.

"You seem rested and relaxed for men who spent the night scheming?" he asked.

Hostilius was quick to respond. "Domitius had already hatched the plan while you were talking to us yesterday, sir. We went to bed early."

He narrowed his eyes. "Tell me."

After hearing us out, he paced back and forth with his hands behind his back for what felt like an age.

Eventually he turned to us, having made up his mind. "Tribune Marcus Claudius, tomorrow you will assume temporary command of the IV Italica assisted by Primus Pilus Hostilius Proculus. In addition, you will command a thousand strong vexillation of the Ala Nova Firma Catafractaria."

"Tribune Lucius Domitius, you will assume temporary command over the three groups of foederati normally commanded by Tribune Claudius."

"I must emphasize that I believe that there is a significant element of risk involved, but I will sacrifice to Fortuna and I suggest you do the same."

That evening, I sat with Cai, Gordas and my foederati commanders, detailing my plan.

They all listened intently and eventually Kniva said: "Brother, have you ever heard of the Germani god Lok?"

I shook my head. "He is the spinner of webs, the trickster", Kniva said. "This is truly a plan worthy of Lok."

Chapter 41 – Battle

I handed the scroll to Pezhman. Vibius and Cai had worked on it for hours.

"You know what to do?" I stated. Pezhman nodded, obviously nervous, yet in awe of the responsibility placed on his shoulders.

"I have instructed Gordas to make sure that the items you have asked for are kept aside", I said.

It was still dark. Pezhman nodded and vanished into the night.

We planned to march the fifty miles in two days. On the eve of the second day, we would make camp as close to Edessa as possible.

Hostilius had readied the IV Italica in the pre-dawn light.

The legionaries marched in full armour with their shields uncovered. The legion's artillery would remain with the rest of the army, as we travelled with wagons loaded with barrels and amphorae of water. Any available space on the mules were used to carry additional waterskins.

The Roxolani and Carpiani formed the vanguard with the legion following close behind. Then marched the Goths and the Heruli with the heavy cavalry forming the rearguard.

The countryside was semi-desert with low rocky outcrops rising above the plains. From time to time the road snaked through shallow ravines, sparsely populated with trees and shrubs. My nomad scouts ranged far and wide to minimise the risk of ambush.

I rode at the head of the column with Marcus. Cai remained in camp. Gordas, Thiaper and Elmanos followed, clearly excited about the coming battle.

Every so often a returning scout reported to me.

"We rode at least a third of a watch in that direction, lord", he said, and pointed southeast. "No sign of the enemy. No tracks, no livestock. Nothing."

Similar reports kept arriving and it continued throughout the day. A watch after midday, we arrived at the site that the surveyors had identified for the marching camp.

A temporary camp was constructed and the night passed without incident.

We filled the ditches when morning came and set off after sunrise. Soon the first scout arrived back to report.

Immediately I noticed the difference in his countenance and I knew what was coming. "Lord, we have spied a patrol of the enemy. Thirty riders, watching us from the crest of a hill.

They did not try to follow us, nor did they conceal themselves."

"You have done well", I said. "Watch them and keep scouting, but do not chase after them. I wish for them to see our numbers." He nodded and rode off.

Reports kept coming in of scouts studying us.

Edessa was located in the northwest corner of a huge expanse of flat terrain, stretching past the horizon to the south and east. The plain, thirty miles from north to south, and twenty across, is hemmed in by rocky hills and ravines. I was very aware of the fact that nearly three hundred years ago, only twenty miles south of Edessa, the Romans suffered one of their most crushing defeats ever. Seven legions and auxiliaries were annihilated on the plains next to Carrhae by a well-led Parthian army consisting of nine thousand horse archers and a thousand cataphracts. I would not repeat the mistakes of Legate Marcus Crassus.

The last couple of miles of the road to the city traversed the hilly terrain that bordered the plain. Three miles from the city the ravine temporarily opened up. It was adequate for the construction of a marching camp to accommodate the legion as well as the foederati.

While Hostilius's men laboured to do the necessary, the Sasanians watched from the hills. We allowed them to do just that.

I doubted that the enemy would try to launch a night attack, but I still posted sentries in the hills to be sure that there would be no assault by archers.

As was the norm, Hostilius woke me before sunrise. He had a spring in his step. "Today is payback time, Domitius. Remember how they tried to stab us in the back at the Gorgan Wall? I just hope that they don't turn tail and run away before we can lay into them."

"They won't run, Primus Pilus", I replied.

He narrowed his eyes in suspicion. "How can you be so sure? Did Arash tell you?"

I produced a small scroll. "I have it in writing from the Sasanian commander."

I gestured to a weary Pezhman, who strolled in from the gloom, having earlier arrived back from his mission.

"Tell him, Pezhman", I said.

Pezhman answered in rudimentary Latin. "Roman lord Primus Pilus, I delivered message from great king Shapur to lord of Sasanian army yesterday morning. Message said for him to destroy our army if he is able to."

Hostilius stared at him with wide eyes.

"Cai removed the seal of Shapur from the scroll he had given us months ago and Vibius had forged a message", I said. "Apparently Shapur is still on his way back from quelling a rebellion close to Gorgan or Chorasmia, according to Timesitheus. Good thing we had a Parthian scout from Gorgan available to deliver the message."

"They ask me much question about Gorgan. I answer and they take message. They give me message to take back to shahanshah", Pezhman said, pointing at the scroll I held in my hand.

"They follow me many watches to make sure I no lie", he said, and grinned. "When they see me on way to Shapur, they leave."

In any event, it was time to test my plan. We left the camp intact and marched through the last two miles of the ravine to reach the plain of Edessa. The Sasanians were already deployed three miles to the south, which afforded enough space for their horsemen to function effectively. The commander of the enemy army had reason to be confident.

The Parthians have always employed a simple, yet highly effective strategy - their lightly armoured horse archers weaken and break the infantry line. Once the line has broken, the heavy cavalry would wreak havoc and crush the enemy.

On the day, the Sasanians deployed their light horse archers in three enormous blocks. The only difference between the groups, I guessed, being the Parthian lord they owed fealty to. Behind the light cavalry waited the cataphracts - the feared men on enormous horses clad in metal scales and chain. They would be patient, ready to strike when the first signs of weakness appeared.

The Roman army deployed in three distinct blocks. In the centre, the mighty IV Italica. On the left flank, the foederati horse archers. On the right, facing the enemy from the front ranks, the heavy cavalry and behind them, the infantry of the Goths and the Heruli. Or so it would seem to the enemy.

In actual fact, only the second and third cohort of the legion faced the enemy at the centre. At their rear, screened from view, I had stationed five thousand horse archers. Today they would be fighting on foot.

On the left flank, two lines of horse archers made up the front rank. Behind them, five thousand legionaries were waiting.

The Parthians acted predictably. The centre of their line galloped towards the Roman infantry. They knew that the pila of the legionaries were only effective up to a maximum of forty paces and if they stayed farther away, they were in no danger. The horse archers raced up to the legionaries to release the first of their deadly volleys when the buccina signalled. Five thousand Scythians released five arrows each into the air within as many heartbeats. The sky darkened and twenty-five thousand arrows fell among the unarmoured Parthians. The Scythians released two more volleys, crushing the enemy charge.

I was only warming up. On Marcus's signal, the Gothic infantry streamed through the ranks of the auxiliary cataphracts, launching a second assault on the Parthian light cavalry. It was impossible to hold any kind of order due to the thousands of dying men and horses littering the ground. This suited the Gothic horde just fine. They swept over the Parthians like a flood.

Marcus signalled again and the left flank started walking their horses in the direction of the enemy right flank.

For the Parthian commander it was an easy decision. He would crush our left flank with his heavy cavalry in order to salvage the victory that was fast slipping from his grasp. Apart from retreating, light and medium cavalry have little defence against a charge from armoured cataphracts.

The Parthian men in metal advanced towards our left flank, first at a walk then at a trot and finally charging at a gallop. They rode boot to boot, an impenetrable wall of metal and horseflesh.

They were eighty paces away when the legionaries rushed
through the two ranks of horsemen and formed a solid wall of
shields, grounding their pila for additional effect. These were
our battle-hardened veterans whom we had trained to repel the
attack of heavy cavalry. The front ranks of the cataphracts
tried to pull back as no horse could be trained to run into a
solid wall. Horses tried to stop or turn, but the rear ranks
collided with them and soon the charge faltered into a milling
mass. Marcus gave the signal and we charged.

Hostilius was next to me in the front rank. "Release pilum",
he boomed.

The spears were thrown at point blank range and reaped a
deadly harvest. Every legionary in the Fourth was issued with
a small, yet heavy, hand axe adorned with a two foot haft.
Armed with these, we charged into the fray.

Most of the legionaries opted to fight with a shield in the left
hand and an axe or a sword in the right. I gripped an axe in
my right hand and my jian in my left. We had trained and
practised to deal with these men clad in iron.

And then we were amongst them. A huge stallion reared up to
my left, its metal shod hooves clawing the air close to my
head. I struck its front leg with the axe, all but severing the
hoof. The horse came to ground and toppled over, pinning the
rider underneath. My jian flashed out, severing his hamstring

under his unarmoured knee. A lithe warrior riding to the left of his fallen comrade, struck at me with his mace. I managed to dodge the blow, the shaft of the weapon striking my armoured shoulder, a flange scoring a line along the side of my helmet. Before he could recover, legionary hands pulled him off his horse. He screamed like a stuck pig as Gordas bashed in his helmet with an axe.

A gap appeared to my right. It gave my next opponent the opportunity to gain some momentum as he tried to skewer me with his fifteen foot spear. I deflected the spear with my jian, clasped the shaft under my armpit and pulled. He pulled back, I pushed, and he lost balance for a heartbeat. My thrown axe's razor-sharp blade cleft his helmet and embedded itself an inch deep in his skull. He toppled forward and I pulled the corpse off the horse. As he fell, I grabbed his metal-flanged mace in my right hand. Fresh legionaries were swarming past us with Hostilius leading the way.

I heard the buccina signal the advance. Knowing what was about to happen, I jumped onto the horse of the man I had dispatched moments ago.

I had never seen the Heruli in battle, but Kniva had explained it to me earlier. "Brother, it is something to behold. The Heruli warriors run to battle alongside charging cavalry. They are nearly as swift as horses. For this, they discard their shields. When within striking distance, they reach for their double-bladed battle axes which they carry on their backs. These axes are wickedly sharp but even when they are blunted, it matters not. The axes are heavy but wielded with great skill. Even when it strikes armour, bones break underneath chain or scale."

The huge beast I rode afforded me a view of the battle. I saw Rodoulphos lead the Heruli against the rear of the Sasanian heavy cavalry. Each warrior had a wolfskin draped over his shoulders, covering the chain. They charged with a swiftness I did not think possible. Where they drove into the enemy rear, they reaped a terrible slaughter. I saw a horse nearly decapitated by a monster of a man. Pivoting on his heel, the axe blade all but disappeared into the chest of a cataphract. Then he clubbed a rearing horse with the flat of his axe, rider and horse falling in the chaos. His bloody axe rose and fell as he finished the job.

I extracted myself from the melee as Marcus gave the next signal.

Although his view was obscured, the commander of the Sasanians would have worked out by then that the battle was not unfolding in favour of his heavy cavalry.

His options were limited. With a third of the light cavalry destroyed and the cataphracts routed, our heavy Germani cavalry charged towards what remained of his horse archers.

Even though our heavy cavalry only numbered a thousand, they could still inflict serious damage on the light horse archers. Predictably, the Sasanian commander decided that on the day, discretion was the better part of valour. They turned tail, abandoned their camp, and fled south towards Carrhae.

Hostilius, Marcus and I had our hands full to ensure that no internal war broke out during the looting. Fortunately my foederati commanders were hands-on. A major benefit being that the diverse groups placed value on different items.

The Roxolani and Carpiani prized the armour of the cataphracts above all. Second came the bows and arrows of the horse archers. Third the horses.

The Goths and Heruli wanted swords, axes and spear points most of all.

The Romans coveted the coin, but above all, the valuable slaves that could be gained.

Gordas coveted scalps. He walked among the corpses for nearly a watch, then came to boast with his gory trophies.

"I have enough scalps to make a full cloak", he babbled on excitedly. "I took only the best. Men who looked after their hair." He held up the grisly harvest, blood dripping from the leather pouch.

I made a mental note not to care for my hair too well. For Gordas, the temptation might just be too big to resist.

Chapter 42 – Carrhae (March/April 243 AD)

Edessa opened their gates to us as the Sasanian garrison had fled with the rest of their army.

Even though we emerged victorious, we had dead to bury and wounded to care for. Damaged armour, weapons and tack needed to be repaired.

Days later, on their arrival, the emperor and his retinue were welcomed as conquering heroes who had lifted the Sasanian yoke from the necks of the people of Edessa. I could not help but wonder whether Shapur received a similar reception years before, as the king who had lifted the Roman yoke. It is doubtful whether the citizenry really cared about which language the yoke spoke. The more things change, the more they stay the same.

In any event, Marcus was the official hero of the battle. The man who took a single legion and some barbarian rabble and did what Crassus couldn't accomplish with seven legions. Although it was my plan that gave us victory, Marcus was a competent commander and a good friend. His good fortune sat well with me.

The Roman army camped outside of Edessa for a few days to take stock and to resupply. It was then that Timesitheus came to see me in my tent.

"Well done, Tribune Domitius", he said. "I know that it was the quality of the Scythians archers that carried the day. That, and the hardened veterans of the IV Italica. You will be rewarded in time. Caesar Gordian feels the same."

Well, to earn the gratitude and promise of reward from the emperor and the prefect of the guard, was more than any man could wish for.

Two weeks passed before the army advanced to reclaim the town of Carrhae. We had hardly set out when messengers arrived from the town, extending an invitation to the emperor, as the garrison of the 'Sasanian oppressors' had fled east.

For days we received no news and my barbarians became restless. Eventually I set out to find the men who would be in the know - my old tent mates from the IV Italica.

Pumilio had heard from his uncle's cousin. "A little bird told me that we will march to Ctesiphon. Only way we can get through this godforsaken desert is to follow the river. We have to march south and then north to a backwater of a place called Rhesaina. From there we can follow the river right up to the gates of Ctesiphon."

"Old Akkas, the slave who cleans out the chamber pots of the Praetorium, said he heard that Shapur is marching this way", Ursa added. "He says them Sasanians will try and cut us off from water. They will be waiting at Rhesaina, he says. But he wouldn't know, would he?"

Predictably, the army marched the next morning.

We slogged south for two days, then turned east. We were headed for Rhesaina, as Akkas had envisaged.

Two days away from our destination the news and rumours intensified.

It turned out that a Sasanian advance force was camped outside the town, although Shapur was yet to join them. He was on his way back from quelling a rebellion of Parthian lords, far to the north.

Marcus rode beside Cai and me. "Lucius, it seems that Fortuna is on our side. Not only is Shapur still on his way, but his army is with him. The force waiting for us will not be large, surely. Maybe Gordian will send a legion or two ahead to chase them away to allow us to set up camp in peace."

His red cloak and magnificent armour was covered in a layer of fine sand-coloured dust. "I could sure use a swim in the river", he said, and spat in the dust. "Even my spit is full of dust."

"If assume, battle lost before fight start", Cai cautioned. "Enemy wish to appear weak. Wait till see with own eyes."

We made camp five miles from the river. When all had settled in, Marcus and I were summoned to attend Timesitheus.

We had to wait outside, as the prefect was engaged. Raised voices emanated from inside the tent, eventually settling down.

Not long after, a dour individual exited the Praetorium and stormed past us. He looked vaguely familiar.

We were shown in, catching Timesitheus in the act of taking a long swig from his goblet of wine.

"Your visitor seems less than happy, sir", Marcus said, and looked over his shoulder.

Timesitheus sighed. "He is the brother of Priscus, Philip the Arab. Used to be prefect of Mesopotamia. He believes that I blame him for the loss of the province. Initially, I did not. Truth be told, his interminable efforts of convincing the emperor otherwise had made me come to believe that he is to blame."

He poured wine and gestured for us to take a seat.

"The army of the Sasanians which is waiting for us close by, is larger than I had expected", he said. "We need to get unhindered access to the river. Our army will attack tomorrow. We leave the camp at dawn."

Marcus and I nodded and stood to leave, but Timesitheus held up his hand.

"There is one other thing." He motioned with his eyes, indicating the way his guest had left moments earlier.

The prefect sighed. "Through his father-in-law, his family wields significant power within the senate. He insisted to be given command of the left flank in order to redeem himself. He had even garnered support from Caesar Gordian via Gaius Priscus. It is not my wish, but I was forced to relent."

He drank deeply. "That is why I am placing you two and the foederati next to him, left of the left flank. If he fails, Fortuna willing, you will still be able to carry the day."

Marcus and I exchanged glances, his face riddled with concern.

I made sure that all my commanders joined Marcus and me for dinner that evening. Vibius had put his command of the local language to good use and managed to procure two sheep, a feat that earned him the gratitude of us all. Cai conjured up two amphorae of red wine that must have been hidden, and the evening turned into a veritable feast.

Before we left Sirmium, I had convinced the legate to requisition twenty-five thousand barbed caltrops from the local blacksmiths. Hostilius delivered it to me at Trimontium. We had practised for weeks, using pebbles, to "sow" these wicked three-pronged spikes. The cavalry would be able to gallop at speed and create a nearly impenetrable barrier. Each one of the five thousand horse archers would carry five of these "thorns of Arash", as they had come to call them.

I spoke to Elmanos and Thiaper. "We may need the thorns of Arash tomorrow. Make sure that the men have them at the ready."

We shared Timesitheus's concerns with them, explaining how the prefect's hand had been forced to entrust the command of the left flank to Philip the Arab.

"In the lands of the Goths, the iudex will never allow a man to command if he is not up to the task", Kniva said. "Even if the iudex allowed it, the men would not follow an incompetent, but appoint the bravest noble from among their ranks to lead."

All my commanders nodded their heads in agreement.

"I can send two of my men to bring you the scalp of this Arab", Gordas suggested.

I shook my head then.

I often wonder how different my life would have been if I had granted the Hun's request. Gordas would not have failed me.

In any event, I was not blessed with the gift of foresight. "That is not our way, Gordas", I said. "We will respect the wishes of the emperor and do our best."

Chapter 43 – Conspirator

We were last to enter the plain at Rhesaina, next to the Khabur River. Near the town water flowed from the soil all year round, giving rise to this main tributary, which snakes south until it flows into the Euphrates.

We could not lay eyes on the river as it was obscured by a mighty Sasanian host.

Like the previous day, Cai was riding alongside us.

"What you say now?" he asked.

Marcus ignored the stab. "By all the gods alive, how is it possible? Their numbers are at least equal to ours. Surely, this must be the army of Shapur's?"

On the far right, the cavalry from Gaul and Germania would protect the flank. Three legions from the Rhine, and Italy, constituted the right flank.

In the centre, Timesitheus had placed the three Danubian legions, the veterans of many campaigns. To the left of the centre I recognised the distinctive blue and gold shields of the IV Italica.

The eastern legions, commanded by Philip, drawn from Syria, Cappadocia and the remnants from Mesopotamia stood closest to us. They formed the left flank.

Behind the centre, as a reserve, the II Parthica and Praetorians stood to attention, reinforced with thousands of Roman legionary cavalry.

The men of the Scythian foederati - the Roxolani, Goths, Heruli and Carpiani bunched together, left of the left flank. To wait in orderly ranks was not their way.

A nearly endless line of Sasanians faced us. I could clearly discern the light infantry by their multi-coloured clothing, milling around on their horses. Many congregating along tribal lines.

Thousands of Dailamite spearmen stood in the centre with their two-pronged spears, conical helmets, large shields and heavy armour.

Across from our position and slightly to the right, mounted on enormous horses, stood the backbone of the Sasanian army - the heavy cavalry. With spears grounded, they stood motionless, like statues cast in iron. The sea of gleaming spear points hinted at their number, in excess of ten thousand.

The Sasanians had learned from the Romans. Across the plain from us, contingents of barbarian horsemen were milling around restlessly. Some of them could very well have been Xionites.

Within the ranks of the Sasanians I noticed strange, shining mounds. At first I could not identify them, but as we drew closer I saw the shapes move.

With shock I realised that the Sasanians had brought their war elephants. They were armoured much the same as the cataphracts. Huge metal monsters that could rout infantry as easily as taking a stroll in the forum.

I gave thanks to Arash that I sat on a horse with a bow in my hand and that I would not have to face these abominations on foot.

Gordas, who sat next to me, said: "Strangest horses I have ever seen. Will the king of the Romans allow me take them as loot? I'll even be content with only one of them." Huns.

At the rear of the left flank, behind the eastern legions, Philip was issuing orders. The commander of the reserves came trotting over to him and I noticed that it was his brother, Prefect Gaius Priscus. A felt a sudden stab of worry in my stomach. Should these men be, as Pezhman had put it "friends with Shapur", then it could mean the annihilation of the Roman army.

Priscus noticed my gaze. He raised his hand and waved at me, smiling broadly.

I ignored him.

I received word earlier that the emperor had decided to employ the Fourth Formation. The entire army would advance. Then, at the signal of the emperor, the wings would advance and attack. It had shock value, but if the initial attack failed, it opened up the centre to flanking attacks.

In any event, Marcus and I were small pieces on a very large gaming board. Today would be about giving it our all and obeying orders. We would not be able to determine the strategy nor the outcome of the battle. Or so we thought at the time.

The Sasanians made the first move. Thousands of light cavalry charged at the centre of our formation. The Scythians were tasked to counter this.

The Roxolani and Carpiani spurred their horses and followed me. Gordas rode at my side.

I had five arrows in my draw hand and at my signal, five thousand arrows darkened the sky. A heartbeat later, the Sasanians released their volley. Before their arrows fell among us, I had emptied my hand. The Hunnic and Scythian bows were superior in range and many of the enemy fell to our arrows.

An arrow clanged off my helmet. Another stuck in my saddle, but I escaped injury.

Many of the Scythians fell victim to the Sasanian arrows, but in return we reaped a larger harvest. The Sasanians turned their mounts and returned to their ranks. I gave the signal and the Scythians aborted the attack. We had successfully countered their first move.

The buccina signalled the advance and inexorably the legions marched forward, towards the enemy. Thousands of men in chain moving as one, emanating a bone chilling sound, like the hissing of some giant serpent.

I called a halt two hundred paces from the enemy. The legions on both flanks received the signal and advanced at a jog. The foederati warriors were not expected to engage, but only to repel an attack on the flank.

Bands of archers broke off from the main body of the enemy and rode towards the flanks of the legion. We slew them with a storm of arrows. A contingent of light spearmen separated from the Parthian ranks and ran towards the legion's flank, our arrows embedding uselessly in their shields. At my command, a mob of Gothic warriors charged forward, washing over them like a wave.

On the far right, I heard vague signals of advance as the veteran killers of the Rhine legions grinded down the enemy. But not all was well. The eastern legions of the left flank were up against the Dailamites, and the battle was bloody. The Sasanian spearmen had spent their stabbing spears and were laying into the legionaries with their terrible axes. Splintering shields and bending the line.

I recognized the signs. I could feel it in my gut. The left flank was about to give way.

I held my breath, waiting for Philip the Arab to provide the signal for the orderly retreat. No order came. I glanced at where he was sitting on his horse and I realised that it would not come.

The left flank was being pushed towards the left and backwards. In the centre the legions had formed the testudo as they were under attack from thousands of archers. But they held their ground. The fourth was trained for this and would not break.

The gap between the centre and the left flank widened and I was certain that at any moment the Sasanians would unleash their cataphracts against the unprotected flank of the centre. The flank occupied by the IV Italica - my brothers.

I anticipated Priscus to send in the reserve to protect the flank. No order was given.

Should the cataphracts penetrate between the centre and the left flank, the battle would be lost. They would roll up the centre, then attack the Rhine legions from both flanks.

Arash gave me a vision of Hostilius and his men being massacred by the iron-clad horsemen.

Priscus and Philip remained motionless. Watching the disaster unfold.

I turned to Marcus who was staring in horror, sharing my thoughts. "My friend", I said, "forgive me. I cannot sit idly by. If I survive, Priscus will have my head for this."

I spurred Simsek and rode to the rear of the formation, circling behind the left flank, into the ever-widening gap, right of the centre.

I rode like never before, like a madman. I looked to my side and there was Cai and Marcus. Gordas and his ten Huns were next to them, howling like wolves.

I turned in my saddle. Five thousand Scythians were trailing in my dust.

Opposite us, I noticed the Sasanian cataphracts peeling off their line, heading straight for the gap. Thousands strong. The opening between the centre and the left was two hundred paces wide and growing by the heartbeat. I gave the signal then, and as we had practised hundreds of times, we sowed the caltrops in a thick line, ten paces wide, to protect the flank of my legion.

We wheeled our horses around, escaping the advancing heavy cavalry by the skin of our teeth. They were unaware of what we had done and charged into the gap, intent on penetrating deep before turning into the legion's flank.

We reined in once we were clear and witnessed as the Sasanians expertly wheeled their horses, lowered their lances and charged into the flank of the IV Italica. Nine out of ten never made it across the path of death that we had sowed. The long spikes of the caltrops penetrated the hooves of the warhorses. Some reared, others fell - the rear ranks bowling into the chaos. The few lone riders who made it to the flank of the legions were dispatched with ease.

Hostilius was aware of what was unfolding. At his signal, the three rear cohorts detached from the ranks and engaged the heavy cavalry. Most of the Sasanians were injured and taken down with ease, but the rest, three thousand strong, regrouped and fought back with a vengeance. But they were in for a surprise. The Heruli axe men ran past us and hit them from behind with the Goths hot on their heels. Caught between the blood-crazed wolf warriors and the iron men of the IV Italica, they did not prevail.

The routed cataphracts had left a gap in the lines of the Sasanians. The Danubian legions in the centre jumped at the opportunity to exploit the situation.

In no time, the advance of the heavy Roman infantry overwhelmed the Sasanians. With the legionaries and Sasanians engaged in close combat, the enemy archers were ineffective, as they did not wish to risk killing their own.

The Sasanian heavy cavalry was no more, and the Roman infantry dominated the battlefield. The enemy had no choice but to abandon their position and flee.

I was overwhelmed by the happenings of the day, staring at the scene of horrific slaughter that had played out around me.

Hostilius arrived at a jog, spattered with blood and gore. I dismounted. "The boys are singing your praises, Domitius", he said. He held out his arm to clasp mine, but then embraced me, which was an action out of character for the burly centurion.

"You have not only saved the Fourth, you have pulled the whole army's arse out of the fire", he said.

He suddenly turned red in the face, seething with anger. "Gods help me or I will do something to Philip the Arab that I will regret. He was watching. Waiting for us to get stuck like pigs. Bastard! It was as if he had tried to help the Sasanians."

I suspected that Hostilius was right in his assessment, but it could not be proven.

Kniva and Rodoulphos joined us as they extracted themselves from the looting. Thiaper and Elmanos arrived moments later.

I heard the approach of horsemen. It was a turma of mounted praetorians, or speculatores, escorting Priscus.

He pointed his finger at me and Marcus in turn. "You will come with us", he sneered. "There is a price to pay for insolence and disobedience."

Hostilius wanted to intervene, but I held up my hands. "I will go with you", I said. "I knew this would happen."

Then Hostilius did something unexpected for the second time that day. He took hold of my arm with his grip of iron and turned to face Priscus.

"Look around you, Prefect Priscus", Hostilius growled.

Slowly, the Heruli and the Goths were filtering back, encircling us. Their axes and spears dripping with blood.

Priscus turned his head this way and that.

"If you take them, there will be blood." Hostilius pointed with his sword towards the legion. "And these boys are certainly not going to intervene on your behalf. Leave now before it is too late."

Priscus realised that he was but a word away from being dragged from his horse and slaughtered like a pig.

Slowly, he backed his horse away and galloped off with murder written all over his face.

"Well, Primus Pilus", I sighed, "you have certainly burned your bridges."

Gordas's stare followed the retreating prefect. "Pity he left", the Hun mumbled, which drew many a questioning stare.

He slid the wickedly sharp dagger back into its felt-lined scabbard, shrugged his scale-encased shoulders and said: "He has nice hair."

Chapter 44 – Friends

None of us were naïve enough to think that the incident would go away. Priscus and Philip were powerful men with even more powerful connections.

On the second day after the battle, a messenger arrived from Timesitheus, summoning Marcus and me to the Praetorium.

I feared some kind of violence so I commanded a reluctant Gordas to remain at the camp.

Marcus and I followed the messenger to the Praetorium where Timesitheus was waiting for us.

He gestured for us to take a seat.

"I have spent much of my time in the aftermath of the battle to find out what exactly happened on the left flank", he said. "According to Priscus and Philip, the two of you ignored his orders and acted against his will, which nearly led to the annihilation of the imperial army."

He sat down heavily and sighed. "Of course, all that is bullshit. Apart from the brothers and their cronies within the guard, everyone hails you two as the heroes of the day."

He leaned in and whispered: "I have a hunch that what Priscus and Philip did was more than just bad leadership. I think they have made a deal with Shapur. The Sasanians get to keep Mesopotamia and maybe they have been promised Armenia? In return, Shapur deals with Gordian after the defeat of the army and the brothers win the purple?"

He sat upright and continued in his normal voice. "It will be impossible to prove, but I have another plan. Three days from now I will launch an official inquiry into your conduct. I will preside over the proceedings. The two of you will be hailed as heroes while Philip the Arab and his brother Priscus will be exposed and disgraced."

"Make sure you report at the Praetorium before the second watch of the morning. Apart from the two of you, I require that you bring along your senior foederati commander as well as Primus Pilus Hostilius Proculus. Just in case I need additional witnesses."

He noticed our sombre looks. "Do not be anxious about this, tribunes. All has been arranged. The outcome is guaranteed."

Without warning, his hand went to his stomach and he doubled over, his face contorted with pain.

He immediately righted himself. "Bloody stomach of mine. I have been struggling with it for a couple of days and it's not getting any better. I will have the surgeon mix me a potion to ensure that I am fit for the proceedings."

Despite the assurances provided by Timesitheus, I woke up in the middle of the night, beset by a feeling of impending doom.

Eventually I fell asleep, but I had learned from experience not to ignore a warning from the gods.

I shared my concern with my friend Marcus. "Your concerns are unfounded, Lucius", he said. "Timesitheus is the emperor for all practical purposes. He is trustworthy. All will be well."

I tried to find comfort in his words, but I could not. I therefore went to seek out Vibius, Gordas and Rodoulphos.

Cai assisted me to don my full Roman armour on the morning of the trial. He had meticulously cleaned and polished it the previous day and I looked the part of a tribune of Rome.

I turned around to leave, but Cai held up his hand.

"I go with you." He wore a look of grim determination, which just added to my concern.

I nodded. His presence always gave me comfort.

We arrived at the proceedings to find a host of senior officers waiting outside the tent. A few clasped our arms, some nodded their heads in acknowledgement, while others stared at us with open contempt. One officer, who I knew to be the legate of the Legio III Gallica, clasped my arm and placed a small scrap of parchment in my hand. I stuffed it in my purse.

Marcus and I were ushered into the Praetorium, while Hostilius, Cai and my barbarian friends remained outside.

Timesitheus was nowhere to be seen. Gaius Priscus came through the door and walked to the front of the assembly.

"Dear friends and colleagues. My fellow praetorian prefect, Gaius Timesitheus was supposed to preside over today's proceedings. It pains me to inform you that he is beset by a most evil stomach malady. He is in much pain at the moment and somewhat delirious, but I have requested my personal physician to attend to him. We expect him to return to health within a week."

The gathered officers turned to leave, but Priscus was not done yet.

He cleared his throat. "Caesar Gordian has requested that I stand in for Timesitheus and deal with the inquiry today as he wishes a speedy resolve. As I am here to serve Caesar and Rome, I have agreed."

What followed can only be described as a farce. Various officers and witnesses called by Priscus attested to our incompetence. Priscus and Philip were heralded as the saviours of the day.

When all had spoken, Priscus excused himself to 'deliberate with the emperor' in order to decide a fit punishment.

He returned a short while later.

"I have spoken to our Caesar Gordian. He is not only a brilliant tactician, but he is also a merciful emperor. Owing to the exemplary record of Tribune Marcus Claudius and Tribune Lucius Domitius, he has decided to spare their lives. They have been leading the foederati for many months, hence they have been corrupted by their barbarian ways and their barbarian gods. That is the reason for their gross incompetence and disregard for the orders of our beloved Caesar."

It was not going well for us.

Priscus lifted Timesitheus's golden goblet to his lips to take a swig. He paused then, smiled and placed the wine on the table without drinking. With a gloating smirk, he continued. "Marcus Claudius and Lucius Domitius, you are stripped of your military rank with immediate effect. You will return to the foederati camp under praetorian escort. You will be allowed to gather your families, but you are hereby exiled to live outside the lands of the Empire. So decrees our beloved emperor, Caesar Gordian the third."

He held up the written decree with the seal of the emperor for all to see.

Four praetorians entered and escorted Marcus and me outside, where a turma of speculatores were waiting to give effect to the well-planned outcome of the hearing.

Marcus spoke under his breath. "It could have been worse. At least we will live."

"I doubt whether Priscus is done with us. Keep your hand on your sword, Marcus", I said.

Cai, Hostilius and Kniva strolled over. "Domitius, that was quick. Come have a drink with me, my throat is parched."

He seemed to suddenly notice our sombre expressions. "By the gods, don't tell me they found you guilty?"

Marcus nodded. "Removal of our ranks and exile. We barely escaped the garrotte."

"Come, we need to do as the emperor commands", the centurion of the speculatores said.

Kniva placed his hand on my shoulder. "I see that the gods are testing you, my friend. Do not despair. Remember my oath. You have friends."

Sixteen praetorians led the way, with sixteen forming the rearguard.

The five of us rode in total silence.

We were camped three miles away, near the river. In order to get there we had to pass through a shallow gorge, overgrown with shrubs. A few lone trees provided welcome shade.

The centurion held up his hand and the leading speculatores turned their horses to face us. They spread out, forming a circle around our small group.

"Please be patient", the centurion said.

Within a few heartbeats, Priscus and Philip appeared, escorted by four speculatores.

Philip walked his horse fifty paces down the road, engaged in idle chatter with the four guards.

Priscus joined the circle of mounted praetorians. He grinned, unable to mask his excitement at having gained the upper hand at long last. "Lay down your swords", he sneered, "or do you wish to see if you can defeat thirty speculatores?"

His comment drew a muted chuckle from somewhere behind me, which died away quickly.

Cai broke the silence. "Let us do as prefect says", which broadened Priscus's grin, as he erroneously assumed that Cai was referring to the first part of his suggestion.

I was about to act when Priscus continued. "A full turma of my men left yesterday to deal with some loose ends near Sirmium. Your shade will not have long to wait in Hades for

390

the rest of your troublesome family to arrive. Your daughter will join you as well."

In the background I noticed Philip's half-smile, revealing his obvious amusement at our predicament.

"You had better start praying to your pathetic barbarian god. What is he called again? Oh yes, Ashar, isn't it?"

Unbeknown to Priscus, I have been breathing deeply for the last two hundred heartbeats, while praying to Arash for guidance.

"Officially, witnesses will swear that you attacked me. That is after I have uncovered your plot to have the men of the Fourth rise up against the young Caesar", he continued smugly. "All of you are implicated. The statements of the witnesses are already signed, filed in my office."

"My brother and I", he gestured towards Philip with his chin, "as the two praetorian prefects, will corroborate the evidence, of course."

"And", he continued, "the barbarian rabble you are so inordinately fond of, I will throw as fodder against the charge of the immortals when we meet Shapur. It is referred to as 'killing two flies with one swat', I believe."

Priscus grinned. "If, er… sorry, when Timesitheus crosses the Styx, Philip will take his place as praetorian prefect."

Priscus made eye contact with the hulking praetorian next to him and gave a nearly imperceptible nod. He mounted his horse and sped away with his brother the Arab, and the four guards.

I readied myself for the inevitable. We would sell our lives dearly.

The speculatores constricted the circle, drew their swords and raised their cavalry shields.

A mounted praetorian spurred his horse towards me, but rather than attack, he slumped forward in the saddle, his corpse sliding to the ground. A spear shaft protruded from his lower back.

Ten arrows were released simultaneously. Ten men died.

Rodoulphos, his wolfskin wrapped around his head and shoulders, rose like a phantom, his vicious axe nearly cleaving a speculatore in half.

It was over in less than three heartbeats.

Priscus's threat against my family had rocked me to the core. I felt confused, even disoriented.

"What do we do now?" I asked no one in particular.

It was Kniva who spoke first. "Now, brother, I deliver on my oath. We gather horses and we ride like the wind."

I suddenly remembered the note given to me by the legate of the Third Gallica. I read the scribble. *"You saved us all. We will not forget. You have friends."* It was unsigned. I stuffed it back into my purse, thinking nothing of it at the time.

We collected all we needed in less time than it would take a man to march a Roman mile.

It was agreed on by all that Elmanos would lead the foederati home. Cai and I took our spare horses and weapons, abandoning the rest.

We rode to Sirmium. Cai and me, Hostilius, Vibius, Kniva, Thiaper, Rodoulphos, Pezhman and Gordas with his nine Huns.

We rode to save an old man, a young mother and an infant daughter.

Chapter 45 – Destiny

Priscus and his brother, Philip the Arab, did not expect the foederati to leave. Even if he wanted to there was not much he could do. The Scythians had the swiftest horses by far. To send the Numidians after them would have been a death sentence for the African horsemen.

When he found out that we had escaped and that the Scythian foederati had abandoned the army, he concocted a story that he had dismissed them, and that he had sent them home due to the lack of feed available to the horses. That, and of course, their inability to follow orders.

In any event, the Scythians rode home, but our small group of desperate men outpaced them.

We did not measure our time in days. We rode until we could ride no farther. We slept during the day. We rode through nights filled with rain, drenched to the bone. We ate half-cooked food, mounted, and rode again - changing horses frequently, and buying or stealing replacements when necessary.

I lost track of time, and with it, a bit of my sanity. We became as close as brothers, forging a bond that would last.

Cai was the only one who counted the days. On the third and twentieth day we rode past Sirmium and I knew the sun would soon rise.

I was tired, my mind weary from carrying the ever-present burden of worry and despair.

We smelled the fire before we could see the thick column of smoke. In my heart I knew that my home was aflame.

I led the way as we raced along the familiar paths of my childhood. I experienced the strange sensation that I was riding back through time and that when the fog dissipated, all would be well again.

We emerged from the trees. In the grey pre-dawn light I saw a turma of mounted praetorians watching the last of the structures collapse in an explosion of bright orange sparks, followed by black puffs of smoke.

I have forgotten the meaning of the word 'mercy' along the road and I yelled: "Keep some alive."

Within heartbeats the ten Huns released as many arrows, emptying half the saddles.

My armour-piercing arrow split the mail of a speculatore, embedding itself deep in his intestines. The speculatores were killers all, but we were delivering a message from Arash and it wasn't gladsome news.

They must have thought us apparitions from Hades as we slew them at will. A handspan of heartbeats later, Rodoulphos was wiping gore from his axe and the Huns were looting.

Three of the speculatores were left alive, albeit badly injured.

I called to Gordas and Hostilius.

Speaking in Scythian, which they both could understand, I said: "Gordas, find out what they know." I held out my dagger to him, but he shook his head. "I would rather use fire", he said, gesturing towards the piles of red hot glowing embers. "These men have done dark deeds. The fire of Arash will purify their spirits to make them acceptable to Tengri."

It proved that Huns could be compassionate when it suited them.

Although there was little hope, I went to grasp at the last straw.

I walked into the trees on my own, to where the hidden door under the soil gave access to the underground escape tunnel. I had the tunnel built years ago by Dacian miners.

I climbed down the ladder, struggling to see in the dark. But then I noticed a flicker of light at the other end of the tunnel.

I ran the hundred paces and found Segelinde, holding a spear above her shoulder, ready to kill, her white dress smeared with blood. I held up my hands and her eyes went wide. "Are you real, or are you a shade?" she queried. I embraced her and both of us broke down momentarily, tears flowing freely.

I heard a groan and in the dim lamplight I saw Felix sitting with his back against the cold, damp wall of the tunnel. A nasty burn scarred the side of his face. Egnatius and a Roxolani sat next to him, both with unidentified wounds.

"They will live", she said.

I spied a small girl with golden locks sleeping soundly next to Adelgunde underneath a fur cloak. My wife smiled and nodded. Relief flooded over me.

Then she took my hand, picked up the lamp and advanced another ten paces.

Close to the door, among the chests of coin, lay my father. His breathing was haggard and I could see that he had taken a serious wound to the chest.

"He killed four of them, Lucius. He was so very brave", Segelinde said. "They would have killed us all, but he cared not for himself. I think he held out for you, Lucius. He kept saying you would come."

Nik groaned then. I walked over to him and laid my hand on his.

He opened his eyes and a thin smile brushed his lips.

"Your god, Arash, gave me a vision, Lucius", he said. He coughed up blood, but continued. "He told me you would come."

I nodded. "All of the attackers have been sent to him."

"Take your family and friends and go north", my father whispered. "Forget all that is Rome and find a home among your mother's people. Live your life away from the evil that Rome has become." He squeezed my hand and closed his eyes. I felt his grip slacken, then he exhaled slowly.

I was sure that he was gone.

I thanked him then. For saving my family. For saving me all those years ago. Even for saving the Empire.

But he found a last morsel of strength, or just maybe Arash came to him. He opened his eyes and studied my face for what felt like hours but could not have been longer than heartbeats.

The great man closed his eyes for the last time and whispered: "I can see the need for vengeance in your eyes, boy. On second thought, go with my blessing and follow your destiny. And if you wish it... kill them all."

Epilogue

I later learned that Timesitheus succumbed days after we departed. Mostly due to the ministrations of Priscus's physician would be my guess.

Philip the Arab was appointed as the second prefect of the Praetorian Guard, naturally at the insistence of Gaius Priscus.

The army marched south along the Khabur to take Ctesiphon, the old capital of Parthia. The fleeing remnants of the defeated Sasanian army of Rhesaina scorched the earth as they fled before the Romans.

Philip and Priscus sent the auxiliary cavalry home, apparently due to lack of feed and continued their march.

Shapur waited for them at a place called Misiche, which was soon renamed Peroz-Shapur, in honour of the thrashing defeat dealt to the Romans.

Gordian was killed in battle. Some say that he was killed by his own soldiers, instigated by the Arab. I have my own view on this.

Philip and Priscus made peace with Shapur, paid him half a million dinars (nearly bankrupting the Empire), and handed Armenia and most of Mesopotamia to the Sasanians. In a stone inscription, Shapur made the bold statement that he had placed Philip on the Roman throne.

Somehow the brothers styled themselves as returning heroes, having made peace with the Sasanians.

Philip the Arab was declared Emperor by the troops. Initially he declined, but they insisted…

But… someone had a score to settle… far to the north, across the mighty River, Arash was whispering into the ear of Eochar the Merciless.

Author's Note

I trust that you have enjoyed the third book in the series.

In many instances, written history relating to this period, has either been lost in the fog of time or it might never have been recorded. That is especially applicable to most of the tribes which Rome referred to as barbarians. These peoples did not record history by writing it down. They only appear in the written histories of the Greeks, Romans and Chinese, who often regarded them as enemies.

In any event, my aim is to be as historically accurate as possible, but I am sure that I inadvertently miss the target from time to time, in which case I apologise to the purists among my readers.

Kindly take the time to provide a rating and/or a review.

The next book in the series will be available early in 2019. I will keep you updated via my blog.

Feel free to contact me any time via my website.

www.HectorMillerBooks.com